PENGUIN BOOKS

BUTTERFLIES

Sylvia Yu is an award-winning filmmaker, author, TV host, and philanthropy adviser. She has led philanthropic initiatives in Asia for some of the world's wealthiest families. She is a trailblazer in the fight against human trafficking, and her three-part documentary series on the subject won her the prestigious 2013 International Human Rights Press Award. Sylvia is the author of five books, including *Fearless: A Guide to Freedom and Fulfilling Your Fullest Potential, A Long Road to Justice,* and *Silenced No More: Voices of Comfort Women*, the only historical journalistic account of Japanese military sex slavery during World War II. She is a highly sought after inspirational keynote speaker.

Matthew S. Friedman is the founder and CEO of The Mekong Club. Matthew is an award-winning filmmaker, author, and philanthropy adviser and has worked for the World Bank, the US State Department, and the United Nations. He is considered the leading catalyst of the anti-slavery movement in Asia's business sector by captains of industry. His expertise has been recognized globally, and he has advised heads of governments and intelligence agencies. Matthew is also a popular motivational speaker who has given over 1,200 presentations to over 95,000 people in 20 nations. He is the author of fourteen books.

ADVANCE PRAISE FOR *BUTTERFLIES*

'*Butterflies* is a highly compelling story. A story that must be told, as it raises awareness that human rights violations, such as the horrors of sexual abuse during World War II, continue in our present times in many places, in different forms, and with new media.

Butterflies also shows us the power of apologies and—if possible—of forgiveness.'

—Kathleen Ferrier, Chairperson,
UNESCO, Netherlands

Butterflies

Sylvia Yu and Matthew S. Friedman

PENGUIN BOOKS
An imprint of Penguin Random House

PENGUIN BOOKS

Penguin Books is an imprint of the Penguin Random House group of companies whose addresses can be found at global.penguinrandomhouse.com

Published by Penguin Random House SEA Pte Ltd
40 Penjuru Lane, #03-12, Block 2
Singapore 609216

Penguin Random House SEA

First published in Penguin Books by Penguin Random House SEA 2026

10 9 8 7 6 5 4 3 2 1

This is a work of fiction. Names, characters, places and incidents are either the product of the author's imagination or are used fictitiously, and any resemblance to any actual person, living or dead, events or locales is entirely coincidental.

ISBN 9789815266368

Typeset in Garamond by MAP Systems, Bangalore, India

www.penguin.sg

This book draws inspiration from true events.

In the quiet corners of history, where untold tales often reside, there is a story of suffering and strength that must not be forgotten. It is up to us to ensure that these untold experiences are brought to light so that we may learn from them and honour those who endured the unspeakable.

This novel is dedicated to the hundreds of thousands of women across Asia who were enslaved in Japanese military brothels during World War II. Legions of women and girls as young as eleven were kidnapped from their families and communities and forced into sexual servitude at the hands of the imperial troops.

These so-called 'comfort women'—a wicked euphemism that masks an unspeakable reality—endured unimaginable hardships in the course of a war that many of them did not survive. Of those who did, most carried the weight of shame, disease, and dark secrets to their graves, often decades later.

We know their stories because of the brave, unbowed few who emerged from the silence and the shadows to share their truth with the world. Their experiences are not only chapters in history but also lessons in human resilience and the enduring spirit.

We dedicate these pages to them with profound gratitude for their courage, their determination, and their unwavering pursuit of justice.

Recognizing the suffering of these women, the deep wounds inflicted on them and their families, and the cultural stigmas that have cast shadows over their lives is essential because, without truth, there can be no reconciliation—a point that seems to have passed the Japanese government by.

Tokyo has evaded the issue for far too long. What we need to bring closure is to hear a heartfelt, unequivocal apology from the Prime Minister of Japan, which would help heal the wounds of history. The sort of apology offered by Willy Brandt, the German Chancellor who fell to his knees in a historic gesture of penance and humility for Nazi war crimes before the Monument to the Ghetto Heroes in Warsaw, Poland.

Unlike Japan, Germany has taken significant steps towards acknowledging and atoning for the atrocities committed during World War II. After the war, the country embarked on a process of reflection, remorse, and reconciliation.

Confronting the past is necessary not only to right historical wrongs, but to see clearly our present and future. Today, only a handful of the original survivors of Imperial Japanese military sexual enslavement are alive—a fact that is not lost on the twisted forces that would rather see them forgotten. History, though, has a habit of repeating, and their plight has a modern echo in the 6.3 million women and girls who languish in sexual slavery today.

The stories and experiences of all these women deserve our attention, empathy, and commitment to justice. We must listen to their narratives, honour their suffering, and learn from history. For in understanding their past, we illuminate the path to a more compassionate and just future.

1

Jeon-Jiju was a small, seedy town with a notorious reputation.

Its traditional Korean buildings had fallen into neglect and disrepair. Their once vibrant colours had faded to a melancholic grey. Cracked wooden shutters hung precariously from their hinges, barely shielding the interiors from prying eyes.

Time had ravaged this place and pride had abandoned it.

The town reeked of decay. Garbage littered the streets; the stench of stale alcohol, cheap cigarettes, and unwashed bodies, mixed together, permeated the air.

The law had turned a blind eye, allowing its dark underbelly to thrive. It had become a haven for criminals, thugs, and deviants. Shady, pungent men in worn-out clothing stalked its streets, glaring at unfamiliar faces with suspicion in their eyes.

Maybe that was why Zoe Kim was feeling so uneasy even though she had seen countless dead-end places like this while covering the vice beat for *The Vancouver Star*.

This was her last day on assignment and her determination to get the story was making her take an unusual risk.

Zoe, thirty-two, had arrived in South Korea two weeks earlier, tasked with uncovering the truth about Jeon-Jiju's vice dens and brothels. She had staked out her targets, planted hidden microphones, and interviewed countless former and current prostitutes, pimps, *mama-sans*, ex-cons, and cops. And all her research pointed to one inescapable conclusion. Women and girls, some as young as twelve, were being trafficked: tricked and physically forced into living and working in these places, in conditions nothing less than slavery. Zoe had almost everything she needed to write an explosive exposé on her return to Canadian soil, but she wanted one more thing: some shocking photographs.

Getting the photographs wasn't proving as easy as she'd hoped. She didn't have a snapper because *The Star*'s budget hadn't stretched that far. As her editor had reminded her, stories of suffering in far off places didn't sell so well in the digital age. 'Take your mobile phone instead,' the photo chief had suggested with a shrug.

Taking her own photos suited Zoe just fine: It would make it all the more worthwhile when she got the scoop. If she got this right, all the media outlets in Canada would want to pick up her story and that meant one important thing to Zoe: she could use the attention to help those poor young women.

Still, now that she was there, on the street, mobile phone in hand, she was beginning to feel nervous about all the ways it could go wrong. What if her photos weren't good enough to run the story? What if a vice den goon discovered her and things turned nasty? Or, worst of all, what if her presence tipped off the brothel overlords and she ended up making life even harder for the women she was trying to help?

Zoe pushed all these thoughts to the back of her mind. She would nail it, she told herself. She was too invested to back out now: She felt an affinity for these women that she couldn't entirely explain.

Her idea had been to blend in. But, judging from some of the looks she was getting, she hadn't been entirely successful. In fact, Zoe's striking appearance made it almost impossible for her to go unnoticed anywhere.

Dressed in jet-black with a fitted blazer that accentuated her sporty figure and a chic bob haircut that framed her delicate features, she exuded confidence, charisma, and beauty—an image that was a world away from the sleazy streets of Jeon-Jiju.

Standing next to Zoe was her young interpreter Jisun, ten years her junior, who, if anything, stood out even more. Zoe hadn't told Jisun where they were heading that day, so Jisun had dressed to impress, picking a hot pink, anime-inspired number that would have turned heads and brought her welcome attention in the trendiest nightlife districts of Seoul. Here, though, it made Jisun feel utterly out of place and dangerously exposed. She followed Zoe like a shadow, her unease palpable.

While more outwardly confident than her interpreter, Zoe too had a growing sense of apprehension as she edged hesitantly along the dimly lit road, keenly aware of how conspicuous they were.

The town's central square, known as the 'Hive', was a gathering place for lowlifes and miscreants, whose shady deals in whispered conversations took place beneath neon signs advertising dubious establishments, cheap thrills, and dangerous encounters.

In Jeon-Jiju, vice was the only business left in town. Stores offering traditional goods and services were all but empty, crumbling, and faded; they barely eked out a living.

The bars and gambling dens hummed with activity. As did the brothels, hidden in the shadows.

As Zoe walked through the streets, she sensed despair, hopelessness, and danger lurking around every corner. Despite her efforts to remain composed, her heart was thumping so loudly that it was echoing in her ears. Her almond-shaped eyes darted nervously from side to side, scanning for signs of trouble.

Her nerves rose as they approached the Dragon Restaurant. She knew the cafe to be an illegal brothel that, in addition to prostitution, hosted a range of criminal activities including unlicensed gambling and drug dealing. Zoe planned to use it as a central case study in her story, and figured that video footage and photos of the underaged girls milling around outside the front of the cafe would be the perfect accompaniment to the piece.

The brothel's outward appearance was that of an unassuming old eatery, though its flickering lights cast an eerie, sinister glow over the dingy street. Its facade was weathered and worn, with wooden panels that bore the scars of harsh winters. Zoe stopped across the street from the restaurant's entrance.

Even from this distance, the air was thick with the acrid smell of cigarette smoke and cheap perfume. Raucous laughter and blaring music emanated from the establishment. Three young teenage girls dressed in revealing tops and short miniskirts sat on display on bright orange, plastic chairs in front. Their faces looked stony despite their heavy make-up—red lips, blue eyeshadow, and pink blush that looked like two spots on either side of their faces.

Mobile phone in hand, Zoe was determined to expose the rotten truth about this place and the depravity that had plagued Jeon-Jiju for more than a decade. Taking a deep breath, she muttered, 'I will do this, no matter the cost,' and prepared herself to face whatever lay ahead. She leaned close to Jisun, her voice dropping to a whisper and her eyes motioning towards the cafe. 'Wait here, I'm going to get some videos of those girls,' she said.

Jisun shrunk back and swallowed hard. Unlike Zoe, she was not used to taking risks, but she was trying to ignore the knot of anxiety tightening in her stomach. 'We can't go any closer,' her voice quivering with trepidation 'There are bad people there. Dangerous. If they think you're doing something to expose them, they'll hurt us. I'm just an interpreter. I can't do this. You don't understand because you're Canadian. You can't understand. This is crazy!'

Zoe's expression hardened, and a determined glint flashed in her eyes. 'I know. I know the risks,' she said, her voice low and steely. 'I have to take the chance. This could be my only shot to expose the traffickers and bring justice to the victims.'

Jisun froze in place and did not respond. She avoided eye contact, shifting on her feet, fidgeting with her hands, and twirling a strand of hair. She had always wanted to do something meaningful, but this situation was too far outside her comfort zone.

'Okay, you go back down the street and wait for me,' Zoe said. 'I'll pretend to take selfies or ask for the time. I can walk back and forth to get my shots. I just need two or three good photos, then we can leave. Would that be okay?'

Feeling relieved that she didn't have to go near the Dragon Restaurant, Jisun turned and scurried down the road. Once she was safely out of sight, Zoe started walking back and forth past the brothel. She tried to appear as casual as possible, pretending to take selfies or read something on her phone.

At one point, the girls sitting in front of the restaurant turned towards this stranger in their midst, their eyes narrowing with suspicion. Sensing this unwelcome attention, Zoe stopped in her tracks and pretended to fix her hair. Then she feigned being lost. After a few minutes, the girls lost interest, turned away, and continued talking with one another.

A surge of adrenaline coursed through Zoe as she realized that she had got what she came for. She struggled to hide her excitement as she swaggered down the street to meet up with Jisun.

'Got it,' Zoe told Jisun with a smug look, her smile extending from ear to ear. Flashing her phone in the air, she added, 'Let's get out of here. With this, I'm officially done.'

Or so she thought. Just as they were walking away, three large men stepped in to block their path out of nowhere. Like predators cornering their prey, the men surrounded the two women, their eyes filled with malice and hostility.

The first man was wearing a tailored suit and might have exuded an air of refinement had it not been for the attention-seeking gaudy outbursts in his attire—a pink silk handkerchief in his left breast pocket and a garish yellow tie that screamed the need for validation.

Standing beside him was a much beefier figure, whose muscular frame bulged out of his leather jacket and whose faded blue tattoos of dragons and snakes with fangs hinted at a violent past.

The third man, who sported a simple fitted tank top and shorts, was smaller than the other two and appeared somewhat out of place. But there was a ferocious intensity in his gaze, and an aura of underlying danger surrounded him. His pasty-white skin contrasted with his yellow-stained teeth, which made him look even more intimidating.

'What are you doing here in this neighbourhood?' bellowed the suited man in Korean, using a venomous tone. 'You're not posting those pictures on TikTok are you? Give me your phone. Now!'

Zoe's heart pounded as the gravity of the situation washed over her. Having grown up in an immigrant Korean household in Canada, she could understand both the thug's words and the implied threat of violence hanging in the air.

Though she did her best to appear composed, a whirlwind of fear and adrenaline swirled within her. Feigning innocence, Zoe responded in English, in a girly voice a few octaves higher than normal and tinged with confusion. 'I'm sorry, I don't understand Korean. I am just visiting from Canada. And anyway, we were just leaving . . .' Playing the role of the clueless tourist had long been one of her favourite get-out-of-jail cards in these types of situations. She hoped at the very least it might buy her a little time.

As Jisun began to plead with the gang in Korean, their glare shifted to her. Zoe's nimble fingers worked swiftly on her phone, desperately trying to erase any evidence that could incriminate them. Her heart raced, and her legs felt like they were going to buckle under her. She knew their lives hung in the balance with each passing second.

Suddenly, the man with the tattoos lunged forward to snatch Zoe's phone. She refused to let it go and braced herself for the confrontation. In a swift motion, he hit her across the side of her face, and Zoe reeled back, stunned and speechless.

Jisun shouted and tried to intervene, but was shoved to the ground like a rag doll. Then she began to scream. The men ignored her.

They closed in on the women, and the one with the yellow teeth stood over the still-screaming Jisun. He smiled grotesquely and reached down to his crotch. Jisun scrunched her eyes shut as tightly as she could. Both women felt their stomachs turn.

Just when it seemed like their fate was sealed, Zoe saw a car emerge from the darkness at the end of the street. It turned towards them. She shouted and waved at it, and the three thugs scattered like startled cockroaches, vanishing into the night.

As the vehicle drew closer, the two women were relieved to see that it was a police car. It pulled up beside them and came to a halt. The two women—still shaking from their encounter—scrambled to their feet and eagerly waited for the car's doors to open, their anticipation building with each passing second.

But that moment never came. After what felt like an eternity, the car pulled away silently.

For a few seconds, the two women stood as if in a trance, bewildered and confused. Zoe was the first to snap out of it. Realizing the three men must still be nearby, she seized Jisun's trembling hand and pulled her young translator along. 'Come on, we have to go,' she said.

Zoe knew that if they could get to the night market area of town just two blocks away, they could find safety in its crowds.

As they ran together, Jisun's voice trembled with confusion. 'Why didn't we get any help from the police? They should have protected us. They were right there.'

'They can't be trusted,' Zoe replied angrily. 'Corruption runs deep in a town like this. We need to get out of here quick, or we won't get out alive. Just keep running! Don't look back.'

Jisun ran several steps in front of Zoe, who turned around and glimpsed the same three ominous figures trailing behind them. Fear coiled within her, but adrenaline propelled her forward.

Despite the women's frantic pace, the three goons kept closing in on them until they were within a few yards. Panic ran through Zoe's veins, her senses heightened to the point of overload as they reached the night market. They ran through narrow pathways between rows of brightly lit food stalls selling dried squid and fish, bright red rice cakes, and fragrant soups full of ivory noodles. Yet still, the men pursued them.

'Run, run, run!' Zoe commanded, her voice infused with sheer terror.

With every ounce of their strength, the two women ran, their legs pumping furiously as they sprinted through narrow alleyways and winding streets.

A sharp pain seized Zoe's right knee, the sort that under normal circumstances would have left her doubled over. But she was running on autopilot now. Her mind had left her body and was watching her from above, detached, as she pushed herself to the limit.

The air crackled with tension, and the echo of their pursuers' enraged shouts spurred them on. Zoe's mind raced, scanning their surroundings for any sign of escape. She spotted a line of taxis parked along the street.

Fate, though, seemed to conspire against them. Just as Zoe reached the taxi line, a thug's hand closed around her shoulder and wrenched her backward. She fought against the powerful grip, her will to survive overriding the pain. Zoe knew she could not win a battle of strength, so she grabbed on to the goon's wrist, stuck out her leg, and twisted her hips around as fast as she could—an old Taekwondo move that had been drilled into her as a little girl.

The thug fell to the ground, landing awkwardly on his buttocks. He looked up at Zoe, completely nonplussed by this woman, half his size, who had left him floored. Zoe and Jisun didn't need another chance. They ran straight to the front of the taxi line, where the first vehicle was about to pull away.

The driver, a middle-aged man with a stern expression, glanced back in astonishment, his eyes widening at the sight before him. Breathless and desperate, Zoe slammed the door shut, her voice filled with urgency as she commanded in broken Korean, 'Go! Drive as fast as you can!'

The car lurched forward, its tires screeching against the pavement as the driver obeyed. In that moment, Zoe didn't know if they would get away or not. Their lives hung in the balance between danger and freedom.

As the car accelerated into the night, leaving their pursuers behind, Zoe and Jisun finally exhaled. It felt like a miracle just to be alive. In that fleeting moment, the traumatized women shared a knowing glance.

They had made it.

Zoe's heart was still pounding in her chest as she turned to Jisun, her voice shaking as she asked, 'Are you okay? Are you hurt?'

'Just leave me alone,' Jisun replied, completely overwhelmed.

'I'm so sorry. I never should have taken you there. It's all my fault.'

As they drove through the dark streets of this small town to their hotel, it dawned on the women that their relationship would never be the same again.

Zoe could see the fear in Jisun's eyes and tried to reassure her. 'We're going to be okay. We're out of there now,' she said, gently rubbing Jisun's back.

Jisun shook her head, tears streaming down her face. 'I thought we were going to die back there. I told you that it was really dangerous. Why didn't you listen to me? I told you. I did. Over and over.'

Zoe felt for Jisun after the trauma she had just endured. 'I'm so sorry,' she said, with genuine regret. 'I didn't realize how dangerous it was going to be. I just wanted to help those girls and capture what's happening in front of those brothels.'

Jisun wiped her tears with the back of her hand. 'I know you meant well, but I can't work with you anymore. I can't put myself in danger like this.'

Zoe nodded and turned to the window. 'I won't ask you to come with me again, Jisun. But please know that what we saw tonight was just a small glimpse of the horrors happening all around us. We can't turn a blind eye to it. My work has the potential to help women like them.'

Jisun closed her eyes, still visibly shaken. 'I'll take the bus home in the morning.'

As the taxi drove through the quiet streets, Zoe felt guilty for putting her young and impressionable translator in harm's way. But she knew her work had only just begun and that she intended to keep going, come what may.

2

Zoe's heart pounded as she stepped into *The Star*'s office for the first time since her story broke. The atmosphere was electric, with the sounds of ringing phones, clattering keys, and chattering colleagues filling the air. The newsroom was a hive of activity. Zoe felt excited, and a little anxious, as she made her way through it. She was looking forward to catching up on the latest stories and getting back to work, but at the same time, she had a feeling that something wasn't quite right.

As she walked, she noticed that her colleagues were pausing their work and turning their attention towards her.

Then suddenly, there was a deafening sound. Every journalist in the newsroom was applauding her. They were cheering, whistling, and banging their pens on the table in recognition of her scoop, a time-honoured tradition reserved for only the very biggest of achievements.

Zoe's face flushed with embarrassment. She had never been one to seek the limelight, and the sudden attention made her feel uneasy. She smiled and waved, trying to maintain her composure, but all she wanted to do was retreat to the safety of her desk.

She was taken aback by the swarm of reporters and editors, all eager to offer their congratulations on her exposé. Everybody agreed that it was an incredible piece of enterprising work that would be a sure-fire winner when awards season came 'round.

Humbled though Zoe was, by their words, she was also secretly thrilled to have her hard work recognized after weeks of risking her life to uncover the truth. One of her colleagues mentioned catching her on ABC News the previous night, marvelling at how she had spoken so candidly and confidently about the harrowing ordeal. Zoe's empathy for the trafficked young girls had shone through in the interview, resonating with millions of viewers worldwide.

After the buzz around her had died down, Zoe headed to her desk and took some time to reflect on her experiences of the past few weeks. Confronting the harsh realities of the modern slave trade had undoubtedly taken a toll on her. She knew that some of it would stay with her forever. That once seen, some things could not be unseen. That there would be quiet moments in her future when it would all come flooding back.

But she also knew her experience paled in comparison to what those girls were forced to endure every day.

She vowed to use the horror she felt at their suffering and turn it into some kind of solution. She would bottle the feeling and use it as fuel. She was determined to never stop fighting for them.

She breathed in deeply, trying to clear her head, and switched on her computer. As soon as it powered up, her boss, Ben, barged into the room unannounced.

The Star's chief editor was a portly man, with a bald head that gleamed in the fluorescent light. He waddled around with an air of superiority that demanded attention. His small eyes, hidden behind thick-rimmed glasses, scanned the room for any sign of vulnerability or weakness that he could exploit.

Ben's voice was a rough and gruff bark, and his words were often laced with a hint of sarcasm that had a way of making even the most hardened reporters feel uneasy. He took pride in his job and believed that he was always teaching his team valuable lessons in journalism. Though he fancied himself to be a gatekeeper of truth, he had a reputation for being a ruthless editor who would twist the facts to suit his own agenda. He had a way of chewing people up and spitting them out without so much as a second thought. Despite this outwardly tough exterior, he showed a softer side when he was dealing with certain reporters, and Zoe was one of them.

Ben slumped into the chair opposite Zoe, letting out a heavy sigh. His hand reached behind to shut the door, providing them with some much-needed privacy. He looked at her for a while before finally speaking up. 'Hey, Zoe. I saw your interview. Great stuff. But you're lucky to be alive. You're pushing yourself too hard. It's only a matter of time before it catches up with you.'

He paused, his face showing a flicker of concern. 'Ever since . . .' he trailed off, not wanting to bring up any painful memories. 'Look, I know you're driven, but you must take some time off. You can't maintain this pace. It's reckless. I know you're pushing yourself to the brink, and I don't want to see you burn out.'

Zoe looked at him, unsure whether she should feel touched or annoyed. Whatever his reputation, Ben genuinely cared about her. But she didn't want to be held back.

'I'm fine. I can handle it. So no need to treat me like a kid,' she said. 'Listen, I have this major lead on a sex trafficking ring operating between Korea and Los Angeles. It's linked to the story I just did. I'm getting closer and closer to the kingpins running these businesses. They're all evil, and I'm going to see them all rot in jail.'

Ben leaned forward and reached towards the bowl of M&M's on Zoe's desk. His fingers quivered as they brushed against the smooth surface of the ceramic bowl. The candy shells rustled against each other as he scooped up a handful of the tiny, colourful chocolates. One by one, he tossed them into his mouth, relishing the burst of sweetness and crunchiness in his mouth. He chewed slowly and let each candy dissolve on his tongue, savouring the pause in the conversation.

His eyes blinked repeatedly as his mind raced, trying to find the right words to say. He felt a bead of sweat trickle down his forehead as he struggled to come up with anything.

'Okay, Zoe,' said Ben, his frustration showing. 'Drop the act. I'm not one of your rivals. I don't want you going OCD on me again. You and I have been there before. It will take a toll on me, on everyone. Take the time off. I'm not asking you. I'm telling you.'

Zoe knew he meant well, but the thought of taking time off made her feel like she was losing control. Her eyes darted around the room, avoiding his gaze as she tried to gather her thoughts.

After a few moments of awkward silence, she spoke up. 'I appreciate your concern, Ben,' she said, trying her best to hide her true emotions. 'But I can handle this. I've been working on this story for months, and I am so close to cracking it wide open. I can't just walk away.'

Ben leaned back in his chair and sighed. 'Zoe, I get it. I do. But you need to take care of yourself first. What good is breaking this story if you burn yourself out?'

Zoe knew Ben had a point; she was pushing herself too hard. But she couldn't give up now. She'd been investigating this scandal for months and had finally uncovered a crucial piece of evidence that could blow the whole thing wide open. The thought of taking time off was unbearable.

She looked away and bit her lip, the words stinging more than she cared to admit. 'I just . . . I can't let this go. Not yet.'

'Listen to me,' Ben said, his tone softening. 'I'm not saying you have to give up on the story. But you need to step back, even if it's just for a little while. Take a breather. Clear your head. Trust me, it'll be worth it in the long run.'

Ben leaned in, eager to gauge the impact of his words.

'Wait a minute,' said Zoe, squinting. She sensed that there was more to this conversation than Ben was letting on. 'What is up with you? You have never told me to put the brakes on anything. What gives?'

'Nothing.'

'Don't lie to me.'

'Okay, there is something else,' Ben said in a hushed voice. 'We've received more of these.' He reached into his blazer pocket and handed over several haphazardly folded notes and letters.

Zoe furrowed her brows. 'More of what?' she asked.

'Threats. Some of them are death threats. Some seemed credible enough for us to call the police,' Ben replied gravely. 'That story caused a stir in Korea. Some of these letters and emails say that you won't leave the country alive if you ever return. Two of them were postmarked Canada.'

Zoe glanced at the letters before handing them back to Ben. 'So what?' she said, doing her best to sound unaffected. 'This isn't the first time I've received intimidating threats. It's part of the job.'

Ben shook his head. 'This is different, Zoe. There's a dozen of them. All it takes is for one of these crazies to act on these threats, and you could be hurt or worse.'

'Listen to this one,' Ben said, reaching for one of the letters and reading it out loud.

You have no business writing stories that disgrace and embarrass Koreans. The topics you write about are shameful. They should be left alone. You don't know what you are talking about. You will need to pay for your disrespect. If I ever see you, I will do the deed myself. Stay out of our country or else.

Zoe stood up from her chair and silently left the room, not wanting Ben to see how shaken she was. She knew that, this time, it was serious.

* * *

Zoe stood in front of the bathroom mirror and stared at her reflection, her eyes swollen and red from crying. She checked her phone, hoping for a message, but there were none.

Winnie, a fellow reporter, entered the bathroom and immediately noticed her friend's distress.

Winnie was one of the warmer characters among *The Star*'s motley crew of journalists. She exuded charm. She was also about a decade older than Zoe and many of the others on staff, which meant that, though she was respected, nobody saw her as competition. People often let down their guard and opened up to her; she was the closest thing the newsroom had to a mother figure.

'Are you okay?' Winnie asked, placing a gentle hand on Zoe's shoulder.

Zoe tried to compose herself. Putting on a brave face, she replied, 'I'm fine—just tired from the jet lag. You know how that feels.'

Winnie sensed there was more.

'You don't seem fine. Is there anything I can do to help?'

Zoe hesitated, before deciding not to confide in her friend.

'Thank you, Winnie. I appreciate your concern. But right now, I just need some space,' Zoe said, trying to maintain her composure.

Winnie looked at Zoe sceptically. Over the years, she had seen many colleagues struggle with PTSD. So many careers and lives ruined. She recognized the look in Zoe's eyes.

'Of course, I understand,' Winnie said, reluctantly. 'But please know that I'm here for you whenever you're ready to talk.'

Zoe nodded gratefully and turned to leave the bathroom. But before she could go, Winnie brought up Jeff. 'Since the two of you broke it off, you've been obsessed with work. We're all worried about you,' she said.

Zoe stopped in her tracks, then slowly turned to face her friend. 'I don't want to talk about Jeff,' Zoe said firmly. 'Please don't bring him up again.'

'I'm sorry, Zoe. It's just that he called me when you were in Korea. He asked about you. He doesn't understand what happened. I think you should call him. He is . . .'

Zoe's heart sank at the mention of Jeff's name. Her fists clenched. She knew that Winnie meant well, but she wasn't ready to talk about him yet. 'I appreciate your concern, but I need time to process everything. Please respect my decision not to talk about Jeff right now.'

Winnie nodded. 'I'm sorry, Zoe. You know I'm here for you no matter what.'

Zoe forced a smile. 'I know, Winnie. Thank you.'

Then she strode out of the room, knocking over Winnie's bag placed on the floor in the process. She swept down the hallway, her heels clicking loudly against the tiled floor. All she could think about was getting out of the office and away from the situation.

She headed straight for the front door, pushed it open with force, and stepped outside, taking in a deep breath of fresh air.

3

Zoe's footsteps echoed through the dimly lit parking garage as she walked towards her car, lost in thought. The sound of her heels hitting the concrete floor was the only noise in the otherwise silent space. As she approached her car, the sudden ringing of her phone startled her out of her thoughts. Fighting the urge to decline the call, she picked up. 'Oh, hi, Mom,' she said, trying to sound cheerful.

'How was your trip?' her mother asked.

'It was good,' Zoe replied slowly, realizing that her mother must not have read any stories of her investigation in Korea. 'I'm happy to be back in Vancouver.'

'Welcome back, and take time to rest,' her mother said. 'Zoe, I just need you to do one thing. Go see your great-aunt, Meera. Her cancer has got worse, and she's in the hospital. She has asked for you.'

Zoe sighed. 'Why me? She never talks to me. Or anyone, for that matter. I just got back, Mom. Do I really have to go?'

'Yes,' her mother insisted. 'She's family. And she's always had a soft spot for you.'

'I have no idea what you're talking about. She hasn't said two words to me in five years.'

'Zoe, please,' her mother said, her voice heavy with emotion. 'Just do it.'

Zoe got into her car and started the engine. She was still uncertain about the visit, but deep down, she knew her mother was right. She had to go see her great-aunt, no matter how hard it might be. After all, family was family.

From as far back as Zoe could recall, Meera had been a regular presence at family gatherings. But while she would always be there, she would remain enigmatic and aloof. Quiet and reserved, she would retreat into a corner, blend into the background, and exchange no more than a few words with everyone.

Over the years, Zoe had made numerous attempts to connect with Meera, seeking to draw her out of her shell, but she had rarely received something more than a 'yes' or 'no' to her questions.

It was as if Meera preferred the solace of her own thoughts and didn't want to be bothered by idle chatter.

For a long time, that made her only more intriguing to Zoe, who often found herself wondering about Meera's inner world. What thoughts and emotions lay hidden behind those silent eyes? What experiences had shaped her into the person she was? These unanswered questions gave Meera an air of mystery.

Eventually, though, Zoe had reluctantly given up trying to engage her. She resigned herself to the fact that Meera was a private person. Wherever her aunt was withdrawing to, perhaps it was the only place she could find comfort.

* * *

Anxiety gripped Zoe as she stood outside Meera's door. The mere thought of seeing her great-aunt locked in a fierce battle against stage four lung cancer was distressing, so she gathered her courage before pushing open the door.

The room greeted her with a hushed stillness, the dim lights casting a soothing calm. The air was heavy with the smell of disinfectant.

Meera was lying on the bed, surrounded by medical equipment. Each beat of her heart was punctuated by the rhythmic beeping of the monitors.

As Zoe approached, Meera's face brightened with an unexpected smile. In a compassionate gesture, Zoe leaned forward to embrace her. To her surprise, the old woman hugged her tightly, as if grateful for the time she had left.

Absent were the usual gifts of flowers and cards; instead, only a few cherished belongings adorned the space—a worn Korean Bible and a crimson notebook, probably revealing snippets of her inner world.

As Zoe stood there, looking at her frail and ailing aunt, memories of their last Christmas dinner flooded her mind. She remembered the warmth of the cosy fireplace, and the delicious aroma of Korean beef, kimchi, and vegetables filling the air. And she remembered Meera, demure as ever. But back then, there had been a certain strength to her aunt's stoicism. The Meera who lay before her now was a shadow of that former self; she had dwindled into a weak and fragile state.

The unrelenting illness had taken its toll on her ninety-two-year-old frame while the gruelling treatments had left her skin pallid and devoid of its once-rosy hue. Zoe felt deep sorrow at seeing Meera so vulnerable. Yet she also saw a glimmer of solace in her aunt's eyes, as if she were relieved the end was drawing near.

Zoe struggled to find the right words to provide comfort to her aunt. She wondered about Meera's mysterious past and the struggles she must have faced throughout her life.

Suddenly, Meera reached out and grabbed Zoe's hand tightly. Zoe was startled by the gesture but allowed her aunt to hold her hand. Meera then picked up the tattered, red notebook from the table beside her bed.

'I'm so proud of you,' Meera said, her voice weak but determined. 'I read your story on the Korean women in the brothels. You know about their conditions. You understand.'

Zoe was taken aback. She had written several detailed articles on sexual slavery in Korea, but she had not expected her aunt to have read any of them. To her, it seemed so out of character. Still, Zoe felt pride and satisfaction knowing that her work had touched someone's life, even in the most unexpected of ways.

Meera thanked Zoe for helping those girls and writing about their tragic lives. She then handed Zoe the journal and made a heartfelt request, 'Please read this. It is written in Korean, but I want you to read it. If you do, you will know. You will see everything. You will understand. No one else does. Read it. Promise me you will read it!'

Zoe looked at the journal. She knew it would be challenging, as she could not read Korean fluently. Yet, she could see the determination in her aunt's eyes and knew that it meant a lot to her.

'Of course, Aunt Meera,' Zoe said, squeezing her hand. 'I'll definitely read it. Thank you so much for sharing this with me. I feel truly honoured.' After a moment of silence, she finally spoke the words she had never said to her great-aunt before, 'I love you.'

Her aunt smiled and nodded in response.

After saying goodbye to her aunt and leaving the hospital room, Zoe hugged the journal tightly. She felt confused about why her great-aunt had given it to her. But she knew she had made a promise, and she wanted to keep it. As she walked towards her car, Zoe's curiosity grew. What secrets would it give up? What effect would it have on her? She put the journal in her bag and drove home, eager to start reading it.

* * *

Having fallen asleep on the couch, Zoe was jolted awake by her phone, its shrill ring piercing the stillness of the hour. After peering at her watch, Zoe knew instinctively that the call could only bring bad news.

She could sense the distress on the other end even before a word was spoken. Her mother's stifled sobs echoed through the phone.

'What's wrong?' Zoe asked.

'She's gone. She's in heaven,' her mother choked out. 'She passed away this morning. I was with her when it happened.'

Zoe's heart sank. Her mind went blank, and the world around her began to seem a little less real. She had seen Meera just the night before—how could she be gone so suddenly?

'Oh my God. I can't believe it,' she whispered softly, her voice trembling with shock and disbelief.

Through her tears, Zoe's mother continued with a heavy heart, 'She passed away peacefully, thank God. And before she left, she took a moment to tell me how grateful she was that you came to see her.'

The weight of those words hit Zoe hard. Emotion overwhelmed her. Her chest tightened as she struggled to hold back tears. She had had no idea that her visit would be the last time she saw Meera.

'I'm so sorry, Mom,' Zoe said, her voice shaking with grief and regret.

The two women stayed on the line for a few more seconds in silence, too upset to speak. Then Zoe's mom hung up.

Zoe's mind drifted back to the journal that Meera had given her. She could almost hear her voice, urging Zoe to read it. Zoe walked over to the coffee maker and set a pot to brew. Then she reached for her bag on the kitchen counter and pulled out the journal, feeling its soft leather cover under her fingertips.

4

Zoe was curled up on her couch, the chilly air nipping at her skin. She had draped a warm wool shawl around herself to keep the cold at bay.

She kept Meera's journal in her lap for a long time before opening it. The cover showed years of wear and tear, and its first page was yellowed with age. She marvelled at the beautiful cursive handwriting. Even just holding it was like going back in time.

Though Zoe had learned Korean from her parents growing up, her skills were rusty. She had to read the words slowly. That allowed her to savour each one. She admired the writer's eloquence and the elegance of her expressions.

The journal began with a statement of purpose:

In these pages, I will document a terrible and unspeakable injustice that many citizens from my home country of Korea have endured, including myself. Though years have passed since these events took place, the memories are as vivid as if the events had occurred yesterday. While once I yearned to bury this painful past and erase it from my mind forever, the demands of justice and truth have compelled me to put pen to paper.

The courage displayed by remarkable women like Kim Hak-sun, the first to bear witness, and others like Lee Yong-soo, Grandma Gil Won-ok, and Kim Soon-duk, has been an unending source of inspiration for me. While I did not in life possess that same bravery, I would like in death to share my story.

The pages that follow document my journey as a young girl, how I was forced into a cruel reality, and, ultimately, how I survived a crime against humanity.

I dedicate this account to my family and hope it sheds light on my distant and reclusive nature. I ask them, please forgive me if this account brings shame upon us. And forgive me for the walls I built around myself; they were my only refuge from the memories.

With deep love and affection,

M

As Zoe read on, a lump formed in her throat. Meera's writing was simply breathtaking. Her words flowed calmly like a river but had the power of a waterfall. She didn't understand what they meant but was intrigued enough to read on.

The Japanese occupation of Korea commenced in 1910 and endured until 1945, bringing profound and far-reaching changes for the Korean people, including my own family. Korea, once a proud and strong sovereign nation, found itself transformed into a colony under the iron fist of the Japanese Empire.

Japanese rule in Korea was characterized by a relentless pursuit of assimilation, a ruthless erasure of Korean national identity, and the violent suppression of any signs of resistance. The Japanese authorities imposed their language, customs, and traditions upon the Korean people, while all banning expressions of the local culture.

The colonial occupation exploited Korea economically, as Japan seized our resources for its own gains. Countless

Koreans were forced to labour in Japanese mines, factories, and plantations, and join the army. In effect, we became slaves in our homeland. Tragically, this brutal oppression befell my own family. My brother was kidnapped from our home and forced to serve as a soldier in the Japanese army during the war. This was the first of many traumatic experiences endured by my family and me. Years later, I learned that he had died fighting for a country that was not his own, for a cause he did not agree with.

The Japanese implemented land reforms that dispossessed Korean farmers of their ancestral lands, fuelling poverty and landlessness. My father, a Korean government administrator, managed to save our family's homestead from this fate by using his connections and bribing the Japanese officials, but few of our neighbours were so fortunate. Many lost everything they held dear.

Even religion was not sacred to the Japanese. They imposed their Shintoism while suppressing Korean practices and all other religions. Churches, temples, and shrines that had been an integral part of Korean religious life for centuries were destroyed and desecrated. My mother, a devout Christian, was so deeply offended by this forced imposition of Shintoism, which went against everything she believed in, that it drove her to an early death.

Intent on controlling every aspect of society from the government to the education system, the Japanese authorities silenced any dissenting voices among the Korean population. Freedom of speech and assembly were stifled, and any criticism of the Japanese regime was met with a demonstration of grotesque brutality.

The education system became a tool to instil loyalty to Japan and its Emperor while undermining or omitting Korean history and heritage. As a result, I did not learn about my own heritage and history until long after the occupation had ended.

As the occupation persisted, resentment and resistance swelled among Koreans, giving rise to protests, uprisings, *and independence movements. The watershed March 1st Movement in 1919 saw Koreans across the nation uniting to advocate for independence and civil rights. Sadly, the Japanese authorities brutally suppressed these movements, executing and imprisoning the leaders and many others. Several of my relatives perished in this strife. Countless Koreans migrated overseas.*

Even long after Japan's defeat in World War II, the scars of its occupation on the local populace continued to shape Korea.

I am giving you this historical context because it would be impossible to grasp the essence of my story without it. I often find myself contemplating what my life might have been like had I grown up in a different time—a time where possibilities and opportunities were not shackled by oppression.

Would I have had the chance to attend school, nurture my mind, and pursue knowledge? Could I have followed my passion to become a university professor, imparting wisdom to eager young minds? Might I have experienced the joys of marriage and parenthood, basking in the love of a family I would cherish? These dreams seem to belong to others, as the harsh circumstances of that period denied me such opportunities.

To this day, my heart aches with the weight of unfulfilled promises and destiny, yet I have not let it crush my spirit entirely.

Instead, I hope that, by educating others to understand and acknowledge this history, we can pave the way for a future where such oppression and suffering is replaced by freedom, equality, and prosperity.

My dreams proved elusive during my own life, but I still cling to the belief that the generations to come might yet set them free. That our future will not be held in chains by our troubled past; and that we will not be doomed to repeat our history by failing to learn from it.

Zoe delicately turned the page of the journal, her fingers feeling the rough edges of the paper as she did so. Her eyes scanned the top of the page, looking for the date, and as they landed on 'November 10, 1959', she shuddered.

The journal weighed heavily in her hands. Every page was divided into neat sections, with each entry marked by a date.

Zoe was drawn to the words on the page. She became so engrossed in her great-aunt's story that she forgot about her own surroundings. With every sentence, Zoe felt closer to Meera, learning her thoughts and experiencing her emotions.

After all those years, her distant relative was finally beginning to give up her secrets.

I can still recall with great detail the day I met Masuki, even though it was many years ago. It was a beautiful summer day, and I had decided to spend my afternoon at the local library. As I was engrossed in a book, I heard a loud thud that made me look up. To my surprise, a young Japanese boy had dropped a handful of books on the floor. I had seen this boy before, but this was the first time I had paid him attention.

The commotion caught everyone's attention, and he appeared shy and embarrassed. I felt the urge to help him pick up the books, which I did. As we gathered the books, I couldn't help but notice his smooth skin, unkempt hair, and bright, expressive eyes that shone with intelligence. Despite his shy demeanour, there was something about him that made him stand out from the other boys in town. He radiated kindness, and I felt drawn to him.

After helping him, I returned to my seat, but for some reason, I found myself repeatedly looking over in his direction.

While I sat there, Masuki put the books on the table and continued to steal glances at me now and then. His curious stares made me feel both self-conscious and intrigued. It was the first time a boy had shown any interest in me, and I felt like I was in a daze. With my thick glasses and plain dresses, I didn't think I was attractive to anyone, but Masuki seemed genuinely interested in me.

The library was silent, but our brief encounter had created a connection between us. As I went back to my book, I couldn't help but think about him and how he had made me feel. I had never met anyone like him before and was eager to get to know him better.

Before leaving, I did something that was unheard of at the time: I approached him. As a young Korean girl of thirteen, it was taboo for me to talk to a teenage Japanese boy, given the hatred between our countries during the occupation. But I didn't feel any animosity toward Masuki. I felt sorry for him since he always looked so lonely whenever I saw him in the library.

I asked him about the books he was reading, and we struck up a conversation that lasted for hours. I was surprised to learn that he loved history and science. He even had a Korean book, which impressed me since it was forbidden for the Japanese to speak or read Korean back then. But Masuki wasn't like other Japanese boys. He was fluent in both Japanese and Korean, and was even studying English under the Canadian missionaries.

We talked about everything that day, from our favourite authors to our dreams for the future.

During our conversation, I also asked him about the reason behind his stay in Korea, but he seemed hesitant to answer. His gaze became distant, and he seemed lost in thought for a moment. After repeating the question, his head hung low as he finally confessed in a soft voice that his father was the Japanese provincial governor. Although his confession surprised me, I didn't want to dwell on the topic and quickly changed the subject.

For the rest of that day, we talked about literature and different languages, and I could sense that Masuki had a genuine interest in learning more. As we continued to chat, he confided in me that he didn't have many friends and spent most of his time at the library reading and studying.

I knew then that our connection was special. And from that day on, we did indeed become inseparable friends.

What I didn't know was that fate had a twist in store for us, one that would change the course of our lives forever.

Zoe stopped reading. Something about this text triggered a memory and she felt a sudden rush of familiarity. As she stared at the journal, she was taken back to the day she met her ex-boyfriend, Jeff.

Zoe remembered flying down the treacherous trail on her mountain bike. Her eyes darted around, anticipating the next obstacle as she weaved through the rocky terrain. Just as she thought she had made it past a pile of sharp rocks, her front tire burst, forcing her into a sudden swerve to miss a tree. She went tumbling down and her bike skidded off to the side of the path. Bruised and shaken, though not seriously hurt, she picked herself up and dusted herself off. Then she inspected the damage to her beloved bike. She desperately hoped it was not beyond repair.

Suddenly, the sound of wheels whizzing towards her made her jump. She looked up to see another biker come barrelling around the corner at breakneck speed, heading straight towards her. He swerved at the last second and crashed through the shrubbery at the side of the trail.

Zoe heard a series of thuds and winced involuntarily as her mind filled in the gaps. Treading gingerly, she followed a trail of broken branches and the occasional piece of ripped clothing to where the biker was sitting in a daze, shaking his head.

Feeling guilty, she began to apologize profusely to the burly figure before her, asking if he was okay.

But the biker seemed unfazed by the crash. In fact, he seemed almost happy to see her. 'Hi. I'm Jeff,' he said, with a broad smile as he brushed down his clothes, insisting that he was fine and that it was just a scratch. He suggested that they find a safer spot to fix their bikes before another accident happened.

Zoe was struck by his kindness and understanding; she had caused him to crash, ruining his bike, yet here he was, wanting to be friends.

He inspected Zoe's blown tire and insisted on escorting her 'back to civilization'. She happily agreed.

As they began walking through the dense forest, he joked about the dangers. 'Lions, tigers, and bears, oh my!' he said, delighting Zoe with a quote from one of her favourite tales, *The Wizard of Oz*. Zoe found that she couldn't help but smile at his zany sense of humour and infectious enthusiasm, and realized that she was attracted to him.

Of course, it helped that Jeff was well over six feet tall with broad shoulders and the physique of an athlete. Zoe could feel her eyes being drawn to his striking good looks. His expressive, kind eyes exuded a twinkling warmth that mirrored his amiable nature, while his wavy salt-and-pepper hair, cut short, added a touch of boyishness to his appearance.

But it wasn't just his good looks that had Zoe smitten. Jeff's gentle spirit radiated an air of quiet confidence and dignity. Zoe was impressed with his patience and chivalry, as they trudged through the rough terrain on a journey that, by foot, would probably take them till nightfall. She felt grateful to be in this situation with someone like him—how different it might have been with someone else—and found herself not wanting their walk together to end.

That day, Zoe sensed this chance encounter might become one of those life-changing moments she would never forget.

She felt exhilarated, and alive, and happier than she had been in a very long time.

Zoe shook her head and snapped back to the present. Her emotions were in turmoil. Her chest felt squeezed as she closed the worn journal that lay in her lap. For several minutes, she paced back and forth on the living room rug to release her nervous energy.

Then she reached for her car keys. There was only one place she knew that could ease her troubled mind—the winding roads that led up to the serene mountainside. Over the years, this scenic route had become her sanctuary, offering solace when life's burdens became too much to bear. This day was no exception, but try as she might, she couldn't keep thoughts of Jeff at bay.

For more than two years, Jeff had been an integral part of Zoe's life, a steadfast companion who shared her passion for exploration. Together, they embarked on countless adventures: hiking through rugged trails, taking long drives into the unknown, or simply savouring each other's company over a cup of coffee. They were inseparable, and their love seemed destined to last forever.

Yet, as the world beckoned with opportunities, Zoe had found herself at a crossroads. As a seasoned journalist, she yearned to achieve great things, but her career had plateaued, leaving her bored. Zoe had tied her identity to her performance at work, and she knew it. It was how her parents had raised her—the traditional Korean way.

Frustration and self-judgment gnawed at her, and she searched for someone or something to blame. Sadly, Jeff fell into the line of fire. She started feeling that he was holding her back. She resented his constant pleas for her to abandon dangerous investigative stories and watched bitterly as the chasm between them grew. Increasingly, their conversations were punctuated with awkward silences and intense arguments.

After months of heated disputes, Zoe reached a breaking point and ended the relationship. She had been struggling with feelings of failure and a low sense of self-worth, and convinced herself that to get out of her headspace, she had to remove all distractions to focus on her work and reach the top of her industry. She felt born to make a difference yet wasn't sure how that would come about. *Jeff had to be jettisoned*, she told herself. And once Zoe set her mind on a path, she found it hard to turn back, even if it meant denying her true feelings.

That was a few months ago now. Since then, Zoe had often tried to convince herself that she had done the right thing, yet thoughts of Jeff continued to creep into her mind. This was one of those times.

As Zoe drove up the winding mountain road, her heart ached with the realization that their once-strong bond had been sacrificed at the altar of her career, because of her uncompromising ego. She longed for the days when they would talk for hours on end, sharing their experiences, hopes, and dreams.

As she reached the summit of the mountain, Zoe parked her car and stepped out, taking in the view of the city below. A breeze washed over her, and she breathed in the cool air.

She sat down on a park bench and gazed into the dazzling blue sky. The ocean, mountains, and skyscrapers in various hues dotted the landscape. Zoe knew how privileged she was. She was well-aware that many people struggled with poverty, ill health, and far greater hardships. She scolded herself for thinking of her own problems and said a prayer for those less fortunate.

Then her thoughts drifted to her late great-aunt Meera, who had lived a solitary life without experiencing the joys of marriage, children, and grandchildren.

Doing so made Zoe's feelings of guilt and emptiness return, even though she knew such thoughts were not productive and even self-indulgent.

Suddenly, she felt a flicker of resolve within her. She had been wallowing in her emotions for far too long, she thought. It was time to take control of her life again. She rose from the bench and filled her lungs.

She felt ready to push through her insecurities and neurotic tendencies and find a way back to the person she truly was. It was as if she had found her second wind, to face the world.

This place is truly special, Zoe thought to herself as she walked back to her car. It had a habit of inspiring answers just when she needed them.

* * *

The moment Zoe stepped into her home that evening, she kicked off her shoes and headed straight to the living room. Her eyes were fixed on the faded journal on the coffee table. As she sat down on the soft, plush couch, she picked up the book and began to read.

Although reading in Korean proved to be a slow and challenging process for her, it only heightened her curiosity and eagerness. Each page was filled with the most intimate details of Meera's life, her thoughts, and her feelings.

As Zoe turned each page, a story of drama, secrets, and love unfolded before her. But amongst the various entries, one leapt from the page. It was the day when Meera and Masuki's relationship turned serious. The entry was written in such detail that Zoe could almost feel the warmth of the sun on her face and the wind in her hair, as if she were there, witnessing the moment herself.

She was happy for the two of them and eagerly continued reading, lost in the world of Meera's journal.

November 15, 1943

On this beautiful day, I was excitedly waiting for Masuki, who had invited me to meet him at the park to celebrate my birthday. It was a different experience for me as we had only met at the library before. He had even given me directions to a secluded spot behind the old water fountain, which was a bit scary but thrilling at the same time.

It was taboo for young people to meet like this, and the fact that he was Japanese and I was Korean made it even more unacceptable.

We had never taken such a daring step before.

As the designated time for our rendezvous approached, my heart began to beat faster in anticipation. I couldn't wait to see him, but at the same time, I was unsure about what to do if he didn't show up. Despite the uncertainty, I waited patiently, hoping that he would arrive soon.

It was a long wait, but he did finally arrive. I could see the beads of sweat on his forehead and the heaving of his chest as he caught his breath. Despite his exhaustion, his face lit up with a huge smile as he walked towards me. I extended my hand to greet him, a gesture that had become familiar between us during our numerous trips to the library together.

My emotions were running high, and I could barely contain myself. I felt like jumping into his arms, but I restrained myself and settled for a warm embrace instead. As I held him, I knew without a doubt that I was in love with him. We had known each other for almost a year, but in that fleeting moment of tenderness, I sensed he felt the same way about me too.

Our hearts beat as one against each other's chests, and we held each other tightly like we never wanted to let go. After a while, we reluctantly pulled away, both of us feeling a little awkward. We had just crossed into new territory, uncharted waters. We sat down beside each other, lost in our own thoughts, savouring the moment, and trying to make sense of it all.

As he handed me the small, beautifully wrapped package from his bag, my heart skipped a beat. I wondered what it was. As I unwrapped the package, I discovered a pen, but it was not just any pen. It was one of those expensive ones that I had once seen in the city centre—one made in Japan. The pen was exquisite, and it was evident how much thought and care he had put into choosing it.

He knew of my passion for writing, and along with the pen, he gave me a notebook, encouraging me to start writing and expressing myself. I was overwhelmed with emotion, and tears streamed down my face. It was an incredibly special gift, from the boy I loved. My heart overflowed with affection.

That day, we held hands and whispered intimate things to each other—words shared between people in love. We didn't need to vocalize those three words; we felt them deep within our hearts.

We had crossed the threshold into a new place, where 'you and I' became 'we'. From that point on, we met at our special spot at least once a week. Some days, we would just sit in silence, my head resting on his shoulder or our hands intertwined. It was always innocent, yet it meant everything to me. He was my one and only, and I knew I loved him. I yearned to spend my life with him, to become his wife.

We had discussed this once before. I had asked him about his aspirations in life, and he had described his dream of becoming a university professor. He spoke of the school that he wished to teach at, the house that he wanted to live in, and more. However, *when he had failed to mention me, I had turned away, feeling disheartened.*

Observing my reaction, he had smiled, taken my hand in his, and said, 'When this war is over, you and I will run away to a place where we can always be together. There, we will start our life.' The mere thought of it warmed my heart. It was clear that he had thought about our future together, and it made me love him even more.

* * *

After several hours, Zoe was still completely absorbed in Meera's journal that lay open in front of her. The yellowing pages of the manuscript exuded a musty smell, blending with the sweet fragrance of the lavender candle that flickered softly on the coffee table. She paused and then lingered at the top of the page—'December 8, 1943'. She tried to imagine what life would have been like back then, as Meera's words transported her to a different era.

The sun had just risen, casting a warm glow on the tranquil Saturday morning. The kitchen was filled with the aroma of freshly cooked food and the sound of utensils clinking against pots and pans. Our trusty servant was bustling around, expertly preparing a delicious breakfast spread that included steaming hot rice, a savoury soup, and perfectly grilled fish.

Mother was setting the table with care, placing plates, glasses, and silverware in their proper places. The kitchen was abuzz with activity, as we all eagerly awaited the scrumptious meal that was about to be served.

The atmosphere was tense as my younger siblings were huddled together, whispering about the Japanese. My sister, who was always outspoken, kept insisting that they were evil devils, but I disagreed, telling her that not all Japanese people were bad. I told my family about Masuki and how he was a good person, but my sister would have none of it.

Suddenly, my mother interjected, her voice low and serious. She warned us not to speak about 'those people', saying that the walls had ears and that great troubles would find us if we said the wrong thing to the wrong person. I felt frustrated with my mother's reaction and asked her about our father's whereabouts.

He had left seven months earlier to search for my brother, Jun-Ho, who was taken away by Japanese soldiers during the war. We had no idea where Jun-Ho was, but my mother seemed sure that he would return soon. She urged us all to pray for his safe return.

As we sat there, I felt a deep sense of unease. The war had taken its toll on our family, and the uncertainty of not knowing where our loved ones were was almost unbearable. My mother was visibly stressed, and there was no conversation. Being the eldest, I helped keep my younger siblings under control when they got unruly.

Yet, despite all of this, we remained hopeful and prayed that, one day, we would all be reunited again.

Soon, the sun was shining brightly, and the birds were chirping merrily in the trees. I eagerly awaited Masuki to come and visit me.

I had promised to meet him at the library, but my mother had not let me go. I had begged her, but she had refused, saying that it was too dangerous. She had even warned us not to leave the yard since there were many Japanese soldiers passing through our village. She had heard that some of them were harassing young girls, and she was worried for our safety.

I was disappointed because I wanted to see Masuki so badly. Fortunately, later in the day, Masuki came to the gate in front of our house. I was thrilled to see him, but at the same time,

I felt guilty for breaking my mother's rule. When he arrived, I explained the situation, and he understood.

We both cherished spending time together, and I could sense the disappointment in his eyes. As our relationship grew, we always tried to find time to be together as much as possible.

I asked him if his father had any information about my brother, but unfortunately, he didn't. We talked about many things, and I showed him the drawings I had made. Through the gate, Masuki handed me a small bouquet of wildflowers that he had picked from the nearby field. In return, I handed him a small, silver butterfly hairpin with three glass stones. It was a gift from my father, but I wanted him to have it now.

Masuki gazed at the pin as if it were his most precious possession, and I told him I would always be his little butterfly. He asked me what that meant, and I told him he would have to discover it for himself.

Then my mother called me from inside the house, and I had to go. I hurried inside, hiding the flowers behind my back. Masuki watched me leave, briefly glancing at the hairpin in his hand . . .

I felt a pang of sadness as I closed the door. But I also felt warmth in my heart, knowing we had a special bond that would never be broken.

As she was reading, Zoe felt a vibration in her pocket. It was a new email from Jeff. She paused for a moment, contemplating whether to check it or not. Despite her reservations, she decided to see what he had to say.

Dear Boo,

I hope this email finds you well. I've been thinking about you a lot lately, and I truly miss us together. It would mean the world to me if we could take some time to work things out.

Today, while I was at Newington Pizza, memories of the good times we had together came rushing back. It made me realize how much I hold dear those moments with you. So, I want to invite you to join me for a relaxed evening over a delicious sausage pizza. We can talk and figure out a plan that works for both of us.

I believe in us, Boo. I believe we're right for each other, and I sincerely hope you feel the same way. Please don't shut me out; give us a chance to mend things. I'll do whatever it takes to regain your trust and support you in all aspects of your life, including your job, which I promise not to bring up again.

Could you find it in your heart to give me that chance? Your response would mean a lot to me, even if it's just a few words. I miss you, and I want nothing more than to get back with you again. Remember all those fun times we had mountain biking together? I'd love to do that again.

Eagerly waiting for your response.

With all my love,
Jeff

She read the message twice. Despite the faint sense of satisfaction that he still cared, she hesitated to reply and ultimately swiped her finger over the delete button. His message disappeared.

Her mind buzzing with troubling thoughts, she made her way towards the kitchen and opened the refrigerator. The cool air hit her face, and she felt an immediate sense of relief. Her eyes scanned the shelves, searching for something to take the edge off things and spotted a bottle of her favourite red wine.

She grabbed at it excitedly and poured herself a generous amount, watching the crimson liquid swirl and rise in the glass. The rich aroma filled her nostrils as she took a sip, savouring the blend of flavours on her tongue. She turned on some soft music to play in the background.

Finally, she felt relaxed and content once more. She found herself enjoying the solitude.

Glass of wine in hand, she made her way back to her reading spot on the couch, where she could lose herself in the journal and forget all her troubles, at least for a little while.

5

Zoe slowly picked up her ringing phone, feeling groggy from the full bottle of wine she had drunk the night before.

She had fallen asleep on top of her blanket in bed in her work clothes, and the sudden ringing made her head throb. Still, even in her dazed state she could sense the urgency in Winnie's voice.

'Hey, it's me,' Winnie said. 'I've been trying to reach you all morning. Where are you?' Zoe checked and saw that she had missed several calls from Winnie and others. She felt a pang of guilt and worry.

'Oh no, what time is it?' she asked, trying to collect herself.

'It's almost 9 a.m.,' Winnie replied. 'Our staff meeting is about to start. Are you on your way?'

Zoe's heart sank as she realized she had overslept and was now running late for work. She jumped off her bed, trying to shake off the remnants of her hangover, and told Winnie she would be there as soon as possible.

'I'll be there in thirty minutes. This story is huge. I need to be at that meeting to pitch it. Tell them to wait for me, please. Don't let them start without me.'

She hung up without saying goodbye, then put her head in her hands and sighed.

She allowed herself only this brief moment to catch her breath, then scurried to her closet to pick out a new outfit.

However, her gaze kept drifting towards the journal on her nightstand. *What other secrets did it hold?* she wondered. She shook her head. *Now was no time to dither!* She grabbed the journal and stashed it in her bag before rushing out the door.

* * *

Zoe burst into *The Star*'s main conference room, her eyes wide with panic. The sudden commotion caught the attention of everyone present, and she could sense her colleagues staring at her as she made her way towards the only empty chair in the room. The chair was two seats away from Ben, the editor-in-chief.

The conference room was the heart of their small newspaper, and it hummed with creative energy every week when about twenty passionate souls gathered for their meeting.

The air was thick with the scent of freshly printed newspapers, and the walls were lined with inspiring quotes and headlines from past issues.

Writers, reporters, photographers, and editors, each with a pressing, unique story to tell, filled the space with anticipation as they waited for their chance to pitch their ideas to the chief.

Some of the journalists had their pitching techniques down to a fine art, talking up every idea as it were a shoo-in for a Pulitzer. They would wave their arms, grandstand with buzzy phrases about speaking truth to power, and wax lyrical about scurrilous—and mostly unprintable—rumours they had heard from their 'sources'. Others seemed content to absorb the conversation quietly, scribbling away at their notepads, asking clever-sounding questions and nodding their heads as they tried to impress the chief with their powers of observation.

Ben had been at this game long enough to see through both approaches. He could tell the gaps in a story before most journalists had finished clearing their throats. After decades in the game, not much impressed him anymore.

Still, he loved the thrill of the chase: He loved being at the centre of the action, setting the agenda and choosing what people read over their breakfast each morning, and loved being able to make or break the careers of his staff. Within this room, the editor-in-chief was a demi-god and everybody else a bootlicker. *Well, almost everybody. That Zoe had potential,* he conceded, *even if she could be a pain in the ass sometimes. Not bad looking either*, Ben mused, *but was the success going to her head?* Perhaps he needed to take her down a peg, for her own good.

'I see you have finally decided to join us,' Ben said with a smirk to Zoe. 'In your absence, we already discussed your story idea. Sadly, it was shot down. Look, the sex trafficking stories were great,' he added. 'It's a big issue and it's good to address it—oh, and great traffic, by the way. We all saw those figures. But we don't want to keep beating the same drum or we'll lose the audience. There are plenty of topics more critical to local readers right now, like homelessness in Vancouver and drug addiction. You can't walk down a street in Chinatown these days without either being asked for change or seeing someone light up a crack pipe. And the whole place smells like a homeless person's ass. What goddamn use is it having such a highly paid police force if we're just letting people spark up on the streets? Now *that's* what we should be investigating. Readers want to know.'

Zoe felt her blood boil at Ben's dismissive tone. She had worked tirelessly on her sex trafficking follow-up and knew that the link to Los Angeles which she was exploring was a potentially explosive development that gave an-already-compelling foreign story a North American link. It would interest any audience. Yet here was Ben, telling her to drop it and move on to something else. It wasn't going to happen.

'I already told you that I'm neck-deep in establishing a link between the trafficking in Korea and Los Angeles,' Zoe shouted, her finger pointed defiantly at her boss. 'Before I left for Korea, you said I could follow this lead. You know it's a very hot topic. I'm not yet done with the series. There's so much more corruption and collusion to uncover.'

Ben didn't even blink an eye at her outburst.

'I changed my mind,' he confessed casually.

This was not the first time they had had this kind of exchange. In fact, it had almost become a regular occurrence between the two of them—a fact that was picked up on by other staff members, as Ben would not have tolerated being challenged so brazenly by any other writer or editor.

'That story has been done a dozen times,' Ben continued. 'People want something new. Let's move on.'

Zoe could feel her anger rising with each word that came out of Ben's mouth. 'We discussed this. I need to go to Los Angeles to meet with those Asian, including Korean, victims. I already scheduled the visit. That was the agreed plan. You can't just change it at the last minute like this. It's not fair. Sorry, but I'm going.'

'No way,' Ben replied, his eyes scanning a document. 'I already told you, I need you to focus on other stories. You were away for weeks, this time in Korea. I don't have that kind of budget anymore.'

'I'm not postponing this trip,' Zoe said, her voice rising. 'It took me weeks to set it up. I won't get another chance.'

'I said no!' Ben exploded, struggling to contain his temper. He looked around, daring anybody to respond, before lowering his voice into a calmer tone. 'And it isn't about postponing. It's about cancelling. Just give it up, Zoe. It's time to move on.'

Zoe opened her mouth to argue but then stopped herself. She was tired of fighting with Ben, tired of being shut down every time she tried to do something important. Maybe it was time to take a break.

'Then I'll . . .' Zoe started but did not finish her statement. The entire room waited to see what she'd say in response. They were expecting the fight to continue. 'Okay, you win,' she surrendered. 'But you told me I should take some leave. So, I am going to take some leave. You are right, I need a break. The stress is really taking a toll on me.'

Zoe stood up abruptly, causing her chair to screech against the wooden floor. She stormed out of the room, her eyes blazing with frustration and anger. She despised it when anyone tried to control her activities. She had a deep-rooted need to be in control of her own life and decisions, and the mere suggestion of someone else dictating her actions was enough to set her off.

As she made her way out of the building, Winnie followed her.

'Zoe, come on. I know what you're planning to do,' her friend said, her voice gentle.

Zoe stopped in her tracks, turning to face her colleague. 'What am I planning to do?'

'You can't just go off on your own like that. You need to stop these crusades of yours. If you keep doing this, you'll get fired. Please don't push your luck. Ben likes you because you're charming and bubbly, and because you're his favourite, you're untouchable. But that can easily change!' Winnie said, her voice laced with concern.

'I'm tired of this hick-town paper,' Zoe said, her voice trembling with emotion. 'To do enterprising journalism, we have to get out there and push the envelope. Ben is always saying no to things we already agreed on. He can go to hell for all I care!'

'Just take a day or two off. You are under a lot of stress from that last trip. I'll talk to Ben. Can you take some time off for me? Please? Don't go to LA. Just don't.'

Zoe stopped to think.

'You're a good friend. I really appreciate you. I'll wait a few days.'

* * *

Zoe sat huddled in the nook of her favourite coffee shop, her eyes scanning the faded pages of Meera's journal. The warm aroma of freshly brewed coffee mingled with the sound of pop music playing in the background. Zoe's fingers traced the faded ink markings on the page as she read Meera's thoughts and emotions, written in her familiar cursive style. She breathed in and closed her eyes, allowing herself to be transported to a world far removed from the chaos of her own life. The journal was a source of comfort for Zoe, providing a respite from the rage she still felt from her disastrous meeting with Ben.

The soft glow of the coffee shop's lights created a warm and soothing ambience as she savoured the bitter taste of the black coffee, and the hum of the chatter around her faded into the background.

December 14, 1943

On this fateful Thursday morning, my life changed forever. Abruptly awoken by a loud knock on the door at dawn, my mother opened it to find two soldiers who shoved her aside and barged into our house.

In the midst of the chaos, one of the Japanese soldiers barked out something in their native tongue. Though I couldn't understand what he was saying, the tone of his voice was unmistakably harsh and commanding, sending shivers down my spine. Suddenly, the other soldier demanded in Korean, 'Where is the girl, Meera? Bring her to us now.' Without hesitating, he and the other soldier began searching for me.

My heart leapt into my throat as I realized with a sickening feeling that they were referring to me and that they were intent on finding me at all costs. Fear and panic coursed through me, making it hard to think or move as I frantically searched for a place to hide. I desperately wanted to retreat to the safety of my room, but I knew there was simply no time. Instead, I ran into my sister's room and closed the door.

A few minutes later, one of the men pushed the door open and walked up to me. Without warning, he seized my arm and dragged me towards the front door and then out of the house. My mother tried to stop them, pleading for my release, but they ignored her desperate cries.

As we made our way through the garden, my mother continued to beg them, tears streaming down her face. She pleaded with them to wait for my father, who was due to return in a day or so. But the soldiers were relentless, showing no mercy or compassion. One of them pushed my mother to the ground, leaving her lying in the mud. Her cries of desperation and terror mingled with my anguished cries as I was taken away and separated from my family.

The Japanese soldiers said that all men and women must work, that the country was at war, and that everyone must follow the National Mobilization Law's Voluntary Labour Corps. But what they forced upon us was far from voluntary. It was a nightmare that would haunt me forever.

On that godforsaken day in 1943, when the war was at its height, I was taken along with nine other Korean captives on a perilous journey to Shanghai.

For two gruelling weeks, we took every truck, train, and boat that could get us closer to the city, sometimes forging ahead on foot, all the while facing the ever-present threat of attacks and bombings.

When we eventually arrived at a military base on the outskirts of Shanghai, we were thrown into a living hell, forced to cook for Japanese soldiers from dawn till dusk, without a moment of respite. We were treated like slaves, and the mere thought of speaking to anyone or even looking at them was enough to earn us a beating with a stick. Fear gripped us all, and we were reduced to silent, trembling shells of our former selves.

Every few nights, an officer would come and select a girl, or sometimes more than one, and they would be taken away forcefully. No one knew what happened to them or where they went.

Night after night, I died a little more inside, wishing for a way to escape. But there seemed to be no way out as soldiers patrolled the area, watching our every move.

This was just the beginning of my suffering, and I was already losing my sense of self—my identity as a carefree daughter, sister, and young woman. I was losing my humanity. I longed to be free, to be with my family again. I began to daydream of my parents, my family, and Masuki. These memories were all that kept me going.

The road ahead seemed bleak. This was my fate now, a reality that no one should ever have to endure.

Throughout her journal, Meera described the day-to-day struggles and harsh treatment that she and the other Korean women were subjected to, explaining that she was just one among hundreds of thousands of Koreans and other nationalities who were forcibly taken to Japan and Japanese-occupied territories.

The women endured abysmal conditions: housed in cramped, unsanitary barracks and forced to work long hours with little rest. Often, they were forced to undertake dangerous tasks, with little regard for their health and safety.

One duty involved cleaning the uniforms that fallen Japanese soldiers had been wearing. The uniforms stank of death and disease, and often, the cleaners would fall prey to infections.

Those deemed not to be working hard enough were vulnerable to physical and psychological abuse by their Japanese overseers, enduring harsh treatment, including beatings, verbal abuse, and harassment. The Koreans were treated as inferior by the Japanese.

Despite the challenging circumstances, many of the women showed resilience and strength. Some engaged in acts of resistance, such as sabotage or work slowdowns, to protest their treatment. This solidarity played a crucial role in their ability to cope with their hardships. But the more they rebelled, the more their captors punished them. One woman was shot in the head, another was disembowelled.

Zoe often winced and sometimes had to put the journal down whenever she read of the wicked treatment and the racist slurs from the Japanese soldiers. They called the Korean women 'chosen pi' or public toilets.

Zoe paused to ponder what she had just read. She was struck by the stark contrast between her own struggles and those of her great-aunt. Meera had been enslaved by the Japanese soldiers, while Zoe's biggest problems were a stubborn boss and a persistent ex-boyfriend.

Zoe read on, captivated by the vivid descriptions of Meera's confinement. As the story unfolded, she learned more about the hardships these women faced, the sacrifices they made, and the resilience they showed in the face of adversity.

She began to feel a sense of gratitude for the life she had. She realized how fortunate she was to have the freedom to choose her own path in life, to pursue her dreams, and to make her own decisions. She also recognized the importance of learning about her family's roots and honouring those that came before her. As much as reading Meera's diary made Zoe feel uncomfortable, it inspired her to be a power for good in the world, to create a better future for generations to come, and to never forget the hardships that her ancestors had faced.

* * *

Zoe was going about her day when suddenly her mobile phone began to ring. She saw her mother's name flashing on the screen and answered the call.

'Hey, Mom, how are you doing?' she asked, eager to hear her mother's voice. She was met with a tense and choked up voice on the other end of the line.

'Zoe, I need you to come to the funeral parlour,' her mother said in a trembling voice, 'I don't want to go there alone.' Zoe felt a lump form in her throat. She knew how difficult this must be for her mother, and she wanted to do everything she could to support her. She tried to keep her voice steady as she responded, 'I'll be there as soon as I can, Mom.'

With a heavy heart, Zoe gathered her things and set out to the funeral home where her mother was making arrangements. As she made her way there, she thought about all the memories they had of great-aunt Meera. She was determined to be there for her mother, despite her own sadness. She knew it was the most important thing to do at the moment.

* * *

As Zoe stood beside her mother, she fidgeted with the hem of her black dress, her mind preoccupied with thoughts of Meera. The funeral home was quiet, the atmosphere sombre and still. The only sound was the shuffling of their shoes on the polished marble floor, which echoed through the halls. On the walls were subdued paintings and old photographs that added to the sense of nostalgia and sadness that filled the air. Zoe's mother was visibly upset, with tear-stained cheeks and a distant expression.

The space was quiet and peaceful, yet it felt as though there was a weight on their shoulders, a heaviness that they were both struggling to bear.

'I can't believe the memorial is happening so soon. After only two days?' Zoe asked, breaking the silence.

'She wanted to be cremated. It doesn't take much time to set it up,' her mother replied sadly.

Zoe looked around the empty room. 'Where is everyone—her other family, friends, neighbours?'

'We were her only family. Your great-aunt didn't have any close friends, even at church. She wrote letters to a few friends in China and Japan. But she was mostly alone.'

Zoe frowned. 'What about her relatives in Korea?'

Her mother shook her head. 'She had relatives there, but she cut them off. She never told us why. She was always very private.'

'That's so depressing,' Zoe said, her voice barely above a whisper.

'She lived a very solitary, lonely life,' her mother said, her eyes filling with tears. 'There were tragic things that happened to her that . . . things I can't talk about.'

There was a long pause, and Zoe could sense the unspoken words hanging in the air as the seconds turned into minutes. She wondered what was going through her mother's mind.

'I know what happened,' she said suddenly.

'What do you mean?' her mother asked, surprised.

'She gave me her journal at the hospital. I started reading it.'

'What journal?'

'Something she wrote. It talks about how she was taken away to help feed the Japanese soldiers and mend their uniforms.'

'That's all it says? It doesn't talk about anything else?' Her mother asked, in a shocked tone.

'I have only gotten that far. My Korean is very rusty, so it's a slow process. What else happened?' Zoe asked, her curiosity piqued.

'If she wrote about it in the journal, you'd understand why she was the way she was,' her mother replied cryptically.

'What do you mean?'

'Your great-aunt suffered a lot,' her mother said, her eyes clouded with emotion.

'How come I didn't know anything about this?' Zoe asked, her voice rising.

'She made me swear never to tell anyone. If she gave you her journal, she wants you to know her secret. It's probably because of the article on trafficked women you just wrote. She told me she read it. She said that you understood. That was all she said.'

Zoe looked straight into her mother's eyes. It was as if they were seeing each other in an entirely new light. Now, the long-held family secret was out in the open between them.

After a few moments of quiet contemplation, Zoe finally spoke up, 'Mom, are you okay? I'm so sorry about Aunt Meera.' She continued, her voice laced with concern, 'Do you have any plans this week?'.

'I'm okay. It's been tough seeing her suffer for so long. On Friday, I have to go to her place and pick up her belongings.'

'That might be good for you,' said Zoe. 'You might find something you want to keep that reminds you of her.'

'We'll see,' said her mother, her voice trailing off as she stared into the distance, lost in the memories of her dear aunt.

6

Zoe was in a tough spot. She had promised Winnie she would spend the weekend with her, but at the same time, she felt an urgent need to head to LA to investigate her sex trafficking story.

She had arranged to interview the founder of Rescued by Grace, a church-run rescue shelter that helped trafficked women in West Hollywood, and she feared that if she cancelled or postponed, her story would lose momentum.

So, without telling her office, Zoe booked a flight to LA and gave Winnie a weak excuse, claiming that she had some unexpected out-of-town visitors. She knew it was risky, but she felt like she was meant to be there.

After touching down in LAX, Zoe headed straight for the shelter. She had met its founder and manager, Sue Lee, more than five years ago through a mutual friend and been impressed by the work the organisation was doing.

Sue was just as Zoe remembered her: a bundle of contradictions. She was wearing a simple, flowery dress that gave off a bright and cheerful energy, with shades of pink and purple that complimented her skin tone, and a pair of running shoes that hinted at a fast-paced life. But on closer inspection, the dress revealed intricate embroidered patterns that spoke to tradition and Sue's Korean roots.

Meanwhile her pretty, heart-shaped face had rosy cheeks that lent a softness to her features, but it bore a constant expression of worry as if she were carrying the weight of the world on her shoulders. Her forehead was creased with anxiety lines, and her eyebrows were furrowed, giving her a look of perpetual concern. She wore rimless glasses that accentuated her facial features and framed her large, almond-shaped eyes, which were a warm, inviting brown that drew people in. But those same eyes betrayed a hint of sadness, as if she were grappling with some deep-seated troubles. There was also a depth to them that suggested she had seen some terrible things. Yet, Zoe had never seen Sue drop her smile. She was approachable and friendly, always and without exception.

Sue moved with a serenity and grace that seemed to belie the weight of her worries. Despite her petite stature, she had a quiet strength and dignity. Clearly, she was a woman who had seen her share of trials and tribulations, and had emerged even stronger, more determined and more resilient for it.

Zoe mused that it was these very contradictions that made Sue the perfect fit for the work she did; here was a modern woman who remained rooted in traditions, a delicate flower wrapped in a tough exterior, a beacon of hope in the darkness.

The shelter was in a seedy corner of Hollywood, concealed within an unassuming building. Had Zoe not known that it was there, it might have been impossible to find. It had been started by a passionate group of Christian activists and social workers, all of whom were committed to restoring dignity to those who had experienced unimaginable traumas. This particular facility specialized in helping Asian women and girls, most of whom were from Korea, China, and Vietnam.

It had calming decor and soft lighting designed to offer survivors a peaceful, private, and safe environment, in which they could process their trauma. Each woman was given her own bedroom as a personal space, in addition to the communal facilities where residents could connect with each other and share their experiences. It contained a fully equipped kitchen and a lounge filled with board games, books, and art supplies.

Rescued by Grace also offered support services to help women who were on the path to recovery. Therapists held group classes and tailored one-on-one sessions, while case managers worked with each resident on personalized recovery plans and connected them with legal aid and medical care. The case managers also did their best to track down the survivors' families and helped to repatriate those from overseas to their countries of origin.

Then there was a whole team of caring individuals—cooks, maintenance personnel, and administrative staff—who all contributed to the smooth functioning of the shelter.

In short, Rescued by Grace was a symbol of transformation and strength, a place where broken people could rebuild their lives.

Sue and Zoe were reuniting after a long time and had a lot to catch up on.

After exchanging some pleasantries, Sue gestured towards the dormitory and said, 'These are just a few of the girls. The rest are at other shelters.' Zoe followed Sue's gaze and saw five teenage girls standing together in an expansive open space.

The girls seemed to be between the ages of fourteen and seventeen, but despite their youthful appearances, they looked sad and disheartened. The energy around them had an aura of melancholy. They wore simple and modest dresses that accentuated their sadness. Most were lost in their own thoughts and emotions. Zoe did not hear a single word escape their lips, but all of them wore expressions that spoke to the pain they were feeling. She felt a pang of empathy for these young girls, who were dealing with such heavy emotions at such a young age. They had experienced hardships that no one should ever have to go through. She was determined to help them in any way she could.

'Seeing them is heart-breaking,' she said, shaking her head in despair. 'They're so young. Where are they from?'

'They're from Korea,' Sue replied. 'But there is a Japanese syndicate involved.'

'Japan?' Zoe was surprised. 'What do you mean?'

Sue explained, 'There's a Japanese gang that specializes in trafficking Korean girls. They deceive the girls into believing that they will become K-Pop stars. They are told that they will be going to Singapore for a photo shoot, but instead, they transport them here to California and force them to work in brothels. It's like it's all happening again.'

Zoe was horrified. 'Again? What do you mean, again?'

'They remind me of the "comfort women" from World War Two,' Sue said.

'What are you talking about? What's a comfort woman?' Zoe asked, confused.

'You're Korean, and you don't know about the comfort women, known as *wianbu* in Korean?' Sue asked, surprised.

'No,' Zoe said. 'I grew up in Canada surrounded by white people and spent half my time hiding from racism. Asian history wasn't taught in schools back then, and even if it had been, I probably would have been in denial that it had anything to do with me. I'm a banana—yellow on the outside and white on the inside.'

Sue ignored Zoe's reference and continued. 'Thousands of teenage, Korean girls and others across the Asia Pacific were rounded up and forced into sexual slavery for Japanese soldiers in rape camps before and during World War II,' Sue explained. 'The details became public a few years ago. Some elderly survivors have been testifying to the United Nations and human rights courts. These women are from China, Korea, the Netherlands, and other countries. The Japanese government denied it, but it happened. The UN calls it one of the worst war crimes against girls and women in modern history, with up to 400,000 victims. They had to be with up to thirty men a day. Can you imagine? And this was all done by the Japanese government. These are the unhealed wounds of history.'

Zoe was shocked and embarrassed that she hadn't heard about this before. But she remembered Meera's reference to Korean women who were rounded up and forced into the Voluntary Labour Corps—as part of Japan's wartime mobilization in Korea that also forcibly recruited men as slave labour.

She began to wonder if there was more to her great-aunt's story and made a mental note to do more research when she returned home.

But for now, she needed to focus on her investigation.

'How does this Japanese gang traffic the girls here?' Zoe asked.

'We believe they are working with some Japanese government officials,' Sue said. 'Most come here on Japanese passports, which are not easy to get. Someone inside the government must be helping.'

'But how?' Zoe asked.

'We don't know,' Sue said. 'All we know is that the victims seem to be everywhere—in local brothels, bars, massage parlours, houses, and on the streets. We've never seen anything like this before. It's an epidemic.'

Zoe's heart raced as Sue told her about the six girls they had rescued. They were found working out of a house only a few miles away after an anonymous tip off. They were all profoundly traumatized. Some had been raped by dozens of men every day for months on end.

'Were you involved in the raid?' Zoe asked. 'How did your team get the tip?'

'Yes, a call came in to our hotline and we passed it on to the police,' Sue explained. 'The raid was set up by this woman detective, Sarah Anderson, and her team of vice officers. We have worked with her on several other cases. When more and more of these girls were identified, they came up with a campaign that they called Operation Liberation.'

Sue stood up and walked over to a counter to retrieve a laptop. Zoe watched as she logged in and pulled up a folder of photographs. Sue pointed to a serious-looking middle-aged Caucasian woman in a black business suit. 'About two weeks ago, Detective Anderson came back to us and said her team was ready to go. They asked me to tag along.'

'The idea was that once her team had done all the rough stuff, I would go in to help the victims, gather personal information, and bring them to our shelter. Some other shelter managers were also brought in. We weren't sure how many girls we'd find. I was so scared. It was so tense, knowing that we were about to come face to face with an international criminal network.'

'To preserve the element of surprise, they surrounded the house just before dawn when everyone would be sleeping.'

Zoe examined the photo of the house. The paint was faded, and the grass and shrubs had taken over the small lawn. Another photo showed where the men who visited the girls parked their cars.

'I got a front-row seat to the whole thing. My heart raced with a mixture of adrenaline and concern for the girls that they were about to find. I've been involved in many of these raids before, but the emotional toll never lessens. It doesn't get any easier.'

'Anyway, as the police team reached the entrance, it split into two groups. One group secured the perimeter, so none of the traffickers could escape. The second group, led by Detective Anderson, kicked down the front door of the house and went in with guns drawn.'

'The thing is though, when we went in, the police couldn't find any of the men who had been holding these girls prisoner. They think someone must have tipped them off. What we did find was a chilling sight. Rows of rooms housed terrified and exhausted teenage girls from Korea who had been held captive, their emaciated faces and vacant eyes showing the horrors they had endured. The air stank of decay and fear. I'll never forget that smell. Take a look at these photos. I'm sorry, I can't look at them again. It is too painful to revisit what I saw that day.'

Zoe scrolled through numerous photos. Each room seemed to measure no more than ten feet long and six feet wide. They only contained a simple bed frame, a mattress, and a fan. In one close-up photo, there were two designated buckets: one for new condoms and one for used ones. Each room looked like a prison with an exterior lock to prevent the women from attempting to flee. One of the photos depicted a shared bathroom which had a wet floor and leaky pipes covered in mould, giving it a dreadful appearance.

'My team, the other staff from different shelters, and I rounded up all of the girls and took them in. Some were too weak to stand, having been starved and abused for far too long. I've never seen anything like this in all my years of work.'

Sue took the laptop and changed folders, revealing graphic photos of the girls. 'Just look at these photos.'

Zoe scrolled through a series of photos showing young women who appeared thin, pale, and lifeless. Their vacant eyes made an impression on her that she couldn't shake.

'But perhaps the worst part of the whole thing is that while Operation Liberation succeeded in rescuing fourteen girls, it failed to identify or arrest a single trafficker. That means that these people are probably still out there, trafficking more women.'

Sue's account of the raid and the photos made Zoe feel sick to the pit of her stomach. It also made her even more determined to do what she could to help.

'Can I interview one of the girls?' she asked.

'I'll see what I can do,' Sue said.

As she went off to set up a possible interview, a call came in from an unknown Vancouver phone number. Zoe hesitated before answering, wondering if it was her travel agent or someone else from her office.

'Don't hang up,' a voice said urgently, making her heart race. 'Please. Just hear me out.'

Zoe furrowed her brows for a second, trying to place the voice. 'Jeff? Is that you?'

'Yes, it's me,' Jeff replied, sounding relieved that she recognized him. 'I'm sorry. I know I've been persistent, but I had to get through to you. Please, just give me a chance to explain.'

Zoe felt frustrated, but curious too. She had been avoiding Jeff's calls for weeks; now, she was intrigued.

'Fine, but make it quick. I'm in Los Angeles on an assignment.'

'I'm sorry,' Jeff said, sounding contrite. 'I shouldn't have kept pushing for you to quit your job. But I was scared for your safety. Those threats that you were receiving were terrifying. I couldn't bear the thought of losing you. I love you.'

Zoe's heart softened at Jeff's words, but she wasn't going to cave. 'It doesn't matter if you love me. You can't just control my life like that. My career is important to me. It's who I am.'

'I know,' Jeff said, sounding defeated. 'But I can't help worrying about you. It's not easy seeing the person you love in danger all the time.'

Zoe sighed, feeling torn. She wanted to be with Jeff, but she couldn't give up taking risks in her job. 'I don't know what to do.'

'I don't either,' Jeff admitted. 'But I'm willing to try to find a compromise. We can work together to make sure you're safe while still doing what you love.'

Zoe was sceptical. 'Really?'

'Yes,' Jeff said firmly. 'I'll do whatever it takes to support you.'

Zoe pondered his words. *He was doing that thing he always did*, she thought. All at once, memories of Jeff's obsessive behaviour came to her. Him staying up to wait for her to come home after an extensive research trip only to pick a fight. Him refusing to see her side of things. Despite his good qualities, his biggest fault was his controlling nature. Once he had something in his mind, he couldn't shake it. His persistence was exhausting, often leaving Zoe angry and frustrated. As often as they had fought about her job and then agreed to never do it again, the topic was ever-present. She felt like this was a deal breaker; that is why she had ended their relationship.

'No, you will not pull that on me again. Just leave me alone. Don't call me again. We are done.'

She hung up.

Jeff was a master at finding an opening in Zoe's heart and exploiting it to win her over. But however much he insisted that he had changed, his actions always proved otherwise. He had a way of saying all the right things but then reverting to his old, controlling self. He was simply incapable of change. Zoe had fallen into this trap too many times before and was determined not to make the same mistake again.

* * *

Zoe and Sue were spellbound by Ji-na's presence. She had an effortless beauty, grace, and poise that belied her young age; strikingly beautiful, long, black hair that cascaded down her back in a smooth, silky wave; delicate facial features; and a soft complexion that gave her an ethereal quality. Her eyes, deep and dark, were full of sorrow.

She had inner beauty too, a magnetism that defied explanation and shone through in her every word and gesture.

She was barely fifteen yet had spent months at the brothel already and was not even the youngest of the group.

'Can you tell me what happened to you?' Zoe asked, softly.

Ji-na looked at Sue, seeking her approval. The shelter director nodded encouragingly.

'I was at a shopping mall when a man approached me,' Ji-na began. 'He said that I looked like a model and that I could make a lot of money as a K-Pop star.'

Zoe's brow furrowed.

'Did you know this man?' she asked.

'No, he was a stranger,' Ji-na replied. 'I was waiting for my friends when he came up to me. He seemed nice and gave me his card, but he told me not to tell anyone until we worked out the details.'

Zoe listened carefully, trying to piece together what had happened. 'What details did he want to work out?'

'He sent me lots of texts with links to magazine articles about rich and famous Korean girls my age,' Ji-na said. 'He said I could be one of them. Then he arranged a meeting with me and two other girls at a coffee shop. He'd described it to me as a talent screening. He told us we could take a trip to Singapore for a modelling shoot and form a girl band. He took our photos and made us sign some forms. He even gave us money. I took that as proof that he was telling the truth. I never had that much money at one time.'

Zoe's heart sank as she listened to the story. 'You didn't tell your parents?'

'No, but I told my best friend, and she said she'd help,' Ji-na said. 'We were both so excited. I said I'd try to get her signed up, too.'

'And then what happened?' Zoe asked.

'He arranged a trip for me to do modelling over a weekend in Singapore. I told my parents that I was staying at a friend's house for the weekend. This is what they told me to say. The man knew my parents wouldn't approve. We met at the airport, and the man gave me a Japanese passport and a plane ticket,' Ji-na said. 'I trusted him, but when we arrived, I thought we were in Singapore. It wasn't until later that I found out we were in the US.'

'Singapore is not far from Korea. The flight would have been only about five hours. The LA flight would have been double that. Didn't the flight time make you suspicious?'

'Yes, but he kept saying that the flight time was normal. I trusted him.'

Zoe couldn't believe what she was hearing. 'You didn't notice any red flags?'

'I only speak and read Korean,' Ji-na said defensively. 'I trusted that awful man.'

Zoe could see the pain and fear in Ji-na's eyes. 'What happened next?'

'After we arrived, the man took our passports and did all the talking for us. He spoke in English with the customs officials. A few times, he pointed to the two of us. We didn't understand what he was saying. We simply followed his orders. When we got into the parking lot, the man completely changed. He was no longer nice. He repeatedly shouted at us. Then, a car pulled up and we were whisked inside. There were two other men—Japanese men. They got angry and began to yell at us. After driving for several hours, they pulled into a building and took us into an elevator. We got off on the fifth floor, where they locked us into separate rooms,' Ji-na said, tears streaming down her face. 'I was so scared.'

Zoe gently placed her hand on Ji-na's arm, 'Are you comfortable describing what happened next? You don't have to . . .'

'After what felt like endless hours of waiting, the door creaked open and two rough men stepped into the room. My heart pounded as their gawking eyes fixed upon me. One of the men, in a low voice, demanded that I undress. My mind was overwhelmed with disbelief. How could this be happening to me? I hesitated for a brief moment, hoping this was some kind of awful dream.'

'But my hesitation only made them mad. The man's hand struck me hard across the face, leaving my cheek burning with pain. The humiliation was unbearable. But I felt terrified. I took off my clothes as fast as I could.'

'There I stood, stripped down to my bra and underwear, while the men circled me like predators, their eyes appraising every inch of my body. One of the men ripped my bra off and tossed it onto the floor. It was all so shameful. All my self-respect had been stolen in an instant.'

'I was so scared, I was shaking and weeping. I was trapped in this twisted nightmare, a victim of their cruel game, unable to escape or fight back.'

'Once they left the room, I could no longer hold back my tears. I wailed, feeling utterly broken and violated. I couldn't breathe. I was angry with myself for trusting that man.'

'After that, they . . . they . . .'

Ji-na broke down and cried. Soft at first, but then with gasping waves. Sue took Ji-na into her arms and escorted her away as Zoe waited patiently on the side. After nearly forty-five minutes, Sue came back.

'You already know the rest, Zoe. They broke her over and over again until she would do whatever they wanted her to,' Sue said, her voice filled with sadness. 'The next day, the girls were taken to those tiny rooms in that house. They were always isolated. This went on for nearly three months before they were rescued. One of the girls said she saw over twenty men in a single day. She said she was so tired, she passed out. And still they used her. I have never seen a gang this cruel.'

Zoe felt her heart sink as she heard the horrific details. 'Do you know anything about the gang? Where are they based?'

Sue paused, and Zoe could sense her hesitation. 'Yes, but you can't share this with anyone.'

Sue walked over to her desk and returned with a large, red ledger. 'After the raid, I found this ledger with the names of the girls in it. It had some Japanese text with account information and phone numbers. These must belong to the people who trafficked them.'

Zoe was shocked. 'Why didn't you tell the police?'

'I thought I'd get into trouble if they found out I took this,' Sue said. 'But I realize now that it was a stupid thing to do. I took it because I thought it would help us find the girls' homes.'

Zoe took the ledger from Sue's hand. 'Can I hold on to this for now?'

'Go ahead,' Sue said. 'Please find those responsible.'

As Zoe flipped through the pages of this strange-looking file, she felt intrigue and trepidation. The content was a perplexing blend of Japanese and Korean notations. Handwritten spreadsheets and meticulously curated lists of names, phone numbers, emails, and other cryptic details hinted at its dark purpose, each entry another thread in a web of illicit activities.

A shiver ran down her spine as the significance of the ledger dawned on her. It was like the Rosetta Stone, which, once deciphered, could help track down every single scumbag involved in the operation, from the traffickers to the pimps to the clients.

As she examined the document, her mind raced with thoughts of what she should do next. Perhaps she should hand it over to the police in Japan. But given her experience with the police car in Jeon-Jiju, could she really trust them to pursue it? Or should she use it for her own investigation, and make sure that justice was served?

Weighing the ethical dilemma, Zoe realized she had to think this through very carefully. She had stumbled upon something that could potentially change the course of many lives. But who could tell what effect exposing this network might have? Could she unwittingly make things worse?

Suddenly she was reminded of her great-aunt Meera, and a thought entered her mind: What if decades ago, someone had taken the time to care about what happened to Meera and the countless kidnapped and trafficked women during World War II? What if a sense of justice had prevailed? Learning about what had happened to these girls and the wicked cycle of trafficking repeating itself motivated Zoe to take action, not just for them, but for Meera.

She closed the document carefully and slipped it into her bag, knowing that she had a choice to make and that regardless of what she decided, there would be consequences.

What she did not know was that this discovery would lead her down a dangerous path where the lines between right and wrong would become blurred and the cost of discovering the truth would be greater than she could ever have imagined.

* * *

Zoe treated Sue to lunch before she headed to the airport. Usually, their intense conversations revolved around the world's pain and suffering, but this time, Zoe made a conscious decision to steer their talk towards more easy-going topics. They discussed their aspirations and dreams, the men in their lives, travel, music, and celebrity gossip.

For once, they were not a journalist and a shelter manager; they were just two single women, enjoying the moment and discussing everything and nothing all at once. The atmosphere was filled with warmth and laughter as they bonded over their shared interests and memories.

The lunch gave them both a chance to recharge their spirits before parting ways. They felt energized and optimistic about the future, knowing that they had each other's support and genuine friendship.

As they said their goodbyes, they hugged each other tightly, grateful for the chance at a little normalcy. Who knew when they would feel it again?

7

After her flight back to Canada, Zoe sat in the back of a taxi, her mind filled with the troubling images and stories she had encountered at the human trafficking shelter in LA. What Ji-na and the young women had gone through had affected her deeply. Meanwhile, she had the creeping suspicion that her great-aunt Meera had been forced into prostitution for the Japanese military during World War II.

As Zoe arrived at her apartment building in Vancouver, the thought of one of her relatives suffering like that was consuming her mind. She knew the issue was much bigger than herself, but she wanted to play a role—however small—in making things right.

She entered her home, made her way to the ivory couch, and sat down. She reached for Meera's journal, which lay on the coffee table in front of her. She had been reading it for days now. She knew that it was a long shot, but she hoped that it would provide her with some answers. Amidst all of these emotions, there was a glimmer of hope.

December 18, 1943

It was a dark and chilly night, well past midnight. We were huddled together on old mats for warmth, our eyes heavy with exhaustion. Suddenly, the silence was shattered by the sound of a door being broken open with brute force. A soldier barged in, followed by three other menacing figures, stepping into the room without a word. Their presence sent a chill down our spines, as we gasped and wondered what was about to happen.

One of the men had a flashlight, which he used to scan the room, its beam darting around restlessly. The light finally settled on one of the girls, Arah, who trembled with fear. We all felt uneasy, as the silence lingered in the air, waiting for the strangers' next move. We knew something terrible was about to happen.

The soldier pointed to her and his companion marched over aggressively, grabbing her by the arm and pulling her away from the group. She cried out in desperation but, after a hopeless struggle, succumbed to their authority.

But the first soldier wasn't satisfied. He remained in the doorway, his gun at the ready, continuing to scan the dimly lit room. His flashlight beam went from girl to girl, each one of us trembling. For a moment, it lingered on the young girl crouched next to me, then it moved on and came to a stop on me. His gaze lingered on me a little longer than any of the others, his eyes narrowing as he scrutinized every inch of my shaking body. I felt like fainting.

As the soldier approached and took hold of me, I resisted, my heart pounding. In response, he slapped me hard across the face, causing me to reel back in pain.

I was dragged away, along with the other girl, both of us helpless and terrified. We were shoved into the back of a Japanese military vehicle. There were already three girls in there, all huddled together and terrified. Arah and I clung to each other. There was a lone soldier too, his eyes watching us like a predator stalking his prey. We could all sense the darkness that awaited us.

Twenty minutes later, we stopped. Each girl was then taken to a different room.

As I walked into my room, I saw a mattress on the floor, and a bucket of water and some rags beside it. Arah was in the room next to me, but we were both alone and vulnerable.

The soldier started shouting something in Japanese, gesturing to the bed and the bucket as he spoke, and then abruptly left the room. I felt dread building inside me as I wondered what was going to happen next.

A few minutes later, a young soldier entered. He placed his rifle to the side and began taking off his pants, leaving only his top on. I froze, petrified, as I realized what was about to happen.

I turned away, not wanting to see such a shameful sight. No girl should be subjected to such horrors. But it was too late. The soldier approached me, and I retreated into the corner like a trapped animal.

I screamed. Yet it was all for nothing. Another soldier rushed into the room, grabbing me before I could even process what was happening. There was a long line of Japanese soldiers outside. And then it began—the nightmare of my innocence being lost over and over again.

I can't write down the details of these events. They are too shameful. Even to this day, I flinch when I think about these things.

Zoe looked up from the journal, her eyes wide, as she finally understood the extent of the horrors that had befallen her great-aunt. Her mind went silent as she tried to process her shock and disgust.

She had guessed the outcome of her great-aunt's story would be grim, but seeing the words on paper made everything more real. She had suffered so much. Zoe thought about her investigation into the trafficking ring in LA and knew she had to push on with it, but it was hard to know where to begin.

* * *

Later that afternoon, Zoe called her mom. 'Mom, I'm back in Vancouver,' she said. 'Have you been to Meera's apartment yet?'

Her mom hesitated for a moment, before answering. 'No, I haven't. I've been putting it off,' she admitted.

'Can I come with you?' asked Zoe. 'Would tomorrow morning work?'

'Yes, that would be great. 9 a.m.?' her mom replied.

'Okay, I'll see you then,' Zoe said before hanging up.

She walked over to the refrigerator and took out a bottle of red wine, her hands trembling slightly. She poured herself a generous amount and sat down on a chair, her gaze landing on a framed photograph of Jeff that was on the stand beside her. Memories flooded her mind as she studied the photo, and a lump formed in her throat. She rubbed her fingers across the image, as if trying to conjure his presence.

Suddenly overcome, Zoe turned the photo face down and left the room, the echoes of her sobs resonating in the empty apartment.

* * *

In the morning, Zoe met up with her mom, and they drove together to Meera's apartment. As they walked in, memories of Meera filled the air.

The apartment was a sanctuary of second-hand books, with stacks of literary treasures filling every available space. Piles of novels, and essay and poetry collections rose like haphazard sculptures, forming narrow pathways through her home. Their well-loved, dog-eared pages held the whispers of past readers. From dusty classics to contemporary tomes, her collection was a diverse tapestry of human stories and knowledge. In one of the corners, there was a worn armchair nestled within the literary labyrinth, where she could immerse herself in worlds far removed from her own.

Together, they spent hours sorting through Meera's belongings, reminiscing about the good times and mourning her loss.

'Mom, what is all of this?' Zoe asked, shocked. 'Have you ever seen these many books in a small apartment?'

'Never,' her mom admitted, shaking her head in disbelief.

'Haven't you been here before?' asked Zoe.

'No. Whenever I picked her up, she was outside, in front. I had no idea she was such an avid reader.'

Zoe wandered amidst the stacks of books. Each stack represented a different world, a new adventure waiting to be explored. She scanned the spines, seeing titles in Chinese, Korean, and English. The Chinese titles included *Dream of the Red Chamber* and *To Live*, while among the Korean books were *Please Look After Mom* and *To the Girl*. English classics like *Pride and Prejudice* and contemporary gems such as *The Night Circus* also stood out.

'I have no idea what I'm going to do with all of these books,' Zoe's mother said, a little overwhelmed.

'I'll make a call. There's a used bookstore in the city. I'm sure they wouldn't mind coming over here and hauling them away. You can just donate them all,' Zoe said.

'Thank you. That would be helpful.'

Having looked through the stacks, Zoe and her mom sifted through the few other belongings in Meera's apartment. There were some clothes and a few boxes of miscellaneous items.

'I guess this explains why she was such a great writer,' Zoe said. 'It must have come from all this reading she did.'

Her mom didn't respond.

'I know what happened to Meera. I read about it in her journal,' Zoe confessed to her mother.

'You know she was a wianbu, a comfort woman?' Zoe's mother asked, her eyes filled with sorrow.

'I learnt about the comfort women during my trip to LA. How come I'd never heard about it before?' Zoe asked.

'Few people talk about it. It's taboo,' her mother explained. 'But a few years ago, some of these elderly women bravely shared their stories with the international media, and it was a big deal in Korea. That's when Meera told me she was a victim too.'

Zoe was consumed with questions. 'I had no idea,' she said softly.

'Not many people do,' her mother said, shaking her head sadly. 'But it's a part of our history.'

'Why didn't you ever talk to me about this?' Zoe asked. 'You know that I write about human rights issues.'

'It's a difficult topic for us Koreans, it's considered shameful. Not something we like to openly discuss. It's hard for me to even think about what happened to Aunt Meera—it's traumatic for her and for the family. I wanted to protect you.'

'In her journal, Meera mentioned some of these women who came forward,' said Zoe. 'Last night, I read an article that said that in South Korea, every Wednesday, a small group of comfort women survivors and their supporters gather in front of the Japanese embassy in Seoul to protest and demand a formal apology and compensation from the Japanese government for the suffering they endured during the war. These protests are known as the "Wednesday Demonstrations" or "Wednesday Rallies". Survivor grandmas, activists, students, journalists, and concerned citizens hold signs, banners, and candles while demanding justice for and recognition of the atrocities.'

'I heard about these protests,' Zoe's mother said. 'The topic sometimes comes up in my women's Bible study group.'

'I'm sorry I never knew,' Zoe said, regretfully. 'You know, this sort of thing is still happening. I'm writing about sex trafficking now. History is repeating itself.'

As they continued to search through Meera's belongings, Zoe came across a shoebox filled with old black-and-white photos. She pulled out a picture of a young Meera surrounded by strangers. Then, she saw a few photos of Meera as a teenager with a young man by her side. He was looking at Meera with affection.

'Did Meera ever mention a boy named Masuki?' Zoe asked.

'No, her mother replied, shrugging her shoulders. 'Not that I can remember. Why?'

'No reason.'

Zoe was rifling through a box of letters when she came across a bundle written in Korean. She immediately recognized the name Arah Cho—the girl Meera had mentioned in her journal entry, about being selected by the soldier. As she went through the letters, she realized that some of them were sent almost thirty years ago, others as recently as three years ago. She also opened one of the envelopes and saw the name Masuki in the return address.

'Wow, it's from him,' she said under her breath, eyes widening as her curiosity piqued. The discovery filled her with excitement, so she asked her mother if she could keep the box of letters for a few days.

'Why are you suddenly interested in her family history?' asked her mother. 'Why do you want it?'

'I'm just curious about my roots,' Zoe explained. 'I'm changing, Mom. I want to know more about where I come from. I want to explore my Korean side.'

Her mother relented. 'Go ahead. But don't take too long. And don't forget to bring the box back.'

While packing up, her mother mentioned that Jeff had called her.

Zoe felt irritated at the mere mention of his name. 'Why would he call you?' She asked, knowing full well that this was one of the tricks Jeff often used—reaching out to her friends and family to get them to plead his case. It was a classic Jeff move that irritated her endlessly.

'He doesn't understand what happened between you two. He thought things were going so well. He wanted my advice,' her mother explained.

'Tell him I don't want to talk,' Zoe declared, her voice firm.

'But why don't you? Maybe you can work things out,' her mother suggested.

'You don't know the entire story. You think he's some kind of saint, but he's not. Just stay out of it,' Zoe snapped, storming out of the apartment.

* * *

Zoe sat at her dining table, surrounded by Meera's old photographs and letters. As she flipped through the pages of Meera's journal, she felt a deep sadness wash over her. Every word on the page seemed to carry the weight of Meera's pain and suffering.

She read about how the men came to Meera every day, one after the other, never stopping. Even while she was eating and sleeping. Meera was trapped, unable to do anything but lie there and endure the torment. She prayed for death every day, and made some attempts, but it never came.

As Zoe read on, she learned about the madam who oversaw Meera and the other women. The old lady would scold and slap them for the smallest mistakes, like wearing make-up that she disapproved of. Zoe couldn't imagine what it must have been like to be at the mercy of someone like that.

But amidst all the darkness, Zoe found a kind of defiance and a steely strength in Meera's story. She read about the bond that formed between Meera and Arah.

Despite everything they went through, they still found solace in each other's company. They whispered to each other through the thin wall that separated them, holding hands through a hole to reassure one another. It was a small act of rebellion against the forces that had stolen everything from them.

Zoe was struck by their resilience. They had been through so much, and yet they still found ways to keep going.

She also discovered something else that she had not expected in Meera's story: an awakening of a deeper sense of purpose. She knew that she had to do something to honour her great-aunt's memory and the memory of all the forgotten women who suffered.

She felt compelled to pick up the phone and call Sue Lee at the West Hollywood shelter. 'Sue, you won't believe what I've uncovered about my great-aunt Meera,' she exclaimed, her voice trembling with emotion. 'She was a former comfort woman.'

Sue gasped in disbelief. 'Oh goodness, that poor woman. The shame and trauma she must have gone through . . .' her voice trailed off.

'I read in her journal that after the first soldier took her innocence away, her fate was sealed. She felt like her life was over.'

'I recently found out that Arah, the girl whom Meera was taken with, is still alive. She decided to stay on in Shanghai after the war and eventually married a local man. In her last letter to Meera, Arah revealed that her husband died a broken man. They were never able to start their own family, because Arah was unable to have children due to the abuse she endured. Her reproductive system was destroyed by disease and trauma.'

'That's . . .' Sue started, before trailing off, unable to say much.

'Now I understand why Aunt Meera never married or had a family. I wish I had known about all of this earlier. I would have spoken to her about it. It's important that we remember the past and honour the memories of those who suffered . . . for peace and a better future.'

Sue's heart broke at the revelation of Meera's tragic past. 'What are you going to do with this information?' she asked.

Zoe thought for a minute.

'I'm going to go to Shanghai and Tokyo to try to uncover more about Meera's life. This is personal, so I'm going to take some time off work. Can you please keep this between us? You already know I'm on thin ice at work. I'm trying to stay out of trouble.'

'Of course, Zoe. You do what you need to do.'

'Thanks!'

'By the way, did you get a chance to review the ledger I gave you?' Sue asked, deftly changing the subject.

'Yes, I used a translation app. The ledger provides detailed accounts including names, dates, and expenses incurred by clients, along with some disturbing information about the trafficked women and girls—things like their ages, bra sizes, and scores for their perceived attractiveness. It mentions a central figure referred to as the "Black Lotus", who appears to be the mastermind behind the operation. I even managed to find his contact information, including a phone number. I'm thinking of reaching out to him discreetly when I'm in Japan,' Zoe replied.

'Be cautious, Zoe. You can't just call someone involved in such a dangerous ring,' Sue warned.

'Don't worry, Sue,' Zoe responded, determined. 'I'll tread carefully and figure out the best approach. We have to get to the bottom of this trafficking ring. Once we have all the evidence, we can pass it on to the special agent you mentioned earlier.'

Sue still seemed unsure. 'Please promise me you'll be careful,' she said. 'These organized criminals are extremely dangerous.'

Zoe hung up the phone and called her office to arrange the upcoming trip. She was in a hurry as she spoke to Mandy, the managing editor's assistant, who usually made travel arrangements for *The Star*'s journalists. She was also one of Zoe's most trusted friends at work.

'Hey Mandy, could you please help me arrange a trip? I need to go to Shanghai for three days and then to Tokyo for a week. This trip is personal, so please keep it confidential and don't tell Ben about it,' she said, hoping for Mandy's understanding.

Mandy could sense the urgency in Zoe's voice and wanted to know more. 'What's going on, Zoe?' she asked, concerned.

Zoe paused for a moment before responding, 'It's a long story. I'll tell you all about it when I get back. But for now, I need you to be discreet and send my itinerary directly to me. Use my credit card for this. Can you do that for me, please? You're a lifesaver, Mandy.'

Zoe trusted her completely, and she knew that Mandy would keep her secret safe.

After ending her call, she was feeling a bit anxious as she dialled her mom's number. 'Hey Mom, it's me. I wanted to let you know that I'll be going on another trip, this time to China and Japan,' she said, trying to sound cheerful and confident.

The concern in her mom's voice was clear, 'Why are you going there?'

Zoe paused before explaining, 'It's related to my job. I'm working on a story that requires me to travel to these countries. I'll be covering some cultural events, interviewing locals, and exploring the cities to get a better understanding of the culture and people there.'

Her mom listened intently, and Zoe could hear her sigh with relief, 'Oh, I see. Please be careful, Zoe. Don't take any unnecessary risks.'

Zoe smiled, 'Don't worry, Mom. I'll take all the right precautions. I'll take my vitamins, watch my posture, and keep in touch with you. I promise.'

'Okay, dear. Just be safe and have fun,' her mom said, sounding more relaxed.

Zoe felt relieved and grateful for her mom's support. 'Thanks, Mom. I'll tell you all about it when I get back. Love you.'

As she hung up the phone, Zoe felt both excitement and apprehension. One way or another, this was going to be a trip that she would never forget.

8

Zoe found herself in a cramped airplane seat, sandwiched between two strangers who seemed oblivious to the concept of personal space. She could hear the dull hum of the engines and the muffled chatter of the passengers around her—background noises that were at once soothing and irritating. Even with the cabin lights dimmed, the bulb above her seat spotlit the pages of Meera's journal in front of her.

She squinted as she tried to decipher the squiggly Korean characters that danced before her eyes. Her progress was slow, and every word felt like a small victory, achieved through hours of tireless study. She was determined to read Meera's words, no matter how long it took or how challenging it was. Zoe's eyes darted back and forth across the page, taking in each character as she struggled to understand the meaning.

Despite the discomfort of the flight, Zoe was lost in her own world, completely absorbed in Meera's life. With each turn of the page, Zoe felt as if she were uncovering a secret, unlocking the mysteries of a foreign culture.

March 9, 1944

That day, the room felt suffocating. The soldiers laughed and jeered outside as they waited for their turn. I tried to block out their lewd comments and unwanted touches, but it was a losing battle. My mind kept drifting back to my family, to the life that had been ripped away from me so cruelly.

As the evening dragged on, I had to endure being with more than twenty-five soldiers. My body ached with each passing moment. It was bruised and battered from the constant abuse; my spirit shattered by the endless humiliation.

I held on to the one precious possession I had left—a photo of my family. I had planned to show Masuki this photo when we met, and so, it had been in my pocket the day I was taken.

My fingers rubbed against it as if that could magically transport me back to a time before this nightmare began. I clung to the photo, staring at it until the faces became blurry through my tears.

The occasional conversation I had with Arah through the thin walls between our rooms was my only other source of comfort. We talked about the old days, our lives before this hell. It gave us both a temporary relief and it was also a reminder of our humanity.

On that particular day, something unexpected happened. A man walked in. I didn't look up. I laid back, closed my eyes, and waited for him to come over and finish his business. He didn't approach me.

When I looked up, I was shocked to see my long-lost friend, Masuki, standing before me. Tears streamed down his face as he gazed at me, frozen in place. His face was filled with worry and grief. Seeing him after all these months felt like a dream, and for a moment, I almost believed that everything would be alright. But reality is a cruel beast.

I turned away with shame. I put my hand out to wave, gesturing for him to leave. He didn't move. He remained standing. I burst into tears.

He walked up to me slowly, knelt, and gently placed his hand on my shoulder. I tried to shrug it off. I was ashamed of the broken, diseased person I had become.

I told him not to look at me. I begged him to go away. I didn't want him to see me this way. I covered my face and crawled up into a ball to hide myself. For me, having my beloved see me this way was more painful than the daily visits from countless soldiers. The feelings of loss penetrated every cell in my body.

In a soft whisper, he told me that he had been searching for me all over China and that he was sorry for what had happened. And then, he said something that I will never forget. He said it was all his father's doing.

Masuki explained how his father had found out about our friendship and been furious about it. He had then used his power as governor to have me taken away and used my capture to torment his own son. Masuki said his father was an evil man.

As he spoke, I felt fury well up inside me. How could his father have done this to us? How could anyone be so heartless so as to tear apart two childhood friends, just because they came from different countries? Masuki's words burned like acid, fuelling my rage and despair.

He then said that after he learned of what had happened, he ran away and signed up for the army. He lied about his age. He used his father's letterhead to draft up some official-looking papers that would allow him to travel from place to place. He said he did this to find me. He said he had visited ten other comfort stations before arriving at this one. He said it was his mission in life to rescue me.

I continued looking at Masuki. I held his gaze for nearly a minute before turning away. He kept telling me that he could get me out. He promised.

Seeing him only added to my humiliation. I didn't want to get out.

I wanted to die.

That was my only escape. It was the only honourable thing to do. I wanted out of this life. When I told him this, he said that

I shouldn't talk this way. He said he could help me leave—I just needed to be patient.

But I knew I was done. I had no hope for a future. By this time, my body was very frail. I was broken in every way. I was beyond hope. I had nothing left to live for. Masuki couldn't understand the shame and pain that had consumed me. How could he? He was a man. He was Japanese. He didn't know my deep sorrow and pain.

He said that I hadn't done anything wrong. That it wasn't my fault.

In anger, I hissed—tell that to my village, tell that to my family, tell that to the world. I asked him if he thought any of them would care how I got here. The damage was already done. I'm now a whore. I want to die, I told him. I explained that if I could have found a way to do so by now, I would have done it.

He finally said, 'I will help you. You are my little butterfly.'

'I am your fallen butterfly,' I corrected him. Hearing him say those words to me made me feel even worse. I told him never to call me that again. That girl was gone forever. She died the moment the first soldier took her. She was no more.

He continued to plead with me. He said that nobody had to know about what had happened to me here.

I told him that I would know! I said to him that if he were truly my friend, he would help me to kill myself.

Then there was silence between us, but it did not last.

I told him that if he had ever cared about me, then he would do two things for me—give me some poison and help Arah, the girl in the next room, to escape. I grabbed his hand and pleaded.

Then the mama-san barged in, furious at Masuki for wasting time talking to me. There was no room for talk. It was simply a physical act. Nothing more. The men were told not to speak to the girls.

She shouted at Masuki, asked what he was doing, and insisted that he finish and leave. Others were waiting.

Masuki stood up, turned, and walked out.

She slapped me hard, calling me a whore. And in that moment, any shred of hope I had felt that Masuki would help me escape this life was extinguished, replaced by a deep, aching sadness.

I broke down crying. I was inconsolable. Even the blows from the mama-san couldn't get me to stop. Masuki's visit had broken my fragile soul to the very core.

* * *

Zoe's arrival at Shanghai Pudong International Airport was a daunting experience. The airport was teeming with people, their voices blending together in a cacophony. The atmosphere was thick with the aroma of Chinese delicacies and the clatter of luggage wheels on the tiled floor.

Every corner of the airport was packed with long lines of travellers, all trying to make their way through security checkpoints and immigration counters.

Zoe felt her patience dwindling as she pushed forward, the shuffle of her feet echoing in the crowded space. It was several hours before she finally emerged from the airport, her eyes bleary and her body exhausted after the long, sleepless flight.

As she made her way towards the taxi queue, a driver approached her with a friendly smile, offering to take her to her hotel. The driver spoke fluent English, but Zoe was hesitant and wary of scams.

Zoe asked him if he used a meter. She had a feeling that she knew what his answer would be.

'Absolutely,' the driver replied. 'Follow me.'

They walked to the airport parking lot, where his cab was parked.

The driver was a young Chinese man named Wang Jun, who had a smooth-talking manner that reminded her of a used-car salesman, but she found herself drawn to his vibe. With his slicked-back hair and charm, he could have sold sea water to a thirsty man.

Zoe raised an eyebrow as he popped open the rear door of the gleaming new Toyota Camry before them and looked at her inquisitively as if seeking her approval. It had been modified with neon under-glow lighting that illuminated the ground beneath it, appearing more like a racing car than a taxi. She walked up to the window and peered inside. *It was hardly the discreet ride she had envisioned*, she thought, *but at least it was impeccably clean.*

Wang Jun opened the glove compartment and showed Zoe the hidden meter inside. Zoe's eyebrow went up even higher. She had heard about scams run by local drivers and wasn't going to fall for it. The meter wasn't genuine at all. It was set up to triple the price of any ride.

'Actually, forget the meter,' said Zoe. 'I'll pay you eighty US dollars if you can take me to this address first and wait for me. Then you can take me to my hotel.'

The driver's smile dropped slightly, and his brow creased as he bent over the piece of paper that Zoe had handed him. The address on it was to Arah's home in the village. 'This place is outside the city. I can't do it for less than a hundred,' he said.

Zoe thought for a moment. She didn't want to get ripped off, but she needed to get to the address. And while Wang Jun's taste in cars might not have matched her own, he had a kind face.

'Okay, how about this? I'll give you ninety, and if you can get me there quickly and safely, I'll give you an extra twenty.'

Wang Jun considered it briefly and then nodded. 'Okay.'

With the deal struck, they set off on their journey through rural China as the sun rose, leaving the bustling metropolis of Shanghai behind them. The landscape slowly transformed into a patchwork of emerald-green rice paddies and misty mountains looming in the distance. Zoe marvelled at the sights and sounds around her and the gentle breeze that caressed her face. The air was filled with the fragrance of blooming wildflowers and the distant calls of birds. Zoe felt truly alive.

All this was in stark contrast to the exhaust fumes and vehicular horns of Shanghai. They passed quaint villages where locals rode bicycles and tended to their crops, their faces weathered by the harsh sun and wind.

Despite all the beauty and light that surrounded her, Zoe found it hard to shake the feeling that something dark and ugly was heading her way. She reached instinctively for Meera's journal, hoping that it would occupy her thoughts, and immersed herself once more.

March 13, 1944

Four days had passed without a sign of Masuki, so I assumed that he had given up on granting my wish.

Late in the day, a woman I had never seen before rushed into my room, carrying a glass of water and a pill. She looked around nervously before handing me the pill and urging me to swallow it quickly. When I asked her what it was, she didn't answer. She insisted that I take it before anyone else came in. I was deeply suspicious, especially at first. I wondered, was this Masuki honouring my request? Or was it some kind of trick, a punishment from the mama-san? As I thought it over, I came to the conclusion that I had nothing to lose. So finally, I swallowed it, the bitter taste lingering in my mouth as I downed the entire glass of water.

Without a word, the woman scurried out of the room, leaving me to wonder what was going to happen to me. I made my way over to the hole in the wall and told Arah that I had taken a poison pill and that I would soon be going to heaven. Arah was shocked and asked me what the pill was and how I had gotten it. I told her that a woman had given it to me and that someone I once knew had arranged it.

But then Arah told me something that made my blood run cold—a woman had come to her too and had given her a small pill as well. She asked if it was poison and if she too was going to die. I was horrified, realizing that Masuki must have misunderstood and given her the same pill by mistake.

I reached out my hand to grab Arah's through the wall, hoping to offer some comfort, but no words passed between us. We both knew that something terrible was about to happen.

After twenty agonizing minutes, I began to feel dizzy and nauseated, my head pounding with a splitting headache. Death was coming for me, I was sure. Arah told me she didn't feel well either and that she thought this was the end. She thanked me for being a dear friend to her and said she was glad that it would all be over soon.

I felt so guilty and ashamed. I had unwittingly dragged Arah into my miserable fate and now she was going to pay the ultimate price. I told her I didn't mean for this to happen to her and that she wasn't supposed to get the pill. I explained that I had tried to get someone to rescue her, but it had all gone wrong.

Arah surprised me with her response. She said that wherever I was going, she would go too. She said she couldn't take the torment and pain anymore and that this was an act of kindness. She was grateful that I had saved her.

Within minutes, we were both vomiting violently, writhing in pain as our bodies convulsed. Two women wearing Red Cross armbands burst into the room, whisking us away to an ambulance parked outside. Then everything turned black.

* * *

The taxi rolled slowly to a stop, and Zoe leaned towards the window to peer outside. She saw a small and ancient village of several dozen non-descript, cement buildings. The paint was peeling, and some windows were broken. The streets were deserted, the only sounds the distant chirping of crickets and the hum of the taxi engine.

Zoe turned to Wang Jun and said, 'I'm sorry, but I don't speak Chinese. I need your assistance. Can you please come with me?'

Wang Jun hesitated. He was about to say something, but Zoe interrupted, 'I know what you're going to say, but I've already paid you more than you deserve, so don't ask.'

He offered a defeated smile, nodded, and took the address from Zoe. As they walked together through the village, Wang Jun would stop periodically to ask the locals for directions to the house. Zoe observed the surroundings with curiosity and awe.

But when they finally arrived, Zoe's hopes deserted her. The house was boarded up, and it appeared that nobody had lived there for years. The paint on the walls was cracked, and the old-fashioned door was locked and rusted shut. Bars stood across the windows and cobwebs hung from the eaves. Zoe was crushed by disappointment and wondered if the woman that she was searching for had passed away.

Despite the let-down, Zoe remained determined to find Arah. She wandered around the run-down, abandoned building, peeking over walls and navigating the piles of bricks. Wang Jun observed with great curiosity. He couldn't understand why someone like her would be in such a remote place. Out of the blue, an old man approached them curiously. Wang Jun translated his words and explained that outsiders rarely came to the village; the old man was intrigued by their presence.

'I'm looking for Arah Cho. Please translate and tell him,' Zoe replied, handing over a black and white photo. Wang Jun obliged.

The old man studied the photo intently and then smiled, pointing to a house nearby. He informed them that Arah's house had been damaged in an earthquake, and she now lived in the house that he had pointed out.

Zoe thanked the old man with a warm smile and walked towards the house with excitement and nervousness building up inside of her.

After knocking on the door, an elderly woman answered, looking confused. Zoe greeted her politely.

'Is your name Arah?' Zoe asked in broken Korean.

The elderly woman took the photo from Zoe's hand and gasped in surprise, taking a step back.

It was clear that Arah recognized the person in the photo and was in shock. Rather than push for a response, Zoe waited patiently and took the chance to observe the woman she had been reading about for so long.

Arah was small and frail, with deep lines on her weathered face that spoke of a lifetime of hard work and struggle. Her hair was grey and wispy, and she wore a faded blue cotton tunic and baggy pants that had been patched in many places. Her feet were bare and calloused from walking on the uneven dirt paths of her village in loose sandals. She had a gentle and kind demeanour. Despite the frailty of her figure, and the struggles that Zoe knew she had faced, she radiated an inner strength.

Finally, Arah spoke, her voice trembling slightly as she asked, 'Where did you get this? Who are you?'

Zoe introduced herself and revealed that she was Meera's great-niece. There was a long pause as Arah's mind tried to make sense of this encounter.

Then, Arah spoke again, this time in perfect English. 'You're from Canada. I know you. Meera wrote to me about her Canadian family.'

Overcome with emotion, the elderly woman suddenly lunged forward and wrapped Zoe in a tight embrace with a warm welcoming smile that crinkled the corners of her eyes. Tears streamed down Arah's face as she rocked back and forth in joy. Zoe felt a surge of grief and amazement. Arah's embrace was comforting and familiar. The connection between them was palpable.

There they stood, lost in their emotions until Arah finally pulled away and looked at Zoe. 'I can't believe this is happening,' Arah said, wiping away her tears. 'Please, come in. There is so much to talk about.'

Zoe smiled and stepped into Arah's humble village home, entering an inviting sitting area positioned just off the entrance. The room was small, but it exuded comfort, with its earthen walls and a tin roof overhead. A single light bulb hung from the ceiling, casting shadows that flickered on the walls, as if they were dancing. At the centre of the room was a low wooden table surrounded by brightly coloured cushions arranged in a circle that seemed to invite visitors to sit and relax.

Against one of the walls, there was a small fireplace made of stacked stones, with a few logs burning brightly in the hearth. The room was decorated simply, with a woven rug on the floor and some traditional artwork on the walls. The fireplace mantel held collections of photos, including black and white snapshots from days gone by that provided a glimpse into the life of the family over the years. The feeling was one of warmth, comfort, and a touch of nostalgia.

As the two women talked together in the modest living room, sipping tea, Zoe was struck by Arah's fluency in English.

After a while, Zoe turned to Arah and said, 'You speak English so well. How did you learn it?'

Arah sat at the edge of her seat and leaned forward as she spoke, 'I spent many years living with a group of missionaries who taught me how to speak English. Meera, who was also part of the same group, learned the language in the same way. I've lost touch with her over the years. How has she been doing?'

Zoe's voice trembled with sadness as she replied, 'I'm sorry to have to tell you this, but Meera passed away just two weeks ago.'

Arah was speechless, tears welling up in her eyes. Zoe reached out to her, but Arah pulled away, too overwhelmed by the news to accept any consolation. Tears streamed down her face. After a moment, she composed herself and confided in Zoe, 'Most of us from the group have gone our separate ways, and now there are only a few of us left. Do you know what happened to Meera and me?'

Zoe responded with gentle compassion, 'Before she passed, Meera gave me her diary. I also found some of your old letters at her apartment. That's how I learned about you.'

'Then you know . . . how . . . you know what the Japanese did to us?' Arah's voice was shaking as she spoke.

Zoe nodded. 'Yes, I read about it. I'm so sorry about what happened to you and my great-aunt.'

'We've spoken to many journalists in the past few years, but nothing ever happens. There is never any justice for us,' Arah sighed.

'I read that people protest in front of the Japanese embassy in Seoul every Wednesday,' Zoe offered.

'The Japanese government still denies that they forcibly exploited us as sex slaves. They accuse us of volunteering as prostitutes and being motivated to make money. Who would volunteer to have thirty men use them every day? No one.

What they say is ridiculous. They're just waiting for us to pass away. That's their strategy,' Arah said angrily.

'Why can't the Japanese government accept responsibility? Why is it so hard for them?' Zoe asked.

'The Japanese people are proud. Accepting what happened would cause the government to lose face,' Arah explained. 'But what about our face? What about our dignity? What about our lives? They destroyed us. They treated us as less than dogs. We were meant to be used. We were slaves. Sex slaves. All we want is an apology from the Japanese government—for them to admit their wrongs. They must accept responsibility and give a healing apology. Girls are still being raped in war and sold around the world. This must stop.'

'What if they don't apologize?' Zoe asked.

'Then we will continue to fight. We will do this until our last breath. Do you think we wanted to tell the world about this? No. What happened brings great shame to us and our families. But we couldn't stay silent anymore. After my husband died, I testified with the others,' Arah said.

'Who are the others?' Zoe asked.

'Chinese women in the neighbouring villages. They, too, suffered in the comfort stations. There is also a supportive Japanese woman, Ms Fujiwara. She helps us with court cases,' Arah replied.

'Was Ms Fujiwara also a comfort woman?' Zoe asked.

'No, but she supports our cause. She is the daughter of a prominent Japanese diplomat. She has a real heart for this topic. I don't really know why. She just seems to care about the issue and about us. She does whatever she can to help with our fight. Our cause is her cause.'

'Do you have her address? I'm going to Japan in a few days,' Zoe said, pulling out her notebook.

'Yes, her address is easy to remember. It is One, Silk Road, in Chinatown, Yokohama,' Arah replied.

'What about the other Chinese women—the other survivors of Japanese military sex slavery? Can I talk to some of them?' Zoe asked.

'Yes. I'll set something up. Would tomorrow work?'

'Should I come back here? I will return to the city, but I can come back again tomorrow. No problem.'

'Yes. We will meet here in my home.'

There was a moment of silence before Arah spoke again. She asked Zoe, 'Do you know who Masuki is?'

Zoe replied, 'Yes, I read about him.'

'It was Masuki who saved us. He arranged for us to get a pill. It made us sick. We thought it was poison to kill us. But instead, it was just a medicine to make us sick, to help us escape.'

Zoe's ears pricked up. 'I wondered about this. I read about the poison in Meera's journal as I was driving here.'

'Did the journal say what happened next?' Arah asked.

'I haven't read that far yet.'

'Do you want to know?'

Zoe nodded and Arah continued, 'We both woke up here in this village. Masuki had set up the whole thing. He had a Canadian missionary friend who ran a church here. We arrived here in an ambulance and hid in a local's home while we recovered. He paid everyone off—the woman who gave us the pills, the medics, the guards, everyone. He arranged the entire thing.'

'Did the pill hurt you at all?' Zoe said softly.

'No, even though it was toxic medicine, it was ultimately harmless.'

Over the next hour, Arah detailed the remarkable journey that she and Meera had shared as they integrated themselves into the network of North American Christian missionaries and Korean revolutionaries who were fighting the Japanese occupation from their base in the village of Shanjia, which was strategically located outside Shanghai. This collective of compassionate individuals had one mission: to help anyone on the run from the Japanese authorities.

The network worked out of a series of buildings, running a haven within this picturesque but unassuming countryside enclave that offered serenity and respite from the relentless violence of the Japanese occupation.

Operating through word-of-mouth, the network did its best to guide anybody in trouble towards the village—to the home that Arah and Meera resided in, where solace and support awaited.

Running this haven were Pastor Lee and his wife, Gwen—two Canadian missionaries whose journey to spread their faith had led them to China in 1938. Caught in the turbulence of war, their return to North America became an impossibility. As part of their efforts to do God's work, Pastor Lee, a compassionate educator, and Gwen, an impassioned social worker, established their operational base within their humble Chinese dwelling. This home, adorned with elegantly arched eaves and weathered timber, underwent a metamorphosis, becoming a beacon of light amid the darkness.

Nestled within this sanctuary lay a safe house. Gwen's boundless compassion, courage, and dedication to those in need drove her to aid local Chinese residents hunted by the Japanese, as well as occasional runaway Korean women, escaping the horrors of Japanese military forced prostitution. Together with her husband, she had designed the safe house to include alcoves in which people could hide when the law came looking for them. Despite sporadic raids by local soldiers, the clever design features kept their elusive quarry of those on the run hidden.

Pastor Lee's ingenuity had also transformed a corner of their dwelling into a modest classroom. Outfitted with timeworn desks and chairs, this room became a space where Arah, Meera, and countless others could learn and nurture their aspirations. It also provided a tranquil place to rejuvenate amidst the chaos. His commitment to education shone through as he taught lessons in English, reading, writing, arithmetic, and practical skills like sewing.

Beyond the confines of the dwelling was a spacious garden that became a flowering symbol of resilience. Despite their scant resources, the missionaries and villagers were able to nurture a patch of vegetables that offered both food and focus to the community. Tending to this garden became a ritual that provided both nourishment and a sense of normalcy for those in hiding. It was a reminder that even in the harshest of times, life could flourish against all odds.

Despite the challenges, the missionaries wove deep bonds with the villagers. Pastor Lee's interactions with the village elders evolved into a cherished routine of exchanging stories and wisdom beneath the sheltering canopy of an ancient, gnarled tree.

Their noble endeavours were not without peril. The Japanese occupiers viewed the missionaries with suspicion, recognizing their activities as a threat to their dominion. Yet, through ingenious communication codes, Pastor Lee, Gwen, and the villagers were usually able to forewarn one another of approaching Japanese officials, giving them plenty of time to hide the people and supplies.

Not a single fugitive was ever found.

When the war finally drew to a close, the village of Shanjia was celebrated as an example of communal solidarity. The missionaries' kindness had turned what was once a modest dwelling into something that radiated hope, healing, and transformation.

Arah told Zoe about how when the missionaries died, they were buried in the outskirts of the village and that she would have passed those simple gravestones on her way into the village.

'It was hard back then,' Arah said. 'We didn't always have enough food. And if the soldiers had found us, we would have been killed. When the war ended, Meera went back to Korea. I stayed here. I made friends and eventually got married to a local. I was an orphan and had no place else to go. This became my home.'

'But Meera didn't stay in Korea—she left. Did she never find her family?' asked Zoe, confused.

Arah stood up and walked over to a small wooden desk in the corner of the room. After sorting through some loose papers, she came back with a letter in her hand. It was from Meera. The paper was faded and yellow. Arah translated the Korean text into English:

Dearest Arah,

I miss you, Pastor Lee, Gwen, and the others so much.

Following a long, arduous journey, I finally made it home to my village in Korea. As you can imagine, both China and Korea are still in complete chaos. So many people are coming and going in every direction that it was hard for me to find any form of transport. I was often forced to walk with countless others, and there were times when there was no food or fresh water. I had to pay five times the price, just for scraps. But thanks to the missionaries, at least I had a little money. Many others had nothing. When I could, I shared what I had. But it was never very much.

After so many years, everything in Korea seemed so different. My once beloved town was run down and no longer pristine and beautiful. Like everywhere else, it was not spared from the ravages of war.

Upon my arrival, I rented a small room near my old neighbourhood. For an entire week, I walked towards my home, stopping somewhere nearby from where I could watch from a distance. I could see my mother, my two sisters, and my younger brother. But whenever I saw them, I noticed that they didn't seem happy. That joy that once thrived was lost; stolen away like everything else. Other relatives were staying in my ancestral home too. But I didn't see my father or my older brother. I feared they were both lost in the war. This thought brought me great sadness.

While I desperately wanted to run through the front gate to reunite with my family, I couldn't bring myself to do so. Every time I thought about this, I remembered what was done to me. The shame I feel is overwhelming. It never goes away. I didn't want to add to my family's loss and burden. I didn't want them to remember me this way—as a whore.

So, I left that place and rented a small room in Seoul. I have a job. I'm working for the war department. I'm helping them relocate families. I don't care much for the work, but it keeps my mind from thinking about other things. I will do this for a while and then find something else.

I have some relatives in Canada. I sent them a letter asking if I could come and visit them. I want to go far away from Korea. Far away from my past life. Far away from the pain and suffering and shame that never leaves me.

I will write again when I arrive there.

With love,
Meera

'Meera never recovered from her experience of being a comfort woman,' Arah said. 'She was often depressed and withdrawn. Even with all of their efforts, Gwen and Pastor Lee couldn't help her. She was completely broken. After receiving this letter, I didn't hear from her for nearly fifteen years. By then, she had settled in Canada. Now and then, we'd write to each other, but she seldom responded to my many letters.'

'What about Masuki? Did you see him again?'

Arah replied with sadness in her voice, 'No. His father caught up with him and forced him to go back to Japan. Years later, he found the addresses where Meera and I were living. I think he was still in love with her after all these years. But she wouldn't see him. She was too ashamed and angry. He tried many times and even flew to Vancouver once.'

Zoe hung on to every word of Arah's account. The more she learned about her great-aunt, the more she admired her strength, and the deeper their connection grew.

* * *

Zoe had just said her goodbyes to Arah and flopped into the taxi, mentally exhausted. The long journey and the emotional visit had depleted her. She couldn't wait to finally rest at her hotel.

Wang Jun was courteous, and as they drove through the rural landscapes, he engaged her in pleasant conversation. Despite her tiredness, Zoe found herself responding to his friendly tone. This was in stark contrast to their ride to the village.

Zoe appreciated how Wang Jun had helped her find Arah's house and asked if he would be available to drive her there again the following day from her hotel. She promised to pay him the same amount as before.

'Of course, I'm happy to help,' Wang Jun responded, without hesitating.

Zoe was taken aback by his supportive response. She had somehow expected him to haggle with her about the fee. She was relieved and grateful, and, for a while, their dialogue lapsed into silence as both of them drifted off into their own thoughts.

Suddenly, Wang Jun broke the silence by politely asking if he could ask her something. 'Go ahead,' said Zoe, curious to hear what he had to say.

'While I waited outside, the older man mentioned to me that your friend Arah was a comfort woman. I learned about the systematic enslavement of tens of thousands of Chinese girls and women by the Imperial Japanese military in school and read about them in newspapers. Is it true? Was Arah a victim of the Japanese?'

Zoe's response was sombre but forthright. 'Yes, unfortunately, she was. What you learned and read about—about the women and their suffering at the hands of the Japanese military—happened to her. They committed serious atrocities against her and so many young women back then.'

Wang Jun delved further. 'I've heard Chinese women were also affected?'

'Yes I believe that is true. Chinese women were also victims. In fact, I'll be meeting with some of them tomorrow,' Zoe said.

His astonishment was evident. 'That's truly awful.'

'It's a dark chapter in Asian history,' Zoe said.

Wang Jun continued. 'My parents have never forgiven the Japanese for what happened in our city during the war. They still boycott products from Japan. Many Chinese still feel this resentment and hatred for the Japanese. I hate them too.'

'Many Asians around the world feel the same. I've also felt resentment as I learn about what happened to my great-aunt.

But it doesn't need to be this way. We need to put the past behind us. But how can we have closure when the Japanese government denies they forced these girls and women into prostitution?' Zoe asked. 'Perhaps, someday, healing and reconciliation will result in some kind of forgiveness among these Asian nations. But only if the apology comes from the top in the government.'

Wang Jun looked at Zoe with gratitude in his eyes. 'Thank you for answering my questions. The local newspapers don't report much about this issue nowadays. Sometimes, the Japanese prime minister visits the Yasukuni Shrine where the Japanese generals and some war criminals are buried and worshipped as gods. That makes our government and many Chinese very angry.'

It dawned on Zoe that many others must harbour similar questions to Wang Jun—and that made her only more determined to shed light on the matter. She was going to tell the world about the plight of countless women and girls who were forced into sexual servitude by the Japanese army during World War II. And if that wasn't what *The Star* and her chief editor wanted—well, then they could go to hell.

9

Zoe arrived at Arah's home the next day to interview the other victim-survivors of Japanese military sexual enslavement. She found Arah sitting cross-legged on the floor while four elderly Chinese ladies were all squeezed together on the couch. Arah beckoned Zoe over and after exchanging small smiles, they began, with Arah translating the women's words from Chinese into English.

A woman whom Arah introduced as Fang spoke up first. 'Those Japanese were devils,' she said with a snarl. 'They took us and never once showed any compassion or kindness. I was there for three years. I was dead inside. I would have killed myself, but I didn't know how.' She paused to collect her thoughts. 'There was one girl—she was Chinese from Taiwan. She was in the room beside mine. She tried running away. When they caught her, she spat at the soldiers and called them bad names. They beat her over and over. Even with her face all bloody, she continued to spit and curse them. They beat her to death that day. That was her way of ending her pain. She knew what they would do to her. She wanted out. I thought about doing the same thing, but I didn't have the courage. I was too weak.'

A second woman, Li, spoke quietly. 'I couldn't have children,' she said, her voice breaking. 'My body was so wrecked with disease. It wouldn't work anymore. I loved my husband. I wanted to give him a child, a boy, but I couldn't. It was heartbreaking for both of us. He knew what happened to me. He understood. But it didn't make it any easier. His parents blamed me for being barren. We couldn't tell them what I went through. It would have brought shame to his family. All I could do was suffer in silence.'

'I hate the Japanese,' said a third woman, Hua. 'They are such great liars. Everyone knows the Japanese government forced us or tricked us. So many women suffered and were killed. They didn't care. We were disposable. I was thirteen when they took me there. I didn't know anything about . . . when they touched me that way, I was so shocked and disgusted. No woman should be treated the way we were. It wasn't right. And yet it was the Japanese government that did this to us. I will never forgive them. Never.'

Fang spoke up again, her voice shaking with emotion. 'I have only a few years left,' she said. 'I don't know how I have lived this long. All I want is for them to admit they were wrong! They must! I don't want money. But the Japanese government keeps saying that all we want is money. I'm too old to spend money. Just give me an apology, so I can have peace of mind. They even say we volunteered to do those things. No woman wants to be with men that way. If I needed money, I would have done anything else. I would have dug ditches. I would have starved to death. I want them to say they were sorry. They owe me that much.'

Zoe listened to their stories, her heart heavy with sorrow and anger. 'I wrote a newspaper story about young girls being trafficked into sex slavery in Korea,' she said. 'More than six million women and girls around the world are forced into prostitution. Do you see this as being the same?'

The fourth woman, Jing, nodded slowly. 'It is terrible that girls are still suffering like this,' she said. 'But we were forced by a government. Governments are supposed to protect people. Governments are supposed to follow rules. Even in war, there are rules. They didn't care. We were nothing to them. We were just warm bodies to be used by their soldiers. If this history isn't acknowledged by the government, it will happen again. We need to draw a line in the sand here . . . now . . . we want justice.'

'I want to say something,' Arah said. 'When I was a small girl, I had dreams of going to school, finding a boy, and marrying him, having children, watching them grow, and growing old with my husband. All Korean girls wanted that life. It was our right. All of this was taken from me. From all of us here. I was kidnapped from my home, beaten, raped, and cast away when the war was over. I have never understood why the world didn't see our pain and respond. We have been in front of the media, on TV. Everyone knows what happened, and yet it doesn't seem to matter. This is what I really don't understand.'

'I feel the same way,' said Zoe. 'I have written several articles on the topic of sex trafficking. There are millions of victims. So many people tell me they feel sad when they read my stories, but nobody ever seems to do anything. I'm not even sure what can be done. I struggle with this question. All I can say is that when I return to Canada, I'm going to try something new. I'm going to reach out to some people I know on social media. They have a large following. Maybe they can help to raise awareness and get people to step up and act.'

'I don't know what you are talking about,' Jing said. 'Who are these people? What is social media?'

'They are called social influencers,' Zoe said. 'It is hard to explain. All I can say is that they are able to reach millions of people with their messages. Their followers listen to them.

Maybe this approach would work. If it could, what would you want people to do? What is your message?'

'I would want them to pressure the Japanese government for a proper apology,' said Arah. 'I would ask them to see to it that governments around the world commit to never doing this again. I would tell them to insist that the millions of women and girls who are forced to do this even now be freed and that laws are put in place to prevent this from ever happening again.'

Zoe felt humbled by the women's bravery and strength in speaking out. As she prepared to leave, she felt determined to bear witness to their suffering. It felt like a watershed moment in her life.

As she stood by the door, she hugged Arah tightly. 'I will do whatever I can to tell the world what I learned,' she whispered into her friend's ear.

'There is one more thing. I received this ledger from a shelter in Los Angeles,' Zoe said, her voice low. 'It has a lot of writing in Japanese and Korean. There are names, dates, phone numbers, and more. I can read the Korean but not the Japanese. I'm afraid to take it with me into Japan. It has sensitive information. Do you know anyone who can translate this? I was able to get some useful details for my investigation, but there is so much more. It might help me to expose a sex trafficking ring between Korea and the USA that is being run by a Japanese gang.'

Arah seemed lost in thought for a moment. Then she nodded. 'Yes, I have a friend who reads Japanese,' she said. 'Her family was stranded in China after the war. She can look it over.'

'Thank you,' said Zoe, relieved. 'That would be a great help to me.'

With that, Zoe left the village, as the secrets of the Chinese women swirled around her head. But the thought of the ledger, which she had left behind with Arah, gave her hope. She was going to get to the truth, whatever it took.

* * *

Back in the taxi, it was Zoe's turn to ask Wang Jun a question.

'Do you mind if I ask you something?' Zoe asked. 'Do you use social media here in China?'

'Absolutely, I'm active on Sina Weibo, WeChat, and Douyin, or as you might know it in English, TikTok,' he said.

'What is Weibo?'

'It is the Chinese counterpart to your Twitter and Instagram. It is used to share information among friends and family.'

Zoe thought about this for a minute. 'I wonder if it could play a role in raising awareness about human trafficking,' she said. 'Are there social influencers in China?'

'Yes, there's many of them. They have a huge number of followers, more than, I would think, your influencers in the West. Some of them have millions, even tens of millions of followers.'

'Do you happen to follow any of them?' Zoe asked.

'A handful, actually. Why do you ask?'

'I've been toying with an idea and was just wondering. Thank you, Wang Jun. You've been very helpful.'

'Anytime. Glad to help.'

10

Zoe's heart was beating fast as she walked through the airport terminal, dragging her luggage behind her. The thought of bustling crowds and the unfamiliar environment had made her anxious the entire flight to Tokyo. She felt like a fish out of water: alone in a foreign country, with no one she knew.

As she left the arrivals area, she noticed a man holding a sign with her name on it. Zoe approached him cautiously. She had not expected anyone to be meeting her here.

'Are you here for me?' she asked, her voice betraying her apprehension. 'I'm Zoe.'

The man introduced himself as Kobe. He had a warm smile that put Zoe at ease.

'Yes, I'm here to take you wherever you need to go during your stay in Japan,' he explained.

Zoe raised an eyebrow. 'And who exactly sent you?'

'A lady named Mandy,' he said. 'She works for your newspaper. She said you'd need my help and would pay me directly.'

Zoe remained sceptical and asked how Mandy had found him.

'I've worked on a few projects with your company. My English is very good. This is not my first assignment with your paper.'

Kobe had a rugged, striking appearance, with sharp features and piercing eyes. His jet-black hair was styled into a spiky mess and a pair of black-framed glasses sat perfectly on his nose. His clothes were a mix of streetwear and casual chic—a loose-fitting T-shirt, a hoodie, cargo pants, and sneakers that rounded off the hipster look. But at twenty-nine years old, he was a little old to pull it off.

Still, something about Kobe's calm demeanour appealed to Zoe.

'Okay,' she said finally. 'Can you take me to the Mercure Hotel in Yokosuka?'

'Of course,' Kobe said, grabbing her luggage and leading her towards the parking lot.

Feeling a little relieved, Zoe thanked Kobe for his help and followed him out of the airport.

As they headed for the car, Zoe felt grateful to Mandy for arranging Kobe's services. Having him there helped to ease some of the anxieties she felt about the dangers ahead. She wondered what other surprises Japan had in store for her.

Zoe settled into the plush back seat of the car and took in the captivating surroundings. As the vehicle made its way from Tokyo's airport to the city, she was fascinated by the sights and sounds that surrounded her. The highway leading to the big city took them past quaint neighbourhoods boasting vibrant foliage, far removed from the bustling metropolis that she was soon surrounded by.

As she looked out the car window, she caught glimpses of daily life: students in pristine uniforms walking to school, salarymen engrossed in newspapers, and traditional temples juxtaposed with modern architecture. The forty-five-minute journey through the countryside was punctuated by moments of tranquillity and anticipation as Zoe caught sight of the glistening skyscrapers in the distance.

As the suburbs slowly faded away, the city came into view. Every inch of it seemed to pulsate with an uncontainable energy, as if it were alive and breathing on its own. Neon lights illuminated the streets, casting a surreal glow that seemed to transcend time itself. Zoe's eyes roamed over the horizon, drinking in the awe-inspiring spectacle before her.

The city's skyline was an architectural marvel, a symphony of towering skyscrapers that stretched towards the heavens, their glass and steel facades glinting under the sun's luminous embrace. Each one seemed to reach higher than the last, competing for the stars while casting intricate shadows upon the bustling streets below.

The sidewalks, alive with a constant ebb and flow of crowds, showcased Tokyo's ceaseless heartbeat. People from all walks of life mingled—locals in impeccably tailored suits, fashion-forward youths wearing avant-garde clothes, and confused-looking tourists carrying maps that they just couldn't understand.

Billboards and screens covered every available surface, casting kaleidoscopic hues that painted the cityscape with an iridescent glow. Advertisements for the latest technological marvels, haute couture fashion, and mouth-watering culinary delights competed for attention in a dazzling dance of light and colour. The city was like a canvas, each billboard a stroke of paint, telling a story of modernity and ambition.

It wasn't only the sights and sounds that captivated Zoe. It was the intangible essence of Tokyo: its electric energy that vibrated through the air, and its limitless potential and determination to be at the forefront of progress and innovation.

It was the sound of traffic, the chatter of people, and the occasional street performer entertaining passersby. It was the smell of restaurant food mingling with the aroma of coffee and freshly baked pastries.

As they pulled up in front of the hotel, Zoe stepped out of the car, excited like a little girl.

'Can you pick me up tomorrow at 10 a.m.?' Zoe asked.

'Yes, I'll be here,' Kobe replied, handing her the luggage.

'Thank you,' she said. She was about to turn away when something tugged at her to stop.

'Your name, Kobe, like the beef?'

'Kobe, like the city.'

As she watched him drive away, Zoe felt grateful for his assistance once again. *Maybe, just maybe, I can make it through this trip after all*, she thought.

* * *

Zoe stood in her hotel room, suddenly exhausted from her jet lag and her excessive range of emotions. She had felt tired since China, where hearing so many heart-wrenching stories had left her feeling drained. Her travel-worn bag seemed to weigh a ton as she carefully placed it in the closet.

She took a moment to look around the room, taking in the modest bed in the corner and the simple decor that surrounded her. The bed looked inviting, and she knew that she needed to rest her weary body. She made her way over to it, her footsteps echoing softly against the wooden floor, and with a deep sigh, allowed herself to collapse onto the well-worn mattress, feeling the softness envelop her. As she lay there, she closed her eyes and felt her exhaustion and emotions start to dissipate and give way to a sense of calm and peace.

Unlike the expansive hotel room she had experienced in China, this accommodation in Japan was compact and confining. She barely had any room to move.

As she rolled about on the micro-sized bed, she began to gather her thoughts. The unusual series of events unfolding in her life converged in her mind. Her run-in with the sex trafficking ring in Korea, her break-up with Jeff, the loss of her great-aunt, the stirring conversation with Arah and the tales of her fellow survivors—all these threads were crossing each other, and she was trying to see a pattern in them.

She let her thoughts swim as she lay back, hoping a solution might emerge as that twilight world between waking life and sleep approached. Inspiration hit just as her eyelids had begun to close. She sat bolt upright.

Forming in her mind were the hazy first details of a plan to bring the sex traffickers to justice. It was risky, foolish, and more than a little impulsive.

'But it just might work,' she muttered.

11

Zoe stepped out of the hotel and basked in the warm glow of the morning sun. She had been waiting eagerly for Kobe to arrive and smiled to herself as she saw him emerge from his car wearing a flannel shirt, skinny jeans, and a pair of retro sneakers.

There was something about the way he dressed that put her at ease. Amid all the drama and danger, it reminded her of youthful innocence. Here was someone who meant no harm, whom she could trust. She could be anonymous and safe behind the tinted windows of his simple Toyota. And he was young enough to do as she said, no questions asked.

Kobe greeted Zoe with a friendly grin and opened the door for her.

'Good morning, Zoe. Ready to explore Tokyo?' Kobe asked, flashing a set of pearly white teeth that only deepened Zoe's appreciation of him.

'Absolutely. But first, I need to get a Japanese SIM card. Then we can head to the Ameyoko market,' Zoe replied, handing him the address.

As they drove through the bustling streets of Tokyo, Zoe's anxiety began to return. What she was about to do was risky, she knew, but she was too far gone to stop. 'You've got this, girl,' she whispered to herself, not entirely convinced.

'Stop!' Zoe shouted suddenly, jolting Kobe out of his thoughts.

'Here?' asked Kobe, looking around in confusion and then pulling over to the side of the road.

'Yes, that shop over there, I think they would sell SIM cards,' said Zoe.

Kobe nodded in agreement.

Zoe stepped out of the car and hurried to the store. She scanned the shelves for a Japanese SIM card, found one, paid for it, and hurried back to the car. Kobe watched her as she swapped her old SIM card for the Japanese one.

'I need you to do something for me,' said Zoe, handing Kobe a piece of paper with English text on it. 'I'm going to call a number, and when the person answers, I need you to translate this into Japanese for them. I'm doing a story on sex trafficking victims and need to make contact with some of the people involved. And please, no questions.'

Kobe looked uneasy.

'I don't feel . . .' he began, but Zoe cut him off.

'Kobe, I'm a journalist. This is what we do. Just help me, okay? Just make the statement and hang up. You don't have to say anything else. Just hang up when you are done. Can you do this for me? They won't be able to trace our call back to us.'

Zoe dialled the number and handed the phone to Kobe, who had, by now, reluctantly accepted his fate. Someone answered the call, and the pair began to speak in Japanese.

'I am from Los Angeles. I run a strip club. I need to get young Korean girls. Let's talk about it. Face to face, not over the phone,' Kobe said, deepening his usual tone of voice. 'Please meet me at Café Tokyo, across from Ameyoko market, today at 1 p.m. I will be wearing a yellow shirt.'

'Who are you?' asked the man on the other end. 'How did you get this number?'

Kobe hung up the phone and handed it over to Zoe, whose heart was racing.

'What did the person say?'

'He wanted to know who I was. He sounded very angry.'

'Thank you for that, Kobe. You did great,' said Zoe, patting him on the arm and doing her best to use a reassuring tone, despite her own unease.

Zoe quickly removed the Japanese SIM card, bent it, and tossed it into a nearby trash bin. She was scared as hell, but there was no way she was going to show it.

She turned her head towards Kobe and smiled slightly. 'Things just got exciting,' she said.

* * *

Kobe and Zoe had been circling the block for what felt like hours, searching for a parking spot near Café Tokyo. Finally, they found one right in front of the coffee shop. Kobe had been anxious about their plan, and his hands were shaking as he turned off the engine. Zoe, on the other hand, seemed confident and determined as she got out of the vehicle.

'Stay here, Zoe said firmly, 'I'll return soon. Okay?'

'I'm just a driver. I don't want any trouble,' Kobe replied, his voice betraying a slight tremble.

'Don't worry. Just wait for me, please. Everything will be fine,' Zoe assured him.

And with that, she crossed the street and disappeared into the cafe.

Zoe had picked the venue—and her attire—wisely. Café Tokyo was a bustling spot in the heart of Tokyo, a favourite on the tourist trail because of apocryphal stories about now-famous writers, artists, and celebrities who all had, supposedly, once hung out here. It was too busy and high-profile to be used in a police sting, so it wouldn't arouse suspicion and the man who Zoe was hoping to meet would arrive. At least, so she hoped. It was also busy enough that she could disappear into the crowd if things took a turn for the worse.

Wearing a loose-fitting, floral dress and comfortable running shoes, Zoe was dressed to blend in as a free-spirited tourist making the most of the scorching Japanese summer. And if things did go south, it was the perfect outfit for her to do a runner.

The scent of freshly brewed coffee wafted through the air, mingling with the sound of chatter and the hum of the espresso machine. Every table was occupied, and a long line of customers was hugging the counter.

After hastily paying for her coffee, Zoe scanned the cafe for a vacant seat. Her eyes locked on to what seemed the perfect spot—a corner table occupied by an elderly couple. She dashed over and circled them like a hawk. The elderly woman was unimpressed. She stared at Zoe while muttering disapprovingly to her husband. The pair resisted the pressure to vacate their seats for the next few minutes, as if they meant to teach this impolite young woman some manners.

Zoe knew she was being rude, but reminded herself of why she was there, and returned the lady's scowls with the biggest smile she could muster.

Finally, the couple stood up and shuffled off, pausing only to give her pointed, reproachful looks and a slight shake of their heads.

Zoe quickly nestled herself in the plush seat. She nursed her lukewarm coffee and waited for the minutes to tick by, and they did, though seemingly in slow motion. As she sat there, she began to wonder if her impulsive decision to investigate this story was the right one.

By 1 p.m., her nerves had started to get the better of her. She waited a further fifteen minutes and was just about to leave when two men, so burly their chests barely fit in their jackets, walked in. A cold shiver travelled down Zoe's spine. They scanned the room, inspecting the faces of several male patrons before each of them shook their heads in disappointment.

Each of the men had his own distinct style. The first man was in a black leather jacket with crimson insignia, ripped jeans, and combat boots. His hair was wild, and a silver chain hung around his neck. The second man was in a tailored navy suit with a red pocket square and a silver chain around his neck. Both men had an aura of menace, and as they scanned the cafe, very few people dared to meet their gaze.

A distinguished-looking man in a tailored black suit then entered and headed towards them. The way he strode oozed power and influence; it was clear he was their leader.

Slightly older than the other two, he appeared to be middle-aged and had a refined demeanour matched by his taste in clothes: a crisp, white dress shirt, a silk tie in cornflower blue, and handmade leather shoes. Standing six feet tall, with a lean, athletic build and jet-black hair slicked back, he exuded confidence and authority through his dark, piercing eyes.

Zoe tried to remain composed and unfazed, carefully observing the situation from a safe distance. As the three men began to converse, she stood up calmly and exited the cafe, making her way to a newsstand nearby while keeping a watchful eye on the men.

Her eyes followed them as they too soon exited the cafe and climbed into a sleek black BMW, a 740-series model, parked outside.

As soon as the car began moving, Zoe climbed back into Kobe's car and instructed him to follow the BMW. Kobe turned and looked at Zoe, as if he was about to object, but thought it over again when he met her gaze.

'Just do it,' she hissed.

They followed the black BMW for thirty minutes, keeping at least a couple of cars between them, so as to not arouse suspicion until, eventually, they arrived at a dimly lit backstreet deep in the bowels of the red-light district.

The BMW came to a stop outside a building, and the three men got out, passed between two imposing security guards dressed in suits, and disappeared inside. The security guards then closed rank, folding their arms across their formidable torsos as if daring anybody to try to get past them.

'Park the car over there,' Zoe directed Kobe, pointing to a nearby spot. 'I'll be back shortly.' Zoe stepped out of the car and made her way towards the building, keeping a low profile. She studied the entrance, taking note of the security guards' positions and demeanour. Her eyes scanned the area, searching for any clues that would help her on her mission.

The red-light district was bustling with places offering every type of adult entertainment known to man. There were absinthe bars, gambling dens, hostess clubs, strip joints, and brothels—a cornucopia of vice and sin. The streets were filled with people whose darting eyes seemed keen to see but not to be seen.

Tourists, salarymen, businessmen, and locals—all were drawn in by the bright neon signs, flashing lights, and billboards touting shady-sounding services specializing in pleasures of the flesh.

The buildings were tall and narrow, with small entrances leading to multiple floors lined with private rooms. Some had large windows with red curtains or blinds, allowing passers-by to see inside. The decor and ambiance varied widely from one establishment to the other, but they were all designed to create a sensual and enticing atmosphere.

Zoe began walking up and down the street, stealthily taking photos as she went. She watched one building in particular, around which young girls dressed in school uniforms were loitering. Occasionally, a car would pull up, and a girl would enter through the back door.

Zoe's eyes scanned the area surrounding the building, searching for the perfect vantage point and doing her best not to stick out. Finally, she found an inconspicuous spot, hidden from view, where she could keep watch. She took out her phone and pretended to be deep in conversation, as she waited patiently for any signs of activity.

About an hour passed before a young girl emerged from the building, looking nervous and uncomfortable in her provocative attire. Zoe followed the girl, from what she assumed was a safe distance, observing her every move. Her stride was purposeful, and her steps measured and deliberate, as she trailed the young girl, who left behind the frenzied energy of the brothel district and turned into a quiet lane. Zoe gradually approached, her footsteps soft and muted on the pavement. She hoped she wouldn't scare this girl away.

She held her breath and reached out, gently tapping the girl's shoulder.

The girl spun around in surprise.

'Konnichiwa,' Zoe said as warmly as she could. When she received no response, she tried the same greeting in Korean. 'Annyeong haseyo.'

The girl looked at her in amazement.

I knew it. She's Korean, thought Zoe.

The girl cut a small but striking figure, standing five feet tall with a delicate, fragile frame. Her heavily made-up face—dark, smoky eyes with thick luscious lashes and a bold, red lip—seemed designed for seduction, as did the revealingly short, school-uniform dress that she was wearing. But behind the make-up, she had child-like features, and seemed lonely and out of place.

The young girl's voice held a hint of suspicion as she sized up Zoe, her eyes narrowing. 'Who are you?' she demanded, in Korean. 'What do you want from me?'

Zoe steeled herself for what was to come.

This was the moment she had been waiting for, the moment that could change everything. She knew that the answer she gave could determine whether she won the girl's trust.

'I'm Zoe Kim,' she said, her voice steady. 'I'm a reporter from Canada. I'm Korean-Canadian, and I'm working on a story about Korean girls being forced into prostitution here in Japan. I want to help put an end to it. Are you in trouble? Do you need any help?'

The girl's eyes widened, betraying her nerves. She lifted her hand to cover her mouth and mumbled, 'Oh my God. I'm going to be in trouble.'

Zoe knew that she had to tread carefully or risk losing the only lead she had.

'Please,' Zoe implored, 'just a few minutes of your time. I promise that I won't use your real name in the article.'

The girl turned and began to walk away. 'No. No. Leave me alone. You can't talk to me.' She waved her hand to shoo the stranger away.

But Zoe refused to give up. Not yet.

'What's happening in that building?' she asked, as gently as she could. 'Can we talk? Just for a few minutes?'

'No. I'll get into trouble.' The girl looked around. 'These men are gangsters,' she said. 'They're dangerous. Nobody can stop them.'

Zoe knew that she had hit a nerve. The girl was clearly scared. So she backed off.

'What is your name?' Zoe asked, changing the subject.

The girl's eyes flickered with uncertainty as she considered the question.

'Pinky. That's my name here.'

Zoe took a step forward and tried to lock eyes with her.

'Just give me five minutes, Pinky. We can talk anywhere.'

'Leave me alone,' Pinky said, shaking her head. She hastened her pace and turned up a walkway leading to what appeared to be an apartment building.

'I know you're scared. Do you have a sister? What if this was to happen to her? Do you want that?' asked Zoe, desperation starting to set in.

Pinky's sudden stop caught Zoe off guard. She turned around, her eyes beginning to tear up. Zoe had hit another nerve. Pinky scanned the surroundings to make sure that no one was watching them and then motioned for Zoe to follow her. Hesitating, Zoe trailed her into the apartment building. She felt a surge of hope, that she was finally getting to the truth.

Zoe spoke softly, 'It's nice to meet you, Pinky. Can we do this?'

Pinky's eyes darted back and forth as she sighed, and weighed the risks and benefits of speaking out. Finally, she nodded her head slowly.

Zoe asked, 'How about if we talk at your place? If we do this interview, you can save others. Girls like your sister. No one will know. I promise.'

She felt the hairs on her arms stand on end and a foreboding sense of danger.

Pinky looked up at her to think of her final decision, then she nodded her head and motioned to Zoe to follow her. They went down a hallway to a room on the third floor.

For a few tense moments, uncertainty filled Zoe's mind. Was it really a good idea to be following her? If someone had followed them, she would be trapped. Could she even be sure that she could trust Pinky? Who knew what this girl had been through, or what was going through her mind?

As soon as Zoe and Pinky stepped inside, a wave of relief washed over her. Pinky quickly closed the door behind them and turned on the only source of light in the room. The dim lamp illuminated the tiny space, revealing grey concrete walls that bore the stains of years of use. The silence was broken only by the sound of their breathing.

The room had barely enough space for two people to stand side by side. A narrow window was set high up on the wall, allowing in some faint light. Spartan though it was, the room felt safe and secure, a haven from the outside world.

There were a few basic essentials: a simple cot with a thin mattress, a table and chair, and a small seating area for applying make-up before a session at the brothel. A heap of K-Pop magazines had been tossed carelessly into one corner of the room. The toilet was outside down the hallway. The flooring was made of cold, hard concrete that seemed slightly damp, making the room feel colder than it already was.

The door was thick and made of solid wood, with a small slot at eye level, through which the security personnel could observe the girls. The air in the room was stale and musty, with a faint odour of mildew. The only decoration in the room was a framed picture of a faded view of Mount Fuji, the lone reminder of the outside world for Pinky.

Zoe watched Pinky. She could see the haunted look in her downcast eyes as she took a seat. Zoe spoke softly as she reached for her notebook, her eyes fixed on the girl in front of her. 'Thank you for taking the time to talk,' she said. 'Can you please tell me more about how you ended up here?'

Pinky's eyes appeared disturbed, as if weighed down by heavy thoughts, and her gaze was faraway, as if lost in contemplation.

Zoe spoke gently, trying to put Pinky at ease. 'I am here to listen to you, Pinky. Can you tell me how you ended up here?'

Pinky's voice was barely audible as she began to recount her story.

'I came to Japan when a man and a woman promised me a modelling job. They said I would be rich and famous. I believed them. They promised I would have enough money to buy anything I wanted, including a new phone. I wanted to buy a new iPhone. They said I would be able to. It was supposed to be a short trip—one day. Then they . . .'

As Pinky spoke, Zoe listened intently, scribbling away in her notebook. She could sense the fear and confusion in Pinky's voice as she recounted how the people who had promised her the modelling job betrayed her trust, leaving her in a foreign country with no money, no job, and no way to get back home.

Zoe's heart ached as she listened, anticipating the extent of the horrors Pinky had endured. She already knew much of the story, which was like many others that she had heard in the course of her research.

'When did you arrive?' she asked, struggling to keep her voice steady.

'Two years ago. They tricked me at fourteen and brought me here,' Pinky replied, her words laced with pain and anger.

'What happened next?'

'I was forced to work in that place. They took terrible photos of me naked. I was drugged. They said I was a bad girl. But I didn't do anything. They said they'd show the photos to everyone at my school. They also threatened my parents and my little sister. They had my address.'

Zoe felt her stomach churn. 'Are there other girls like you from Korea?' she asked, trying to keep her emotions in check. 'Others your age?'

'Yes, so many,' Pinky said, her voice strained. 'The passport they gave me says that I am twenty. But I don't look twenty. No one seemed to care about this when I entered Japan.'

'How do they stop all of you from running off?' asked Zoe.

'They have photos of girls who tried. Awful pictures. They were beaten to death. Bad things were done to their bodies, unwomanly things. We can't run. They have eyes everywhere. They said they'd do this to my sister, too, if I tried to run off. They know where my family lives. They have people there. I am trapped here. There is no escaping.'

Zoe could see the fear in Pinky's eyes. She saw how her pupils dilated, and her hands shook as she recalled her story. She was truly terrified. Zoe felt anger build up inside her. She felt for Pinky and the situation she was in, yet she knew she must not let her own emotions get in the way of helping her.

'Have they hurt you?' she asked.

'They hit us all the time. But not on our face. They're so cruel. I've been so scared, but now I don't care. I just want to die. I want out.'

A knot formed in Zoe's throat. She remembered how Meera, Arah, and several of the other survivors had said the same thing.

'I am deeply sorry to hear about what you're going through,' Zoe said. 'But please, remember that you are not alone in this.

You have a wonderful family who loves you unconditionally and who will always be there for you. You have so much to live for. There's always hope, even in the darkest of moments. There are brighter days ahead . . .'

'They tell us if we hurt ourselves, our entire family will be killed,' Pinky continued, ignoring Zoe's statement as if she hadn't heard it. Her voice was barely above a whisper.

'Do you believe that?'

'Yes. They're ruthless. They'll do anything to make money from us.'

Zoe's phone dinged, and a jolt of fear shot through her. She looked down and was surprised to see a text message from Jeff.

She put the phone aside, not wanting to be bothered by one of his pathetic pleas to get back together.

As Zoe turned back to Pinky, her phone dinged three more times in rapid succession. Feeling annoyed, she thought she would put a stop to this. Tell him once and for all to stop texting her. But before she could start, she saw a series of messages that read:

Danger. Danger. You are in terrible danger. Get out of there quickly. They are coming for you in the building you just entered! Run for your life!

Jeff's messages made no sense. She was completely confused. But she also knew that however annoying Jeff could be, he never lied to her.

As she looked up from her phone, she saw terror in Pinky's eyes as she too read the messages. Pinky was shaking uncontrollably.

'We have to get out of here,' Zoe said, grabbing Pinky's hand. 'Is there a back door?'

Pinky nodded, still trembling. 'Yes, down the back staircase. Oh my God. They know about us. I'm dead. They'll kill me. They'll kill us both. Why did I listen to you?' she cried.

'No, I won't let that happen. I promise,' Zoe said.

Zoe held Pinky's hand and led her towards the back staircase, their footsteps echoing ominously in the empty building. As they descended the stairs, they heard voices speaking in Japanese. They had been discovered. Zoe knew that they had to act quickly, so she led Pinky up to the higher floors of the building.

With the gangsters in hot pursuit, they climbed ten sets of stairs, their legs burning with exertion, until they finally burst out onto the roof. Zoe noticed an old, rusty deadbolt that allowed her to lock the door. *Hopefully that'd hold*, she thought.

Zoe looked around frantically, scanning for an escape route. But there was no way out that she could see which didn't involve jumping to the adjacent building. Zoe ran along the roof's edge, her eyes fixed on the gap. It was risky, but she knew that there was no other option but for Pinky to jump.

Pinky looked at her, terrified.

'You have to jump, Pinky,' Zoe urged again, her voice frantic. She could hear the men pounding on the other side of the door, at the top of the staircase. With each blow, the door slowly succumbed to their brutal force.

'I can't,' Pinky said, her eyes wide with fear. 'It's too far.'

'You must. That's the only way. Once you're on the other side, run along the top of those roofs. You'll find an exit somewhere. All these buildings are connected. Then go to the nearest police station. I'll come find you later. I know people in Seoul who can help protect you and your family.'

'Where are you going?' Pinky asked.

'I'll stay here. I have to hold them back until you can get away. I'm a foreign journalist. They won't do anything to me,' Zoe said naively, trying to reassure herself as much as Pinky. 'I got you into this mess, I'll get you out. Now, go!'

Pinky stared at the street below and then back at the gap between the buildings. She knew she had to commit fully, or she was dead. She took several steps back, breathed in, and rocked on her ankles before breaking into a sprint and launching herself across the chasm. Zoe watched as she flew through the sky, as if in slow motion.

Pinky landed on the second roof, hard, and her momentum sent her tumbling over. She stood up and brushed herself down briefly before turning back to look at Zoe.

Zoe waved her on, urging her to run. 'Don't stop,' she yelled.

With trembling hands, she deleted all the notes and photos from her phone. She then picked up her notebook and threw it off the side of the building. Nobody could know her sources, or all the people she had spoken to would be at risk.

Moments later they burst through. There were four large men in ill-fitting dark suits who did not look at all sympathetic.

For a brief moment, they almost appeared confused as they took in their new surroundings. Then their eyes landed on Zoe.

She knew that if she was to survive this encounter, she had to act fast.

As they walked towards Zoe, their sharp and chiselled features caught her attention. They had cold and unyielding expressions on their faces, and their bald heads poked out from the necks of their black suits. To Zoe, they looked like giant vultures.

As they closed in, she could see that each of them had a knife in their hand. *Men like these stopped at nothing to get their way*, she thought, fighting the urge to run.

'Where is she?' asked one of the men, casting his eyes around the rooftop.

'Where's who?' said Zoe, trying her best to look puzzled by their question.

'Pinky. The girl that was with you earlier,' the man said.

'I'm afraid I don't know what you mean,' Zoe replied calmly. 'I'm by myself, no one else is here. It's just me.'

The man lashed out, slapping Zoe across the face. Two of the others grabbed her by the arms and dragged her toward the stairwell.

She didn't resist. How could she?

12

Zoe was taken down the street and into the brothel. The men had bent her arms behind her back, making it easy to control her movements. The slightest resistance from her and it felt like her wrists would break.

Once inside the brothel, they took her down a long corridor on the ground level and into a large, spacious room. The room was filled with military antiques, samurai swords, and old, black-and-white photographs.

They pushed her forward until they were roughly in the centre of the room. She was now standing before a grandiose mahogany desk, the sort a head of state might sit behind in a television drama. To each side of it stood two large stern looking men. *They must be the enforcers for whoever is running this place*, Zoe thought. And then she saw him.

Sat behind the desk was a smaller man, writing something with slow, methodical movements. Zoe recognized him as the same man she had seen in the cafe. *So he* was *the boss*, she thought.

He looked up and asked one of the men, 'Did you find Pinky?'

'No, sir,' the enforcer replied, with his eyes looking down.

'Get on it,' the boss snapped back. 'You know what to do.'

The man turned toward his two companions, motioning with his head for them to follow him out.

As he finished writing, the boss took off his glasses and turned his attention to Zoe. 'I read your story in the Canadian newspaper,' he said, his English perfect and accented with a hint of formality. 'It was quite an interesting article. I'm told you received a lot of praise for it.'

Zoe was surprised by the reference to her work and his impeccable English. She remained silent, waiting for him to continue.

The boss carefully studied her as he cleaned his glasses with a small cloth, then returned them to his face. 'What you don't seem to understand, Ms Zoe, is that some things should remain unknown. When you shine a light on a business like this, you create a lot of problems. Problems for me. And I don't like that.'

Zoe bristled at his words. 'What do you want me to say?' she said with an edge to her voice. 'It's my job. I'm a journalist. This is what we do.'

'Is it really your job, though?' the boss asked. 'Why this story? There are so many other important, global issues—endangered whales, the environment, poverty, gun violence. When I was at Oxford, many clubs raised awareness about these other subjects. Why not write about those stories? Why do you keep focusing on these women? It is not your place.'

Zoe felt her anger rise. 'Women? Are you kidding me?' she said, her voice rising. 'These so-called sex workers in your brothels are barely women. They're trafficked children, exploited and abused by men like you!'

The boss's expression remained impassive, but Zoe could sense annoyance in his tone as he spoke. 'You misunderstand, Ms Zoe. These girls are not being exploited. They are making a choice, a choice that is better than the other options available to them back in their country. And as for me, I am merely providing a service. A service that is in high demand.'

Zoe shook her head in disbelief. 'That's not a service, it's a crime! These girls deserve better than this!'

The boss reclined in his plush leather chair, the rich mahogany creaking beneath him, and fixed his intense gaze on Zoe. The only sounds were the hum of the air conditioning and the soft ticking of the antique clock on the wall.

'You may think that, Ms Zoe, but you are a long way from home, and we have a different way of life here in Asia. A different culture and a different set of values. Foreign reporters like you do not respect that, and that is why you are not welcome here. You may look Asian, but you are not. You have been hypnotized by Canada's misinformed, racist ways.'

As he leaned forward against the desk, Zoe could smell his breath. It had a foulness that belied his sophisticated appearance. His pen twirled between his fingers as he paused to gather his thoughts, his every move calculated and deliberate. He seemed to be weighing his next words.

'In many countries across Asia, girls marry at the age of twelve. Some of them have two children by the time they are fifteen. They're not children. You are imposing a Western standard on this part of the world. You don't understand anything. You do not understand your own culture. You are white inside,' he said, his voice cold and condescending. 'You are a banana—yellow on the outside but white on the inside. That's what they say where you're from. Am I right?'

His words knocked Zoe sideways. Fury began to build inside her, like a rush of hot blood that turned her muscles into coiled springs. Her body bristled with anger and resentment. He had insulted and belittled her, zooming in on her most vulnerable spot. She was struggling to keep her cool.

'I understand that selling young girls' bodies is wrong, no matter where you come from,' she said, trying to convey a sense of calm confidence. 'There is nothing Western about this truth. It is universal.'

As he leaned back in his chair, the sound of creaking filled the air. His face remained stoic, but his eyes narrowed and were fixed on something intently, as if examining it under a microscope. The silence in the room was unbearable; he was using it as a weapon against Zoe. She felt her pulse quicken, adrenaline and fear gripping her as she waited for him to speak.

'So how do you know these girls don't want to do this work? We help them to leave Korea to live here in Japan. Korea is a dump—not even fit for dogs. There is a better life here. That is why they willingly choose this profession.'

Zoe's eyes grew large as she stared in utter disbelief. Her mind struggled to comprehend what she was hearing or the fact that she was sitting before this grotesque monster.

'These teen girls choose to sell their bodies? Are you out of your mind?' she exclaimed, her voice rising. 'The girls I met in LA had no idea where they were going. No one would have agreed to go there to be raped and used by so many men. They were all deceived by your people. The same is happening here in Japan.'

The boss remained reclined in his chair, a smile spreading across his face. He began to rock back and forth in a steady rhythm as his eyes fixed on something in the distance. He seemed at ease, relaxed and content. The soft creaking of the chair was the only sound in the room.

'So, that's how you found us here. Someone in the USA linked us to something happening there? Who was it?'

Zoe was visibly agitated. She'd had enough of his questions. It was as if something had been boiling inside her and she could no longer contain it.

'The day after those young girls arrived in America, they were sold. They're like the girls forced into Japanese military prostitution, the comfort women, the sex slaves your government provided for your soldiers during World War II. It's happening all over again,' she said through clenched teeth.

He tilted his head, studying Zoe with a hint of curiosity and a slight smile playing on his lips. His eyes locked on to hers with an intensity that made her uneasy. She felt like a mouse in the presence of a cat, waiting for him to pounce. He grinned back, enjoying the power he held over her.

Zoe shifted uncomfortably. Despite the fear that was creeping up on her, she was fascinated by the man in front of her. He held a kind of power and confidence that she had never seen before; she wondered what drove his narcissism and sadism, his need for control.

'You have heard of the comfort women?' he said. 'Once again, you have it all wrong. Those women volunteered to service our brave soldiers during the great war. They did it for the money. Some women are just whores. It is just the way things are,' he said in a playful tone. 'They are "chosen pi"—public toilets,' he added with a glint in his eye.

He knew exactly which words would hurt Zoe the most.

'You think they just woke up one day and decided that they wanted to be raped by thirty soldiers a day?' screamed Zoe, her anger exploding.

'Yes. How would you know anyway? They were living in desperate times. There is nothing written about this. No proof. It is fake news. Just a myth that liberal Japanese and foreigners like you have repeated so often that you've begun to think it's true. You want to bring shame to Japan and our traditions.'

'I know because my great-aunt was one of them. She lost everything!' Zoe spat out angrily. 'She was dragged away from her family in Korea and forced into prostitution in China. I was just there. I interviewed four others who were taken and raped by your government and military. I heard it from their own mouths. None of them volunteered. None of them would have done this shameful work. You forced them. You turned them into slaves.'

'Then I guess your aunt was a toilet too. A fucking whore,' he hissed.

'You racist, bastard pimp! Go to hell!'

The air in the room turned heavy. Both of them had lost the tempers they were trying so hard to hide from each other.

A silence descended for several long and uncomfortable seconds. Both knew the slightest noise or movement could shatter the fragile balance and send the situation spiralling out of control. Neither of them wanted to make the first move, the tension building with every passing moment.

'Enough of this,' the boss said eventually. 'So, did someone in the USA tell you about our operation? Who was it?'

'No one told me anything. I just found out some things,' Zoe replied, her tone defiant.

With a renewed air of authority, the boss leaned forward, his elbows planted firmly on the desk before him.

'What things?' he asked, in a low voice.

'I have information—an audit ledger. It relates to your business. It's safe in Canada, I sealed it away in an envelope and gave it to my colleagues. They'll open it if they don't hear from me soon,' she bluffed, trying to sound confident.

He squinted his eyes and steepled his fingers in front of him. 'You're lying,' he said flatly.

Zoe locked eyes with the mob boss, determined not to blink. She was prepared to stand her ground no matter what.

'I'm not,' she said. 'How green do you think I am? I've written a thousand stories about people like you. They won't hesitate to turn it over to the authorities if you don't let me go.'

His lips curled up slightly, and he emitted a low, quiet laugh. 'You think you can blackmail me? You have no idea who you're dealing with. But perhaps I'll play along. What do you want in exchange for this ledger?'

Zoe was at a loss for words. She had not thought this far ahead, and was flustered and unsure of how to proceed.

'I want you to stop trafficking these girls. Let them go free, let them live their lives.'

'You know, you're just like so many other clueless people who don't understand anything,' he said sadistically, a cruel smirk planted on his face. 'You are young and naive, and think you can change the world. But the truth is, you're powerless. You're nothing but a pawn in my game.'

The hot lava of emotions that had been welling up inside Zoe was ready to erupt.

'You're the one who's going to regret messing with me,' she said, shaking with anger.

'I don't think so. I hold all the cards. Ms Zoe, what you said to me is already a bit ridiculous. Think about it. If I let you go, you'll use the media against me. So why should I let you go? Wouldn't that be a grave mistake on my part? If you were me, would you let you go?'

Zoe's heart was pounding, her head throbbing as she frantically tried to see a way out of the dangerous situation that she had found herself in. The man's words echoed in her head, taunting her with the horrors that awaited her. She couldn't believe that she had let her guard down so easily. She knew what fate awaited her if she couldn't find a way out. Meera, Arah, the sex slaves for the Japanese army, Pinky . . . they had told her all about it.

But she refused to give up hope. She scanned the room for any possible means of escape. She racked her brain for ideas, wondering if she could somehow distract the guards and make a break for it. But her mind was slowing down, and she had to be quick if she wanted to survive.

Suddenly, there was a knock on the door, and a man entered the room, holding a large, red ledger in his hand. He approached the desk and bowed deeply, his head almost touching the ground. The boss acknowledged him with a curt nod, then his cold eyes shifted back and fixed on Zoe.

The ledger seemed almost identical to the one that Kim had given to Zoe in LA. Zoe watched in silence as the boss signed the ledger in several places. The other man then took the book and walked over to a wall safe. He opened it and put the book inside. Then he turned around and quietly walked out the door.

Zoe realized then that perhaps the book she had left with Arah was more important than she had originally thought.

'Just let me go,' Zoe demanded.

'You're not going anywhere,' he said menacingly. 'I've decided that you're going to be one of my girls.'

'You're insane,' she spat out. 'I won't be a part of your sick game.'

'You are young and pretty, a sexy little banana,' he said, taunting Zoe. 'I'm sure those Canadian men love getting under your skin. But I suppose you must be bored of white cock after all these years.'

'That's why I'm so pleased that you've chosen to come here to service some real men. Japanese men. They'll show you how it's really done. And I appreciate you volunteering for the job, just like that comfort woman aunt of yours. You'll be a modern-day comfort woman, just like all those others. You can replace Pinky. After we find her, she'll be of no use to anyone.'

It was the reference to Pinky that disturbed Zoe the most.

'You want to truly understand what it is like to be one of these women?' he asked, pausing for a moment as if carefully choosing his next words. 'You can find out first hand. Let's call it immersive reporting,' he snorted.

'You won't get away with this. You'll get caught, and I'll expose you and your evil business.'

'And how will you do that? You are here, now. As my guest. You will be for a long time. You need to understand something. You don't get to win in this game.'

He turned to the two thugs on each side of his desk. 'Take her to one of the rooms upstairs.'

Then he turned back to his desk, as if he had lost interest in Zoe all of a sudden and began reading one of the papers on his desk.

Without looking up, he added, 'Oh, one more thing. Give me her phone.'

One of the thugs walked over, took it away from Zoe and handed it to him. He looked it over.

'Have someone unlock it.'

The other thug grabbed Zoe's shoulders to escort her out. She tried to resist but he was too strong. As he dragged her out of the room, dread and uncertainty threatened to consume her.

But she was not beaten, not yet. Zoe did what little she could to resist: she focused on her surroundings, doing her best to memorize every detail. She told herself she would use these memories one day to help her escape, or to give evidence in a court of law, to bring these people down.

She kept repeating to herself that, somehow, she would find a way out of this place, that she would make it out alive.

She closed her eyes, breathed in deeply to keep the panic at bay, and tried to imagine a future where she was safe and free from harm.

13

Zoe ascended a narrow set of stairs that led to a large lounge area. She walked through the space with one of the thugs holding her arm to guide her forward. The air was thick with the pungent scent of tobacco and cheap cologne, almost suffocating her senses.

The room was dimly lit, with only a few scattered lamps casting a warm glow on the red and gold accents that adorned it, adding a seedy glamour to the atmosphere. On the walls, traditional Japanese art pieces depicting geishas, samurais, and cherry blossoms were juxtaposed with lewd posters and suggestive photographs.

At the tables sat men smoking cigarettes and drinking sake. Some of them wore expensive suits and loosened ties, while others were dressed more casually. Their eyes roved around the room, scanning for their next conquest.

In one corner, a group of well-dressed businessmen were huddled together, their faces flushed with the effects of the various cocktails scattered on the table before them. They laughed and joked, their voices rising above the din of the other patrons. They were there to let loose, to forget their troubles and responsibilities, and to revel in the pleasures of the flesh.

Amidst the ambient thumping of music, the businessmen gestured wildly, exchanging anecdotes with animated expressions. Slurred words and innuendos punctuated the air, adding to the camaraderie and carefree revelry among the men. All the girls could do was look on and try to hide their sadness.

With every cheer, glasses clinked. This was the light banter that played out before they molested girls young enough to be their daughters.

Their businesslike facades dissolved a little more with every sip of sake into a more primal energy. Crisp, white shirts were untucked, collars were unbuttoned, and ties hung like forgotten trophies. This was a moment of shared indulgence.

The girls, strategically situated throughout the lounge, were dressed in form-fitting outfits, some in schoolgirl uniforms, others in short dresses. They giggled and flirted with the men, their voices high-pitched and girlish. This was how the men liked it, and every girl knew she had to keep the men happy—or else.

Zoe felt out of place, a foreigner in a world that she didn't understand. The hallway that followed the lounge was narrow and claustrophobic, lined with countless doors on either side. Each door had a number on it, and Zoe could only imagine what horrors lay behind them.

As she walked, a drunk man stumbled out of one of the rooms, his shirt untucked and his eyes glazed. He was accompanied by a girl in a school uniform, her hair tousled and her makeup smudged. Zoe felt her stomach churn, as she thought of what had just happened to that girl. She was just a teenager—no more than fourteen or fifteen years old.

Zoe wondered how many girls were trapped in this world, forced to sell their bodies by these terrible men. She was witnessing a dark side of Japan, one that few people on the outside would ever believe exists behind the majestic brownstone facade of this building.

When they reached door '23', the thug stopped, unlocked it, and pushed Zoe inside before locking it from the outside.

The room was small and suffocating, damp and dark. Its walls were made of rough, grey stone, and from its high ceiling hung a large, dilapidated fan that looked like it might fall at any moment. The only source of light came from a tiny window high up on the wall, which was covered in grime and barely let in any of the sun.

The bed in the corner was old and creaky, with a thin, tattered mattress, which was stained with unknown substances. The pillow was flat and lumpy, and the sheets were threadbare and torn. The table and chair were made of rusted metal, and the surface was covered with scratches and dents. There was no other furniture in the room.

The air was thick with a musty, smothering smell. The walls were slick with moisture, and there were several spots of black mould. The only sound was the constant dripping of water from an exposed set of rusting pipes, echoing through the cramped space.

The wooden door was heavy, with a small peephole that allowed people to peer in from the outside. The door had been reinforced, making it impossible to break down.

It was a dingy, dark prison cell, designed to isolate those within from the outside world. Zoe had no hope of escape.

Having taken stock of her surroundings, fear crept over Zoe as she paced the room. The mob boss's threat lingered in her mind, making her feel helpless.

'What have I gotten myself into?' she mumbled out loud to herself. 'How do I get out of this mess?'

Zoe's mind was a whirlwind of fear and uncertainty—for her own safety and that of Pinky. She blamed herself for having put Pinky in such danger. She knew now that if the mob boss managed to find her, she would face a slow and painful death.

The guilt gnawed at Zoe's insides: If only she had been more cautious.

Something else was playing on Zoe's mind too: the mystery of how Jeff had learned about her crisis. She kept recalling the text message:

They are coming for you in the building you just entered! Run for your life!

She had been trying to come up with possible explanations but couldn't be certain of anything. She also couldn't shake the feeling that there might be other factors at play here that were hidden from her understanding. The more she thought about it, the more uncertain she became.

Trapped within the confines of the brothel, she started to think of all the strange men who would be sent in to rape her and she started to feel out of breath—the beginning of a panic attack. She could be sure the mob boss would handpick the vilest creatures in his books. He wanted to break her.

Zoe's chest tightened. She felt suffocated, as though the walls of the room were closing in on her. She frantically thought of how to escape, but all she could see were Pinky's terrified eyes staring back at her. Zoe grappled with her regrets and her worries, as she constantly replayed scenes in her mind of how she had become ensnared.

She couldn't believe that she had been so careless. How had she ended up here, in this dark and dingy room, with no way out? She desperately needed to escape, so she could protect the innocent girl that she herself had endangered. She couldn't let Pinky suffer because of her mistakes.

She had to be strong, for both of them.

* * *

Zoe had been pacing the room for several hours, consumed by worries, when, suddenly, she heard the sound of the lock being fiddled with. The door swung open, and she was surprised to see a small, elderly Japanese woman enter with a tray of food. The tray held two bowls and a can of Coke, with a straw sticking out of it.

As the old woman walked towards Zoe, Zoe noticed the fragile grace in her movements. Despite her age and obvious frailty, she moved with a quiet dignity. Her pallid face was lined with the marks of a life she hadn't chosen, and her once-lustrous hair was now threaded with strands of grey. *Was this woman a slave too, or was she here voluntarily as a paid worker?* Zoe wondered as she tried to strike up a conversation with her.

'Konnichiwa.'

The woman studiously ignored her greeting and shrank from her gaze.

Against the vibrant colours of the brothel's decor, the woman's faded pink dress made her appear like a delicate flower adrift in a sea of garish opulence. Her nervous frown betrayed the turmoil that lay just beneath the surface, and her downcast eyes held secrets that Zoe couldn't even begin to guess. The woman's hands trembled as she held the tray of food out to Zoe, her fingers delicate and thin. One of the bowls contained some watery vegetables and the other, some rice.

Zoe didn't take the tray, so the woman walked over to the table and set it down shakily. Each step was hesitant, like she was walking on eggshells.. Her fear was evident. The woman's presence reminded Zoe of the wickedness and vulnerability that lay beneath the surface of the brothel's decadence. She was a soul trapped in a world of dark shadows.

Zoe tried to ask her what was going on, but the woman shook her head to indicate she didn't understand. A muscular thug stepped inside and scolded the woman, and she scurried away. The door was slammed shut and locked.

For a long time, Zoe ignored the food, but her thirst got the better of her, and she drank the Coke. Then, she sat on her bed to think. Within minutes, she began to feel dizzy. All at once, a terrible thought crossed her mind. She had heard the story so many times. Girls were drugged by strangers who then took advantage of them.

Realizing she would soon lose consciousness, Zoe desperately searched for a way to buy herself some time. She locked the two deadbolts on the inside of the door—put there to give clients privacy presumably—and pushed her bed against the door.

Struggling to stay awake, she sat on the bed and waited. Fifteen minutes later, she heard the lock being opened from the outside. When the thug realized the door had been bolted from the inside, he began to shout and pound on it. Zoe could hear people talking and arguing. Knowing that it would only be a matter of time before they broke the door down, she prepared herself.

She sat perched on the edge of the bed, a maelstrom of emotions raging within her. As she struggled to keep her eyes open, the world around her seemed to shift and twist in a dizzying display that mirrored the chaos of her thoughts. It was as if her surroundings were engaged in a bewildering dance, one that she found impossible to follow as she battled to stay awake. Her mind was consumed by a tumultuous storm, a tempest of conflicting emotions and thoughts that threatened to overwhelm her at any moment. Despite the struggle, she fought on, determined to stay alert until the end.

Amid her desperate fight for consciousness, recent events played before her like a movie being fast-forwarded in her mind: her voyage to Korea, the sketchy alleyways, Pinky, and the ever-present undercurrent of danger. And then there was her great-aunt Meera, the loss of whom haunted her. It was a profound sense of loss intermingled with the remorse of never having truly understood her.

The shards of her shattered relationship with Jeff added yet another layer of anguish to Zoe's inner turmoil. The love they once nurtured had not withered away; but this period of separation had left behind an ache of emptiness and disillusionment. Their arguments reverberated like a haunting sonata, a terrible reminder of the dissolution of a once-beautiful connection.

Her clash with her boss also resurfaced. She was amazed to find that, even in her present, dire circumstances, just thinking about him caused a rush of frustration and a sense of injustice to well up anew. The memory of their heated exchange replayed in her mind: she remembered the cutting words so clearly. A sensation of helplessness clawed at her again.

As the spinning sensation grew, an irresistible undertow merged these memories and emotions into a terrifying whirlpool. Zoe was engulfed—a hapless bystander drawn into the uncontrollable swirl of her foolish mistakes and regrets.

Unable to keep her eyes open from the effects of the sedative, the darkness finally consumed her.

14

Zoe's eyes slowly fluttered open, as she gradually regained consciousness. A sharp, throbbing pain emanated from her skull, as if her head were about to explode. The room felt disorienting, with the objects around her appearing as blurry shapes that refused to come into focus.

Her memory was foggy, and she struggled to remember what had happened to her, leaving her confused and somewhat alarmed. The headache pounded away like a drumbeat. She groaned in agony as she tried to rise.

As she sat up, she realized that she was still trapped in the same room where she had been held captive. Panic set in as the events of the previous night began coming back to her. But to her surprise and relief, it seemed like they hadn't managed to get in while she was unconscious.

She stood up and felt her vision somewhat improve. Her eyes looked around the small room in search of a way out. She moved towards the window and dragged the chair over, her hands shaking as she climbed up to inspect it. To her dismay, she figured out that it was nailed shut from the outside. She felt like she was in a nightmare, trapped in a small cell with no hope of escape.

Suddenly, there was shouting outside the door. It was in a language she didn't understand, but the tone was urgent and frantic. The noise grew louder and more chaotic, the sound of people rushing up and down the hallway filling her ears. Her chest felt constricted, as her breath grew shallow and rapid. She braced herself despite her feeling of helplessness, being alone in a foreign place. Her eyes were fixed on the door as she waited for the worst.

There was a pounding on the door. Someone shouted something in Japanese. She could see the door handle being turned frantically.

'Go away!' Zoe shouted, her voice shaking with dread. 'I'm not letting you in!'

Suddenly, the head of a huge axe plunged through the door. It was drawn back and then rammed in again and again, destroying the wood. Zoe recoiled in horror, certain that she was going to die. She backed away as far as she could and crouched in a foetal position against the wall.

Having completely obliterated the door, someone pushed hard against it to move the heavy bed behind it away. What was left of the door finally swung open, and there, standing in front of her, was a fireman.

The fireman was clad in a traditional, indigo *hanten* coat and *hakama* pants. He stood in front of Zoe with a look of determination on his weathered face. Eyes ablaze, he walked up to her. Grabbing her hand, he looked around carefully before motioning for Zoe to follow him. She could see smoke billowing into the room from the hallway.

As she was ushered out of the building, she was wrapped in a damp blanket and taken to an area where there were many half-dressed girls milling around in front of the establishment. They had assumed she was one of them.

The space directly in front of the building buzzed with an eerie blend of anticipation and curiosity. A large crowd had gathered outside, drawn by the wailing sirens of fire engines and the pulsating red and blue lights. The burgeoning crowd watched with a mixture of concern and fascination.

A subtle tension hung in the air as people craned their necks to catch a glimpse of the unfolding spectacle. The brothel, an unassuming six-story building, emitted an otherworldly glow from the neon signs above its entrance, casting flickering lights on the faces of the curious onlookers.

To the crowd's surprise, the firemen discovered that the smoke billowing into the air was caused by nothing more than a metal can that had been set ablaze.

As she entered the street, Zoe could see groups of young prostitutes whispering amongst themselves, their painted lips forming delicate curves of curiosity. Salarymen found themselves unexpectedly captivated by the pretty girls standing before them. Tourists, wide-eyed and bewildered, fumbled for their smartphones to capture the moment. Sirens wailed an unbearable jarring shriek.

In these moments, Tokyo's red-light district had been laid bare. The fire had stolen the spotlight from the hidden desires and pleasures that thrive in the darkness, stripping them of the aura of mystery. It had left the spectators feeling peculiar, confused, dirty, and exposed.

Off to the side, some of the thugs from the brothel were watching Zoe closely. But with so many police and firefighters around, they kept their distance.

Suddenly, someone grabbed Zoe from behind. She panicked, thinking it was one of the gangsters. Then she realized that it was Jeff. She had never been so relieved to see anyone in her life.

Jeff held his index finger to his lips, telling Zoe to keep quiet, and gently pulled her into a side street. Some of the thugs saw what was happening and started to head over.

Kobe's car was waiting for Jeff and Zoe. They both jumped in. Just as they thought it was safe to leave, two of the thugs ran in front of the car, blocking it with menacing expressions on their faces.

'What do we do?' Kobe shouted in panic.

'Run them down,' Zoe responded.

As the two men approached the front doors, Kobe twisted around to look back, slammed the car in reverse, and sped down the side street like an experienced race car driver. Before the thugs had time to catch up on foot, Kobe had whipped the car around and was flying down an alley to safety. As the thugs disappeared from their view, they all breathed a sigh of relief.

'I didn't see that coming,' said Jeff, exhilarated by Kobe's masterful driving. 'How did you learn to drive like that?'

Kobe was too shocked to respond. All he could do was focus on the road. His entire body was shaking from head to toe.

Zoe was in a daze, still struggling to recover from the effects of the narcotic she had been given the night before. She was confused and disoriented, unsure of what was occurring around her.

'What just happened?' she asked Jeff.

'You are safe now. We rescued you from that place,' he said, his voice soothing and calming. 'I watched you enter that building yesterday, but we didn't see you come out. Are you okay? Did they do anything to you? I'm so relieved you're safe. I was so worried.'

'What are you doing here in Japan?' asked Zoe.

'Your mom called me before you left for this trip,' Jeff confessed sheepishly, unsure how she would react. 'She was really worried. She had this gut feeling that you were going to do something that would put you in danger. She couldn't explain what it was. She just felt it in her heart, so I decided to come and make sure you were safe. I had some time off from work. So, I just came. It was a whim, but I'm so glad I tracked you down. We could have lost . . .'

Zoe felt a wave of emotion wash over her. She was so grateful to have him there and relieved to be safe.

'Thank you,' she said, tears streaming down her face. 'It's so good to see you.'

Jeff didn't know what to do, so he just held her close, his arms wrapped around her. He felt her body shaking, and he knew that she was still in shock. He wasn't used to seeing her this vulnerable. She always seemed strong and impenetrable.

After some time, Zoe pulled back, wiping away her tears.

'Have you been here all this time?' she asked him, trying to make sense of everything that had happened.

'I arrived the day before you came,' Jeff said, his voice calm and reassuring. 'I hired Kobe to make sure you were safe. Your company recommended him.'

Zoe gasped, 'That's how you knew I was here?'

'Yes,' Jeff admitted, his expression serious. 'I've been following you since you got here. I sent you the text message when I saw those men going into the building. The one you went into with that girl.'

Zoe's face crumpled as she remembered the terrifying events of the day before.

'After you were taken to the brothel, I wasn't sure what to do,' he continued. 'I went to the police. It didn't go well. They thought that I was the problem. So I spent all of yesterday walking around the building. I found that the back door to the brothel was unlocked, and there was no one around. I peered in and realized that it was a storage room. It had a lot of cleaning supplies. That's how I got the idea to start the fire. I put some old rags in a large metal bucket and lit it on fire. It created a lot of smoke but no flames. I then had Kobe call the emergency number. And the plan worked. I'm so happy you are out safely.'

Zoe stared in wonder as she realized how far Jeff had gone to help her. 'Wow. I can't believe it. Where are we going now?'

'My hotel,' Jeff replied. 'These guys will be looking for you. Kobe told me that they're one of the most notorious gangs. The mafia boss is Kiyotaka Suetake. He comes from a major crime family linked with local police and corrupt government officials. We're in big danger.'

Zoe shivered as she recalled the past few days. She was struggling to gather her thoughts after all this new information.

'I can't believe you got me out of there,' she said. 'Thank you.'

Maybe Jeff had been right. He wasn't controlling—he was just trying to look out for me, she thought. 'I'm sorry I've been so awful to you. Can you forgive me?'

'For what?' Jeff asked, his voice gentle. 'I love you. I'm just glad you're safe.'

Zoe felt a warmth spread through her. 'I love you too,' she said softly.

They soon arrived at the hotel, located in the other side of town. Jeff and Zoe headed straight for their room.

Once inside, Zoe collapsed on the bed, her body shaking with the aftershocks of her ordeal. Jeff sat beside her, stroking her shoulder, offering comfort and support. Within minutes, she passed out again, this time in the safety of Jeff's hotel room.

* * *

Several hours later, Zoe woke up. She still felt groggy, and her head was pounding. She realized that Jeff was still sitting next to her, watching her intently.

'Are you doing okay?' he asked.

'I'm not sure,' Zoe croaked, her voice barely above a whisper. 'What happened?'

'You passed out on the bed when we arrived at the hotel.'

Zoe's mind was still foggy, but she remembered enough to feel a deep sense of unease. She was scared and unsure of what to do next.

'Did they do anything to you?' Jeff asked hesitantly. This was the second time he had asked this all-important question. She did look disturbed to him.

She was still struggling to recover her memories. Zoe closed her eyes, trying to remember what had happened before she had been rescued. She remembered being locked in and then feeling dizzy, nauseated, and scared out of her mind, but then her memory went blank.

'I don't . . . I don't know.'

She kept pushing herself until the memories all rushed back.

'No, they didn't do anything to me,' she finally said, opening her eyes. 'The door was still locked when I woke up in that room. This was just before the fireman arrived.'

Jeff put his hand gently on her shoulder. 'That's good to hear.'

'We need to get out of here,' she replied, her voice soft but determined. 'I want to go back to Vancouver.'

Zoe couldn't explain the feeling of fear that was gripping her. She was safe—safer than she had been in days—but her mind was clouded with confusion and uncertainty, leaving her with no clear direction to move forward. The only thing she felt certain about was her desire to return home to Canada.

'Where's your passport?' Jeff asked suddenly with concern.

'It's in my hotel safe,' Zoe replied. 'But we can't go there. They have my phone. They'll know where I'm staying. What are we going to do?'

'Give me some time to figure out a plan,' Jeff said, looking up at the ceiling.

As Zoe sat there with her thoughts, her mind feverishly conjured up ideas about how to proceed. It suddenly hit her that she needed to find Pinky, who she knew was in grave danger. Zoe remembered that she had told her to go to the police, and she had promised to meet her there and help her.

'We have to go to the police,' Zoe said, urgently. 'I have to find Pinky.'

'Who is Pinky?'

'That young sex trafficking victim from the brothel, who I was interviewing.'

Jeff shook his head. 'I told you, I tried to get help from the police. I don't trust them. Kobe says the police and gangs all work together, especially in this part of the city.'

'Then what do we do?' Zoe asked, feeling lost.

'We go to your hotel, try to get your passport, drive to the airport, and take the first flight out of here and go anywhere else,' Jeff said.

'But what about Pinky?' Zoe asked, feeling desperate. 'I put her life at risk. I'm responsible for her.'

'You can't help her from here,' Jeff replied gently. 'Let's get out of here first. You can try to help her from Canada, maybe write her story.'

Zoe began to sob, and Jeff pulled her into his arms. He had never seen this side of her before: scared and vulnerable. It was so out of character.

As they were getting ready, there was a soft knock on the hotel room door. Jeff peered through the peephole and saw Kobe standing outside. He opened the door.

'Kobe, what's going on?' Jeff asked, ushering him into the room before quickly shutting the door.

Kobe handed Jeff an English newspaper. There was a photo of Zoe on the front page.

'What is this?' Jeff asked with concern.

'Read it,' Kobe said, his voice urgent. 'You two are in very big trouble.'

Jeff stood at the desk, his eyes scanning the article in silence. As he read on, his brows furrowed and his expression grew darker with each passing word. Zoe approached and peered over Jeff's shoulder, attempting to read along with him, but the words were too small and blurry for her to make out.

'What does it say?' she asked impatiently.

'Monday afternoon, Tokyo Police put out a bulletin for the capture and arrest of Zoe Kim, who is wanted in connection with the murder of a Korean prostitute in Tokyo,' Jeff read aloud. 'Ms Kim is a radical, Korean-Canadian journalist who works for *The Vancouver Star* and is on the run with her accomplice, an unknown Caucasian male. Ms Kim was last seen with the Korean murder victim before her death. The young girl, who investigators have identified only by the name "Pinky", died after falling from the roof of a three-storey building.'

The colour drained from Zoe's face, leaving her as pale as the freshly laundered white sheets on the hotel bed. 'No,' she whispered. 'This can't be happening.'

'That's not all,' Jeff said grimly. 'They're accusing you of spreading lies about Japan. They say that you're trying to plant a fake news story claiming the government forced girls into sex slavery during World War II and that you're trying to slander businessmen by falsely linking them to organized crime. It says that it's not clear why you're doing this. Apparently, some people think you're working for the Korean deep state, others say you're being paid by rival criminal gangs. It says the authorities are considering charging you with violating the Ethics and Information Falsification Act 506.'

Zoe's eyes bulged in disbelief, as she struggled to comprehend the unexpected turn of events. 'That's ridiculous,' she said, walking over to the bed to sit down—her legs were suddenly feeling wobbly. 'It's all lies.'

'We know that,' Jeff said. 'But we have to be careful. The police are looking for us.'

'This is Mr Suetake's doing,' Kobe said carefully. 'He is good friends with the police, politicians, and many conservative writers in Japan. Discrediting you is his way of covering his own tracks. His fingerprints are all over this. I told you—he has a lot of power and influence. He's very dangerous.'

Kobe shifted uneasily and cleared his throat. It was his way of trying to alleviate his nervousness. 'I'm sorry to leave after bringing you such news,' he continued, 'but I have to go. I don't want to be involved in this. If they find you, I'll be arrested too. Japanese people who get involved in things related to these people—people like Mr Suetake—disappear. I have a wife and child to take care of.'

'Wait,' Jeff said, reaching for his wallet. 'Let me pay you first.'

But Kobe had no interest in receiving the money. He walked towards the door without looking back, 'No, it's okay. I don't want any part of this. Good luck.' He waved with his hand before closing the door, leaving Jeff and Zoe alone.

Her breathing became shallower as she turned her gaze to Jeff's laptop, hoping to find some shred of information that might help her understand what was happening. Her hands trembled as she grabbed the laptop and opened it. Her fingers hesitated, unsure of how to frame her search, but she finally started to type. Each tap sent a jolt of fear through her body.

As she hit enter, her face contorted into an anguished expression, scanning the screen frantically for any clues. She felt a knot in her stomach as she saw her photo and text on the screen, and frantically copy and pasted it into a translation website. She was struggling to make sense of it.

'Look at this. They have CCTV footage of Pinky and me together, on the roof of the brothel's apartment building. They killed her and now they're trying to frame me!'

Jeff read out the headline, '"Korean Prostitute Found Brutally Murdered in Central Tokyo".' He clicked through several Japanese news outlets, each one more damning than the last. Then he started looking at English news sites. Many appeared to have copied the details from their Japanese counterparts, rehashing and embellishing along the way. With each new telling, the tale became even more lurid.

'Oh my God. We're all over the internet,' Jeff said, his voice thick with anger. 'One media company said you were last seen with the murdered prostitute and is all but accusing you of doing it. It says here that you're part of a communist group, which has a manifesto on how to bring down the government of Japan. It's completely twisted your work, saying that you're trying to stir up racial tensions by spreading a conspiracy theory about the Japanese government sponsoring the systematic rape of Koreans. They're framing you with these lies. Both of us. It's all fake news.'

Zoe's eyes narrowed as she spoke. 'When I was in China, I heard about these right-wing nationalists in Japan. They're in cahoots with the media, police, and the mafia. They're very conservative—they go after anyone who says anything critical about their country and discredit them. It happens all the time.'

Jeff's mind raced as he considered their options. 'We need to get ahead of this. We need to find out who's behind this and clear your name before it gets any more out of control.'

Zoe nodded in agreement, her eyes fiery with determination. 'Let's do it. Let's bring these people down.' But as she picked up the newspaper Kobe had brought in, she felt her spirit waver. 'This is a nightmare,' she said. 'How could they do this? It's insane!'

'I don't know,' Jeff said, gently holding her arm. 'But we have to figure out a way to get out of here and then clear your name.'

'I know,' she said. 'But how?'

A strand of hair fell in front of her face as she sat hunched, tears streaming down her cheeks. The tears left rivulets in their wake, tracing a path down her skin and dripping onto her clothes. She sighed, grateful for Jeff's support despite the sadness and fear consuming her. She looked at him.

Jeff's eyes met hers, and he reached out to take her hand, their fingers interlacing. He could feel a slight tremble in her fingers, a telltale sign of her anxiety.

'We'll find a way,' he said. 'I promise.' His touch reaffirmed his words: He was there for her, he would stand by her side no matter what, and that together they could face any challenge that lay ahead.

* * *

Zoe threw herself into researching the Suetake family on the internet. Surprisingly, many newspaper articles and historical blogs had been written about them over the years. She discovered that the family's lineage spanned centuries and had been intertwined with Japan's criminal underworld from the very beginning.

The first mentions of the Suetake family dated back to Japan's Edo period, to seventeenth-century Osaka, where they played a prominent role in bringing together street vendors and gamblers to form alliances, which developed into, what are now known as, Japan's Yakuza organized crime gangs.

Those gangs, like the family itself, were founded on the principles of loyalty, honour, and hierarchy. In the mid-eighteenth century, both the family and the gangs expanded into managing brothels and gambling establishments, services for which there was a high demand.

But the Suetakes were not always outlaws. In eighteenth-century Japan, when the country was under the rule of the Tokugawa Shogunate, prostitution was tolerated and regulated. It also played a significant role in the rapidly expanding urban centres where there was a strong demand for all forms of entertainment.

In fact, Zoe learned that prostitution had played a big role in the nation's cultural life during that period, when patronage of brothels was seen as a status symbol. Brothels were frequented by samurai, merchants, and other wealthy urban residents. There was even a hierarchy in the brothels: At the top sat the courtesans, whose skills in music, dance, and conversation made them highly sought-after. Many famous artists, writers, and poets drew inspiration from these women.

While prostitution was an accepted part of urban life, the women themselves were socially marginalized. They lived in isolated districts, and their children often faced discrimination due to their mothers' profession.

In the nineteenth century, the fall of the Tokugawa Shogunate saw the decline of the traditional system of prostitution as Japan modernized and adopted Western values. Around this time, the Suetakes expanded their business to Tokyo, with the blessing of the Yakuza.

The family appeared to have thrived through the turmoil and upheaval of World War II. During this period, Suetake's family members were active in both politics and government, and Zoe found multiple sources alleging they had been involved in the same military brothels that had hosted hundreds of vulnerable girls and women—victims who were coerced, and deceived into forced prostitution in 'comfort stations', though these claims were fervently denied by prominent government officials over the years. Japan's defeat in World War II appeared only to have fuelled the family's expansion.

Capitalizing on the chaos of the post-war period, the family expanded into smuggling and political intrigue. They also began running their first brothels outside of Japan, establishing offices in Korea, Vietnam, and China.

By the latter half of the twentieth century, the Suetakes appeared to have diversified their portfolio into legitimate enterprises such as construction, real estate, and finance—a strategic shift that allowed them to launder their dirty money while further infiltrating Japan's economic and political landscape.

* * *

Zoe's eyes were fixed on the laptop screen as her fingers tapped away on the keyboard, creating a rhythmic clicking sound. Jeff sat beside her, observing her with interest but careful not to interrupt her flow. Time crawled by as she carefully crafted her message, taking nearly an hour to complete it. She scanned the email one last time before finally hitting the send button. A triumphant grin spread across her face as she turned to Jeff.

'What did you just do?' Jeff asked.

'I wrote my manifesto,' Zoe replied. 'The mob boss had said to me, "You don't get to win." We'll see about that.'

Oh no, thought Jeff. 'What did you write?' He knew that Zoe had a defiant streak in her DNA. The more someone tried to control her, the more rebellious she became.

'Read this,' said Zoe, beaming with pride, as she handed the laptop over to Jeff. 'This should gather some interest. I'm sending it to a bunch of K-Pop influencers that I know. I did a series of articles about them six months ago. For some reason, we all hit it off. They have millions of loyal followers. They will help me get the word out. What do you think?'

Jeff took the laptop and began to read the manifesto. As he read, his uneasiness turned to alarm.

The issue of forced prostitution at the hands of the Japanese imperial forces is one that has plagued Japan for decades. It is a stain on the country's history that cannot be ignored, and it is a matter that the Japanese people should care deeply about.

The victims were young Korean and Chinese girls, who were used as sex slaves during World War II. They were deceived and recruited under false pretences, taken from their homes, torn from their families, and subjected to unspeakable horrors by their captors. An estimated 200,000 to 400,000 women and girls, some of them as young as eleven years old, fell prey to these war crimes.

For years, the Japanese government refused to acknowledge the existence of these women or the atrocities that they endured. It was not until 1992 that the Japanese government finally and reluctantly admitted to the existence of Japanese military sex slaves, known by the euphemism 'comfort women', and issued a weak, insincere, ambiguous apology but did not accept any moral or legal responsibility. However, this apology is not enough. Many of the remaining victims are yet to receive a formal admission of guilt or any form of reparations for the suffering that they endured.

This is why the Japanese people, the rest of Asia, and even the world should care about their stories. These women are their fellow citizens, and they were subjected to unimaginable cruelty. Some were forced to service up to thirty men a day. The traumas that they endured left many of them scarred forever, physically and mentally.

It is the responsibility of the Japanese people to acknowledge this dark chapter in their history and to do everything in their power to make it right.

This is more than a matter of history. The Japanese military sex slaves of yesterday have a modern equivalent: the sex trafficking victims of today. Across the world, the buying and selling of women and girls continues. Millions of women and children around the world continue to be forced into sexual slavery, just as the countless victims of sexual enslavement, who were subjected to repeated rapes and other forms of sexual violence by the Imperial Japanese army, were.

As part of my investigation into sex trafficking, I stumbled upon a ring that extends from Korea to Japan and the USA. It is run by a notorious crime boss named Kiyotaka Suetake, whose family has been involved in this business since the early eighteenth century. In 1936, they set up and ran dozens of the Japanese military's comfort stations and trafficked women into forced sexual servitude across Asia.

These victims are vulnerable and powerless, and they need our help. We must shine a light on people like Mr Suetake if we are to avoid repeating the tragedies of yesterday. It's time to step up and take a stand.

I, for one, will not stop until this is done—and that is why so many lies are being spread about me in the Japanese press. Mr Suetake, along with the police and politicians who are paid off by him, is desperate to disgrace me, to keep me quiet.

But I will not be silenced. I implore you to stand with me. Please reject these lies, and help me right the wrongs of the past.

Zoe Kim

Jeff could see that the document was filled with explosive accusations against the Suetake family and the Japanese government. He understood that Zoe needed to bring attention to what was happening, but he also knew that it could get her into even more trouble.

'I don't know, Zoe,' he said, returning the laptop. 'This is pretty damning material. Are you sure you want to send this out?'

'Too late,' Zoe replied defiantly. 'I sent it already. I have to fight back somehow. And besides, if something happens to me, at least people will know what I stood for. I have another dozen people that I'll share this with. That should get the word out.'

Jeff sighed heavily, his shoulders slumping in defeat. He knew all too well that arguing with Zoe was an exercise in futility once she had made up her mind. He could already feel the tension building between them, but he forced himself to stay calm. All he could do now was support her, even if he didn't agree with her decisions. With things finally going well between them, he didn't want to upset the delicate balance that they had achieved.

15

Later that afternoon, as Jeff opened the door to his hotel room after running an errand, he was met with a disturbing sight. There was Zoe, holding a mug of coffee tightly, as if it were the only thing keeping her anchored to reality. A grey blanket was draped over her.

Jeff had observed that Zoe's mood swings were erratic, fluctuating between determination and defiance, and feelings of defeat. He also noticed that when she lacked research to occupy her mind, her thoughts would spiral out of control. 'How are you holding up?' Jeff asked softly, not wanting to startle her.

'What do you think?' she responded with her head lowered. 'I killed that girl.'

'It wasn't your fault. They did it to her, not you.'

Zoe lifted her gaze, and, for a moment, there was hope in her eyes. 'I'm not okay,' she replied in a barely audible whisper. 'I'm scared, Jeff. I don't know what's going to happen to us. Are we going to make it out alive?'

Jeff knelt beside her, taking her hand in his. He felt her fingers trembling in his, and he knew that he had to stay strong for both of them. He was convinced that the terrifying events that took place at the brothel had triggered an episode of PTSD.

'We'll figure something out. I promise,' he said, and handed her a small package.

She looked at him quizzically. 'What's this?'

'It's a nun's outfit,' he explained. I have one for a priest. We need to disguise ourselves and get out of here. I went to a costume shop, and this was the best that I could find. This is the only thing they had that wasn't a zombie or an anime character, or something else obviously made for Halloween.'

Zoe looked at the outfit doubtfully, but Jeff's determination was infectious.

'Okay,' she said slowly. 'What else do we need?'

'I got a shaver,' Jeff said, pulling out a small bag. 'We need to cut off my beard and hair. There's CCTV footage of us together, and it won't be long before they figure out who I am.'

Zoe bobbed her head up and down. 'Can we really get away with this?'

Jeff gave her a lopsided grin. 'We'll be a priest and a nun. Nobody here in Japan will look twice. We just need to get to your hotel room and find your passport. We can figure out the rest later.'

Zoe nodded, and they quickly gathered their belongings. Jeff stuffed his computer, passport, and all his money into a small knapsack.

'What about your suitcase?' asked Zoe.

'I'll have to leave it behind. It'll just slow us down. We can't come back here,' he said. 'They'll be looking for us.'

'I had no idea that you have the mind of a CIA spy.'

* * *

Jeff was startled by his own reflection as he looked in the mirror. The man staring back at him was unrecognizable. He had shaved off his beard and cut off most of his hair, leaving only a buzz-cut. Zoe had been there to help him with the transformation. She had guided the razor across his skin with a gentle hand and offered words of encouragement, as he had found the process unsettling. However, now as he donned the priest's black cassock and white collar, he felt a sense of purpose and renewal.

Zoe, too, had undergone a transformation. She had exchanged her everyday clothes for the traditional habit of a nun. As she fastened the veil around her face, a sense of calm descended upon her. They looked like entirely different people.

The two of them stood side by side, gazing into the mirror as they adjusted their garments. Jeff marvelled at their reflections. They had shed their old identities and taken on new ones, like snakes sloughing their skin.

As they prepared to leave, Jeff was a bundle of nervous energy. He was about to embark on a perilous new adventure, one that would require him to be a pillar of strength for Zoe. With her by his side, he knew that he could face whatever challenges lay ahead.

Zoe followed him out the door, and they made their way to a side exit. Just as they were climbing into a taxi, two police cars screeched to a halt outside the hotel. Jeff's heart quivered as he watched several men jump out of the cars and rush inside.

'That was close,' Zoe said, her voice shaking. 'They must know who you are now.'

Jeff nodded grimly. 'We need to stay one step ahead of them. Let's get out of here.'

* * *

Zoe and Jeff arrived at Zoe's hotel. As they made their way over to a set of chairs off to the side, they noticed a policeman standing in front of the elevators, closely examining every guest that entered. The officer briefly glanced at Zoe and Jeff, then quickly looked past them.

Zoe whispered to Jeff, her voice laced with anxiety, 'Yikes. They're waiting for me.'

Jeff, trying to remain calm, responded, 'We'll have to come up with another plan.'

Zoe took a moment to think. 'We can go to the Canadian Embassy. They'll help us.'

'I already called them yesterday morning,' Jeff said. 'They said if we committed a crime, we need to sort it out with the Japanese authorities first. They had a call from the foreign ministry. Their hands are tied.'

'They won't help us?'

'No, we're on our own.'

'Then what do we do?' Zoe asked. 'Without a passport, I can't get out of here.'

Jeff looked around the lobby, searching for inspiration. 'Let's take a train to another city. They'll be looking for us here in Tokyo. But maybe not elsewhere.'

'They'll find us eventually. We can't do anything without our documents,' said Zoe, sounding defeated.

'We'll come up with something,' said Jeff, trying to sound optimistic.

Zoe was growing increasingly worried, 'You know, the Japanese always convict foreigners, even if they haven't done anything. Everyone knows that.' Just then, she had an idea. 'Arah gave me the name of a Japanese woman who also works for the cause of Japanese military sex slaves. Ms Fujiwara. She's in Yokohama. Her address is One, Silk Road in Chinatown. I remember thinking that the address is so cliché.'

'What makes you think she'll help us?' asked Jeff sceptically.

'Arah said she wasn't a fan of the Japanese government. I have a gut feeling about her. We can take the bullet train there. What other option do we have?' said Zoe.

'Okay, it's worth a try,' said Jeff.

Zoe was beginning to think that they might have a chance after all.

* * *

Zoe felt a sense of anticipation as she and Jeff settled into their seats aboard the bullet train. Its sleek, futuristic design was a far cry from the old-fashioned passenger trains that she was used to in Canada.

The two of them sat in silence for a while, lost in their own thoughts. Zoe's gaze roamed around the train, noting the many, different passengers sitting around them. She also became self-conscious of the priest and nun outfits that she and Jeff were wearing. They had largely forgotten about the costumes, but she wondered if they stood out to the people around them.

As the train sped up to breakneck speeds, they watched in awe as the vibrant cityscape of Tokyo became a blur of neon lights and towering skyscrapers, disappearing with each passing mile. The landscape slowly transformed into a blur of green as the train entered and zipped through the lush countryside.

Inside the train, they were surrounded by the soft hum of conversation alongside the sound of the wheels on the tracks. Zoe noticed how the train's interior was designed with comfort in mind. The seats were plush and comfortable, and the ride was incredibly smooth, with no jolts or bumps to disturb their peace.

Halfway through their journey, Jeff decided to broach the topic that they had both been avoiding. 'You know, we've never really talked about our separation. Maybe it's time we address what happened between us.'

Zoe shifted uncomfortably in her seat, her gaze fixed ahead. She knew it was a conversation that they needed to have, but she wasn't sure if now was the right time. 'Jeff, we have so much on our plate right now. Let's save this discussion for another time.'

'But I just . . .' Jeff started, only to be swiftly interrupted by Zoe.

Zoe raised her hand, signalling for him to stop. Her eyes pleaded with him to understand. 'Please, Jeff, not now. I just can't handle it at the moment. I don't even understand why I did what I did. I'm sorry. Can we put this conversation on hold for now? Is that okay?'

Jeff could see the pain in Zoe's eyes and nodded in agreement. They sat in their seats, barely speaking.

As they approached Yokohama, the train gradually slowed down, and they caught a glimpse of the shimmering coast and glittering skyline. The sun had started to set, and the sky was painted in shades of pink and orange. Zoe glanced over at Jeff, catching his eye, but said nothing. She thought to herself, *If it all ends tomorrow, at least I have lived.*

A few minutes later, the train came to a full stop. Jeff and Zoe exchanged nervous glances as they waited for most of the other passengers to disembark before making their move. Their hearts were pounding. They knew they had to be cautious in taking their next steps.

'What now?' Zoe asked, her voice quivering as she scanned their surroundings, trying to figure out their next move.

'Taxi?' Jeff suggested, but uncertainty hung in the air. 'Shouldn't we see if that lady can help?

'Yes,' Zoe replied, nervously. 'That's the plan.' Her eyes looked around the train station.

Jeff paused to open his knapsack, searching for the tourist map that he had picked up from the station in Tokyo. He found it after a moment of fumbling and carefully studied it. The map was old and faded, but it had all the information they needed. He then stuffed it into a pocket of his knapsack, a little carelessly, ready to be used when needed.

As they cautiously made their way toward the exit, Zoe tightly gripped Jeff's arm, her fingers trembling. Then they froze. Two stern-faced police officers were staring directly at them.

'What do we do?' Zoe whispered urgently. 'They're coming right towards us. I can't run in this outfit.'

Jeff instinctively moved in front of Zoe, fists tightened. He had never punched anyone before, but he would do it if it meant keeping Zoe safe.

'Stay back,' Jeff said under his breath. 'On my signal, run to the exit as fast as you can.'

The two young officers approached purposefully until they were standing right in front of the duo. They paused, their expressions inscrutable. Jeff was about to raise his fist just as one of the officers pointed at the floor behind them.

'Paper,' the officer said in broken English. 'On the floor. See the paper.'

Jeff turned and followed the officer's finger, realizing that the map had slipped from his pack. He felt a wave of relief as he retrieved it, profusely thanking the officers for their unexpected assistance.

They walked away without any trouble.

* * *

Zoe and Jeff stood in front of the door to Ms Fujiwara's house, feeling a little apprehensive. Jeff rapped on the door gently, but there was no answer. He tried again, this time with more force, and they heard the sound of footsteps.

The door creaked open, revealing Ms Fujiwara. Though elderly, she had a youthful energy and vitality that was reflected in her demeanour. Her features were exquisitely sculpted and delicate, giving her an elegant and refined appearance. Her dark hair was tied in a bun with a flower hairpiece that framed her face. Her yellow dress was simple, stylish, and tailored to fit her slender frame. The colour matched her warm skin tone, while a blue scarf added a touch of contrast. She glowed with a subtle radiance.

Zoe began to introduce Jeff and herself, but Ms Fujiwara cut her off, speaking in clear English. 'There's no need for introductions,' she said with a gentle smile. 'I've been expecting you.'

Zoe was taken aback. 'You know who we are?' she asked, incredulous. 'Of course,' Ms Fujiwara replied with a smile. 'Everyone in Japan knows who you are. Haven't you been following the news? Besides Arah told me you would be coming to Japan. She said I should expect a visit from you to discuss the issue of the Japanese military sexual slavery system.'

For a while, none of them said a word.

'I see that you've been through a bit of trouble. Please come in.'

As Zoe and Jeff stepped inside, they took off their shoes to show respect for her home. Ms Fujiwara led them to a small sitting area, carrying herself with an air of quiet confidence and sophistication, moving with elegance and grace.

The home had an atmosphere of restfulness as if it had been crafted as a haven for its visitors. The room was designed with minimalist aesthetics, featuring low, cushioned chairs and *zabutons* placed on *tatami* mats. The large windows allowed an abundance of natural light in, illuminating the space and highlighting the carefully placed, decorative *ikebana* flower arrangements and hanging scrolls. Japanese ceramics added to the sense of peace and serenity.

As they sat down, Zoe confessed, 'Yes, we are a bit confused by everything that the police and media are saying about us. We could use some advice.' Her voice betrayed a hint of vulnerability.

Ms Fujiwara smiled warmly, her eyes filled with understanding.

'Very clever disguises,' she remarked, nodding in approval. She gestured towards the low chairs, inviting the visitors to sit down and make themselves comfortable.

'Thank you for seeing us,' Zoe said, feeling relieved to have found someone they could trust.

'You have come up against the mafia and the nationalists,' Ms Fujiwara continued without missing a beat. 'They are fiercely proud of their country and will not tolerate any criticism. There is no limit to what they'll do to maintain our national honour. It's very political. Someone wants to discredit you, and it appears that they have combined the murder of the young, Korean woman and the cause of the comfort women survivors with a personal attack on you. This will neutralize anything you say in the newspapers or on social media. It's a common diversion tactic. Sadly, it works. Do you have any idea who you might have offended?'

'I am writing an investigative article on a brothel run by a mafia boss in Tokyo. He traffics girls from Korea to Japan and the USA. His name is—'

'Kiyotaka Suetake?' Ms Fujiwara interrupted.

'Yes, how did you know?' Zoe asked, surprised.

'He is a notorious nationalist. His family has been running many brothels for decades now. They were the ones who set up some of the Imperial Japanese military rape stations in China on behalf of the government. Mr Suetake is connected with some prominent police officials and politicians. He runs a sex slavery ring trafficking Korean, Chinese, and other Asian girls all over the world. He says the women do it voluntarily, but they don't.'

'That's the one,' Zoe said grimly. 'I think he's out to stop my story because of a ledger I received in LA. It has all kinds of names, dates, phone numbers. I think the story could prove dangerous to his business,' Zoe said.

'That would explain a lot. He is trying to discredit you before you can reveal the truth. Where's this ledger now?' Ms Fujiwara asked.

'Arah has it in China. She was helping me to make sense of it,' Zoe replied.

'So, what will they do to us?' Jeff asked, changing the subject.

'When they find you, and they probably will, they'll come up with some false evidence to frame you and then make a big deal about it in the media. The process has already begun. Jeff, they just identified who you are from some random CCTV footage. You have been described as a "Canadian radical". These extreme articles about you in the press are obviously false. But many will believe it. If you want to leave Japan, you'll eventually have to apologize and accept that whatever they have said is true,' Ms Fujiwara explained.

'I'll never do that,' Zoe said, defiantly. 'The truth must be told.'

'Then you'll be stuck in jail for a long time. Most people eventually recant because they have no other choice. A Japanese jail is a terrible place to be,' Ms Fujiwara warned.

'How do you know all of this?' Jeff asked.

'I have been a vocal critic of the Japanese government's policies for a long time,' Ms Fujiwara replied.

'Why haven't they gone after you?' Zoe inquired.

'My father is a highly respected statesman. I am protected because of who he is,' Ms Fujiwara explained. 'They cannot touch me. I'm completely insulated.'

'What are our options?' Jeff asked.

'You have two choices—wait for them to catch up with you, or find another way to leave Japan,' Ms Fujiwara advised.

'But how? I don't have my passport,' Zoe said, her tone desperate.

'Japan is a series of islands. If you can find a way to get on a boat that is leaving, you can escape,' Ms Fujiwara suggested.

'I'll look into it,' Jeff promised.

'But where should we go now?' Zoe asked, feeling completely lost.

'You can stay here with me, but you'll have to leave and then return. I'm sure my neighbours are already curious about why a nun and a priest have come to see me. If they don't see you leave, they'll gossip. There is an internet cafe a few blocks away. Stay there until later this evening, then come back. Just don't check your emails or do anything that can be traced online. Intelligence officers will be trying to track you that way,' Ms Fujiwara cautioned.

'Thank you, Ms Fujiwara,' Zoe said, grateful.

Jeff and Zoe followed Ms Fujiwara's directions to a narrow, deserted alleyway in Yokohama where they stumbled upon an unassuming but charming tea cafe, tucked away in a corner. The air was filled with the aroma of freshly brewed tea and warm scones.

As they entered, they were struck by the delicate cherry blossom paintings that hung on the walls and the tatami mats that covered the floor. The soft lighting and gentle background music made for a peaceful, calming, and welcoming atmosphere.

The owner of the cafe, a kindly looking, elderly woman dressed in a kimono, greeted them with a warm smile and welcomed them in. They opted for a quiet corner in the back to maintain their privacy. She recommended her personal favourites from the menu, and they ordered a pot of fragrant green tea and a plate of warm scones with whipped cream and strawberry jam.

So hospitable and friendly was the owner that Jeff and Zoe felt like they were old friends rather than strangers.

As they sipped their tea and nibbled on their scones, Jeff and Zoe began to relax for the first time in days. For a few precious moments, they were able to forget their worries, and their ridiculous outfits, and just appreciate each other. But soon the comfortable silence between them turned sombre. Zoe had started feeling restless and anxious, and after a while, she suggested, 'Let's just spend a few minutes checking our social media and emails?'

Jeff hesitated but agreed, 'Okay, but only for a few minutes. You heard what Ms Fujiwara said.'

As they both scrolled through their feeds, Jeff chuckled at some of the articles written about them. He read aloud a few lines that he found amusing, 'Listen to this one—they make us out to be comic book super villains.'

Zoe, on the other hand, was struggling to see the funny side to the lies being spread against them. She was shocked to see how quickly the media had picked up the story, twisted it, and sensationalized it.

'The media has your name and a photo,' Zoe said.

Jeff shrugged. 'Yeah, I saw that. Not a great photo. Not my best side.' He was trying to lighten the mood, but Zoe wasn't in the same headspace. She couldn't stop thinking about how serious the situation was. They were being hunted, and just one slip-up could mean going to prison.

'Jeff, this is not a joke. We need to be careful about what we do and say. We don't want to make things worse.'

Jeff put his phone down and said, 'I'm sorry. You're right. We need to be careful.'

They sat there in silence, lost in their thoughts.

'Ms Kim and Mr Jacobson are working with anti-government organizations to discredit our government,' Jeff whispered in a comic-book voice. 'Our paper has uncovered emails and text messages that state their intention to spread vicious lies across social media through South Korean influencers. They are using a false narrative about so-called "comfort women" and other lies that question the integrity of our people. They have tried to discredit some of our most respected businessmen. The police have launched a manhunt for these two fugitives.'

'Wow. They really do have it in for us,' Zoe admitted. 'How are they able to see our emails and text messages?'

'I don't know,' Jeff admitted. 'They seem to have ways to track these things. We better get off the internet. They could be shadowing us right now.'

'Okay, but just give me a few more minutes. I have to check some things. I'll be quick.'

Zoe's eyes were glued to the laptop screen as she scrolled through her inbox. Her heart rate quickened as she checked for any urgent messages, fearing the worst. But to her relief, there were no pressing matters to attend to. With a sense of calm restored, Zoe took a moment to email her mother. She wanted to tell her that she was safe and would be on her way home soon. As she typed out the brief note, she felt a connection with her mother, even though they were miles apart.

Then Zoe turned her attention to her social media accounts. She had recently reached out to a few influencers that she had written stories about in the past, seeking their advice and support. To her delight, each response was filled with encouragement. She eagerly read through each one.

> Oh god, this is so terrible. I'll share it with my peeps.
>
> —Nina

> I did a blog post on this and your situation. I asked my Korean community to act. Hang in there. We are all with you.
>
> —Jin-Soo

> People are reaching out to me and asking how to help. What do I tell them?
>
> —Emily

> There will be a protest in Seoul. You and Jeff are heroes. We are there for you.
>
> —Alex

Reading the messages made Zoe feel grateful for the connections that she had made through her career. With a little help from her famous friends, she felt ready to take on whatever challenges lay ahead. 'Going to the influencers seems like it's working,' she said to Jeff. 'I've received some incredibly supportive emails. I don't know if it will amount to anything, but at least I tried.'

'Glad to hear it,' Jeff said. 'But come on, let's go offline now. We don't want them to track us down.'

Zoe closed Jeff's laptop and looked up. 'This is getting very serious, Jeff. They are spreading so many lies to try to discredit us.'

'I know,' Jeff sighed. 'This whole thing is so surreal.'

'Do you trust her?' Zoe asked.

'Who?'

'Ms Fujiwara, who else?'

'I guess? Who knows? And what other choices do we have?' Jeff paused. 'Maybe she can help us to get out of Japan. She did say that this was an option. She may be our only hope.'

'What do we do now? I mean over the next few days.'

Jeff looked at her gravely, 'Let's see what she has to say. We'll have to think of something. But for now, we should focus on staying safe.'

They sipped their Japanese tea, trying to pass the time, but every minute felt like an eternity.

At 8.50 p.m., they left the cafe and headed back to Silk Road, unsure of what the future held.

* * *

They walked down the quiet streets holding hands, their fingers entwined. The sound of their footsteps was the only noise to be heard. The evening air was cool and refreshing, carrying a sweet scent from the nearby gardens. Zoe's thoughts were consumed with doubts. It suddenly dawned on her that it was inappropriate for a priest and a nun to be holding hands, and she abruptly let go. In that moment, Jeff also recognized that their actions were out of place given the circumstances.

As they turned into the small walkway that led to Ms Fujiwara's home, Zoe suddenly became aware of a group of plain-clothes police officers emerging from the shadows. They were shouting orders in Japanese, their faces grim and angry, batons in their hands.

Before she could process what was happening, the police slapped cold metal handcuffs around her wrists and tightened them. She looked up to see several reporters snapping photos, their cameras flashing in the night, zooming in on Zoe and Jeff's shocked faces.

One of the officers stepped forward, his face stern and unyielding. He spoke in rapid Japanese, his words not registering in Zoe's mind. This felt like a performance for the media—not for the benefit of the foreigners who didn't speak a word of Japanese. It all felt surreal to Zoe, like a bad dream she couldn't wake from. She looked to Jeff for support, but he was being led away by another group of officers.

Ms Fujiwara appeared out of nowhere, her expression stern and disapproving. She spoke to the police officers in Japanese, her voice sharp and commanding.

Zoe couldn't understand what was being said, but she could tell that Ms Fujiwara was scolding the officers for their treatment towards Jeff and herself. The officers lowered their heads respectfully, acknowledging her authority. Yet they continued with the same procedures.

'I'm so sorry about this,' Ms Fujiwara said to Zoe as she approached her. 'I'm not sure how this could have happened. Did either of you use any electronic devices or computers?'

Zoe looked down without responding. Despite all the chaos unfolding all around her, she seemed quite calm. At some level, she accepted that this outcome was inevitable.

'I was afraid you might. That must be how they found you—they can see everything online,' said Ms Fujiwara. 'I'll come by after they process you. We'll sort out the details later. It may take a few days. The justice system is very slow and cumbersome.'

Zoe nodded, grateful that Ms Fujiwara was helping them. 'What are we accused of?' she asked.

Ms Fujiwara spoke to the main police supervisor in Japanese, her words rapid and forceful. Zoe had no idea what they were talking about, but the long response from the officer implied to her that the charges were serious.

'They said you are being charged with sedition, and you may be an accessory to the murder of the young Korean prostitute,' Ms Fujiwara translated for Zoe. 'I know this may sound ridiculous, but it doesn't surprise me. I told you they'd come up with something like this. This is what they do.'

Two police cars pulled up. Jeff and Zoe were split up and manhandled into each vehicle. But before the doors shut, their eyes met in a fleeting exchange of love and unity. A moment later, Zoe was whisked away.

As she sat in the back seat of the speeding patrol car, her hands still cuffed, Zoe wondered what was going to happen to them. Would they be imprisoned for years? Would they be deported?

Zoe bit down on her lip as these questions swirled around in her mind. She was sure of just one thing: She needed to find a way to clear their names—and quickly.

* * *

Zoe was taken to a secluded white-collar prison on the outskirts of Tokyo. As she entered the cell, its small size and the solitary bed in the corner reminded her of the room that she had been confined to, in the brothel.

The whitewashed walls, bright and unyielding, seemed to stare back at her, making her feel even more alone.

A metal toilet and a sink were the only other amenities in the room.

The air inside the cell carried the subdued whispers of those who had been here before, and the shadows that danced and played on the floor were testifying to their presence. They were cast by a single light dangling from the ceiling, which emitted a muted glow.

The passage of time was marked by the rhythmic ticking of an unseen clock, which served as a metronome for the inmates' muted existence. Everything in the cell was neat and tidy, a silent code of orderliness that everyone seemed to follow. The soap, toothbrush, toothpaste, and towels were meticulously arranged with precision, and every surface was unblemished, as if to prove a commitment to maintaining order in the face of captivity.

To her surprise, the cell still bore the traces of its previous occupants. On one of the walls, Zoe noticed a set of initials with a year carved into the plaster—MSF 2017. Under the bed, she found a key chain and a foreign coin, relics of former inmates that hinted at their lives within these unforgiving walls.

For the next three days, Zoe was completely isolated in the cell and did not receive a single visitor. The only contact she had with the outside world was when a tray of food was brought into the cell and then removed. Since she didn't speak Japanese, she was unable to communicate with the person who delivered the tray. Time seemed to stretch on forever, and the boundaries between Zoe and her confined space began to blur—she was becoming another feature of her cell.

The cell was a mind-bending crucible where despair and solitude coexisted, a realm defined by haunting memories and regrets. Within these suffocating confines, Zoe found herself ensnared in the unforgiving clutches of isolation and an unbearable loneliness. The narrow space, cold and unwelcoming, echoed with the hollow whispers of her own breath. With no one to talk to, her stream of consciousness became a spontaneous, dissonant song that reverberated through the silence. Zoe couldn't tell if days had passed or weeks. The endless expanse of time before her seemed to stretch on interminably. With nothing else to occupy her, she counted the hours by etching marks on the damp walls surrounding her, desperately trying to anchor herself in the relentless flow of this monotonous existence and create some sense of structure. The ever-present solitude gnawed at the edges of her sanity, leaving her adrift in a sea of her own ruminations. Her mind, once a lively marketplace of ideas and dreams, had withered into a desolate wasteland, devoid of any meaningful stimulation. To keep her mind sharp, she tried to sing every Korean childhood song that she could remember and recite the holy poems and Bible verses that she had memorized at Sunday school.

With nothing to look forward to, each passing day was a torture without end.

16

Ben was struck by the oppressive atmosphere as he entered the small interview room in the Tokyo jail. He was shocked to see Zoe, his star reporter, sitting alone with her hands cuffed in front of her.

Ben could tell she was exhausted from her long journey, her face pale and drawn. Her hair was unkempt, and her clothing rumpled, as if she had been travelling for days.

Zoe did not meet his eye, her mind lost in the depths of regret. Her head was bowed in recognition of the trouble she had put her company and herself in. She waited for him to speak.

Ben knew she would be giving herself a hard time and tried to break the heavy silence between them by lightening the mood. 'This is my first time in Japan, you know. I don't know how you manage these long-haul flights, but I couldn't sleep a wink. Phew!' he said, pulling the chair out from the desk and dropping down onto it, across from her.

Zoe remained quiet, her thoughts elsewhere.

'How are you and Jeff holding up?' he asked, looking for something positive in this bleak situation.

'I'm sorry, I don't know,' Zoe said softly, looking up at him. Despite her response, Ben could see in her eyes that they had not yet broken her and that made him feel proud of her.

This was a woman who had faced adversity before and had always come out on top. She continued, 'I haven't seen Jeff since the day of our arrest. In fact, I haven't seen anyone else either. You're the first person to visit me. I've been completely alone in here, with no idea of what's been happening outside.'

'Well maybe it's time I brought you up to speed,' Ben said, with a sudden hint of amusement in his voice and a glint in his eye. 'Because quite a lot's been happening outside these walls. Out there,' he said, gesturing with his arm, 'you're something of a celebrity these days.' He seemed pleased with himself, as if he were just waiting for Zoe to ask him to explain.

'What do you mean?' Zoe asked suspiciously, her anxiety momentarily on hold.

'The "Jeon-Jiju Two", that's what they're calling you.'

'The Jeon-Jiju *what*?' asked Zoe. 'And who's calling us that?' She was perplexed and a little annoyed. This wasn't the time for Ben's *humour*.

'Everyone, Zoe. Everyone's calling you that,' Ben said. 'People are demonstrating in the streets, demanding that you be freed. Your work has really touched people, and so your arrest hit a nerve.'

'What do you mean?' Zoe asked. 'We haven't even published my story yet. Come to think of it, you shouldn't even know I'm here. I wanted to surprise you with it. I knew that if I got it done, you'd see how big of a deal it was. That's why I came here without telling you.'

'I know, Zoe. And I can see how special a story it is. I think everyone can. Your arrest has really lit a spark. Think of it like Asia's finally having its MeToo moment in relation to the comfort women or Imperial Japanese military sex slaves, and it began with your arrest. People are fired up. The demonstrations are getting bigger and more intense every day.'

Ben pulled out his phone and began showing Zoe a series of media clips capturing the protests happening in various parts of the world.

She recognized the first one as the Wednesday movement outside the Japanese embassy in Seoul that she had read about. Only this protest was much larger than the ones she had seen on YouTube during her research. Ben's clips showed similar demonstrations taking place in Korea, China, Canada, and the Netherlands, where protesters were holding banners demanding that Japan apologize to the comfort women. People were chanting and marching through the streets, carrying makeshift copies of the comfort women memorial statue in Seoul. The energy was electric.

Ben also showed her a clip of a CNN interview with an elderly survivor of Japanese wartime forced prostitution. The banner underneath her read, 'Comfort woman speaks out after Japan arrests Canadian nun activist.'

'What the hell? How did all this happen?' she asked as she watched the clips. She realized that she had become part of the story—that was not something she was used to.

'Let's call it the power of the media,' Ben said with a large, self-satisfied grin on his face. 'See, when we splashed the front page with your arrest, Zoe, it was big news—*big* news. But I didn't realize how big. Of course, I knew some networks would pick it up too—we journalists stick together, right—but I figured the fuss would die down after a day or two. I mean, who cares really if a journo goes to jail?'

'But you, Zoe, that cute little face of yours dressed up in that nun suit, plastered all over the media, that really pushed some buttons, just like I knew it would. Man, you should have seen our Chartbeat figures. It was like someone had lit nitroglycerine under our readership stats. I've never seen anything like it . . .'

Ben shook his head in amazement and drifted off. He still couldn't quite believe it.

'So, all this is because *The Star* wrote about me?' Zoe asked, dubiously, bringing him back to earth.

'Well, yeah . . . I mean, it wasn't just us, Zoe. Like I said, all the big TV networks picked it up. What really got the ball rolling was those influencers you tipped off. I gotta hand it to you, that was a very canny move. Once something like that gets out, there's no stopping it. Guess it's called viral news for a reason.'

Zoe nodded slowly. *So the plan had worked*, she thought.

Ben continued, 'I think what really did it is the details of what you were investigating when you were caught. Not just the bits about the Japanese military sex slaves, but those young girls. Korean girls, Chinese girls, still suffering the same fate as the grandmas. Disgusting. It just hit all the right buttons . . . sex, race, crime, the whole thing. Nitro-fucking-glycerine . . .' he said, trailing off again.

Zoe stared at him, reproachfully.

Ben coughed self-consciously and adjusted his tone. 'So the thing is, every time a network covered your arrest, it just dragged up all these painful wartime memories again and again. People in Asia still have so much anger against Japan and what it did in the war, you know that. It's like your arrest shoved it all back in people's faces. It all came flooding back.'

Ben snorted and shook his head as if appreciating the irony. 'And then, as you know, it's like a self-feeding doom loop. The more outrage there is, the more the media covers it and the angrier everyone gets. Classic!'

Zoe fixed Ben with an unblinking stare. As gross as he sounded, the explanation made sense. And she could forgive him his gruffness—she knew it was a show, a tough-talking exterior that shielded him from confronting unpleasant realities.

'Sounds like I owe you one, Ben,' Zoe said, half-heartedly.

He shifted uncomfortably.

'Well, like I said, all those K-Pop friends of yours helped. I think a lot of them reached out to their audiences on TikTok and Instagram and whatnot, and on Chinese social media, of course. Boy, I heard one message by a guy on Weibo in China got like—fifty million reposts, was it? It was some really pithy quote about how Japan was up to its old tricks, defending wartime sexual slavery by the military and erasing and revising this history by calling the victims of rapes—many of whom reported that thirty to fifty Japanese soldiers raped them every day—voluntary prostitutes who wanted to make money. That really fanned the flames, helped bring people out on the streets. Boy, fifty million.'

She raised an eyebrow, but he kept talking regardless.

'With all those K-Pop stars talking about it, all the Asian politicians have really jumped on the bandwagon. They get to show they're down with the kids while also bashing Japan. It's a no-brainer for them. But it's even being tweeted about by government ministers in the US, Canada, Australia, and the EU. Even the UN has called a session on it. Word is Angelina Jolie wants to make a film about it. Shit, there's been like a hundred articles just on her. Everyone is talking about this.'

He looked back at Zoe, thoughtfully.

'And it all started with that picture of you dressed as a nun. What was that about anyway?' he asked with a slight grin.

Before she could answer, he pulled his phone back out and showed her a picture of a poster that had Jeff and her in their disguises, superimposed on top of a Mao-era propaganda poster from China.

'This has become a meme on Instagram. People post it and then make up their own captions. There have been some really funny ones . . .'

Zoe could hardly believe what she was hearing. But it was all too surreal for Ben to make up. And he had the pictures to prove it.

Ben could see that she still wasn't entirely convinced, so he tried one more time.

'Zoe, remember how the Arab Spring started? That one guy set himself on fire, despairing because he couldn't buy bread . . . how that just ignited all these other dormant issues and resentments that had been simmering away, how people started off angry at his death, then just used it as a springboard for all their frustrations. How it all kept snowballing, growing bigger and wider, and angrier and more violent. By the time the governments were falling, nobody could even remember that guy's name.'

'Mohamed Bouazizi,' Zoe responded. 'I remember.'

Ben nodded slightly in acknowledgment. 'What I'm getting at is that a similar thing's happened here. Your arrest provided the spark that ignited a fire, but all the kindling had been set in place a long time ago. It's just been waiting to go up in flames.'

Zoe thought of Meera, and the hairpin Masuki had given her. 'It's like the butterfly effect,' she murmured.

'You got it, kid,' said Ben, looking at her triumphantly. 'You're a symbol now, Zoe, whether you like it or not. A symbol for fighting for oppressed Asian women everywhere.'

The idea of her newfound fame was too much for Zoe to take in, so she shut it out and tried to think of something else.

'Have you heard anything about Jeff? How is he doing? Have you seen him?'

'No, I haven't,' said Ben. 'But I'm doing my best. I know where he's being held, and I've requested a visit. Since I'm not family and he doesn't work for me, they denied my request. But I'll keep trying.'

Zoe's eyes filled with guilt. 'It's all my fault. He's in this mess because of me. I shouldn't have come here. I should have just left the story alone. I should have stopped when I could . . .'

'Don't beat yourself up,' Ben said, sympathetically. 'That's what good reporters do. They keep going. I get it. I bet Jeff gets it too, that's why he loves you. I'll do what I can to talk to him. I think I can work this out. Then I'll let you know how he's doing. Okay? Give me a few days.'

There was a long silence before Zoe spoke again.

'They murdered that girl, Pinky, the one I was interviewing,' Zoe said, changing the subject. Her voice was filled with a mixture of sadness and anger. 'It was my fault. I was the one who put her in danger.'

'I heard about her,' Ben said, mirroring her sadness. All traces of his earlier bravado had evaporated.

'Who do you think did it?'

'I know who did it,' Zoe said. 'A brothel owner who I met here in Tokyo. A sadist who punishes anyone who goes against him. Because Pinky dared to talk to me, she was killed. He's the mastermind behind all of this. He has strong ties with the Japanese government and those nationalist extremists. He needs to discredit me to avoid any backlash. I have something he wants. That's why he's going after me.'

'What do you have?' Ben asked, intrigued.

'A ledger. Someone gave it to me in Los Angeles,' Zoe said. 'It has names and phone numbers associated with his trafficking ring between Korea and Japan. I didn't realize how important it was until I mentioned it to him. His reaction helped me understand how damaging to their business it would be if released.'

Alarmed, Ben asked, 'Where is it?'

'It's in China. I left it with someone. We need to retrieve it. It can serve as leverage,' Zoe replied.

'After we sort things out here for you, I'll look into it,' said Ben, writing down something in a small notebook. 'What was this guy's name?'

'Kiyotaka Suetake,' Zoe said, mouthing the syllables as if she was tasting something foul.

'Okay, I'll see what I can dig up on him. I'm on it.'

'So, what about the murder charge against me?' asked Zoe. 'Do you think the accusation will stick? I know that foreigners don't always get a fair trial in this country. Are they going to be able to actually pin this on me?'

Ben's expression turned serious. 'Nobody believes it, Zoe. It's their desperate attempt to divert attention and discredit you, everybody can see that. I don't think this charge will hold up. I'm told there isn't a shred of evidence.'

Zoe felt relieved but only momentarily.

She went back to scrolling through the visuals on Ben's phone, absorbing the magnitude of the movement. She refocused her thoughts and turned to Ben, desperation in her voice. 'How bad is it? I mean all the other charges. Can you get us out of here?' she asked, her eyes searching his face for signs.

'You know, it's always hard with the Japanese. In most other places, I could get you outta here in no time. Most countries like to avoid the publicity. They cut some deal to let you out and make it go away. But the Japanese don't always think the same way.'

'The more the world pushes this agenda, the more the nationalists dig in. They are a small but very influential group. They are proud and don't like losing face. They are using their entire media machine to discredit you and know precisely which buttons to press. But as I said, your supporters are really pushing back. Every time one of their articles goes after you, the response in your favour is ten times stronger. At some point, I think the government will intervene to stop this group of people from pouring gasoline on this fire. They know where fires like this end. With Bozizi.'

Zoe nodded and corrected him, 'Bouazizi.'

The silence that followed lasted for several minutes before Ben spoke again.

'Listen, we managed to find a local lawyer who appears sympathetic,' he said, trying to ease Zoe's worries. 'It was challenging to find someone willing to go against the nationalist tide. For a while, I thought we wouldn't find anyone, but she came to us out of the blue. She is offering pro bono services, which surprised me. She is smart and tough. I think you'll like her. She said it is really important that you follow everything she says. You can't be all self-righteous in this country. You have to be quiet and respectful. Do you understand? When you meet her, please do what she says.'

Zoe's eyes welled up with tears. This time she had taken things too far and it had cost an innocent girl her life. She had been selfish and made choices based on her own needs and desires . . . all for a story and a few rotten column inches. It was a painful pill to swallow but, in prison, all she had was her thoughts and they were beginning to attack her.

She accepted all the blame. It was her fault. Her life was over. She accepted that now.

As she sat in the cold, sterile room, she realized how much she missed Jeff and wanted to be with him. Not just now, but forever.

Her voice was barely audible as she whispered, 'I'm so sorry for causing all this trouble, Ben. I just want to go home with Jeff. I'll do whatever I have to do.'

Their conversation was abruptly interrupted by the entrance of a guard who had come to get Ben. Their time had come to an end.

With a heavy heart, Ben exited the room with the guard, leaving Zoe alone with her thoughts.

She sat there and looked around the room: the stark white walls, the metal table and chairs, and the small window that barely let any light in. It was all so oppressive, suffocating, as if the room itself was trying to crush her spirit—break her down and make her give up.

She tried to calm these troubling thoughts, to banish her longing to give up, to silence that voice inside that said she'd be better off dead.

Zoe was getting desperate and knew she needed to muster some inner strength somehow, but how? She had nothing left and was at the end of her rope.

* * *

Zoe was back in her cell, sat down on the cold, hard bed, when she heard the footsteps approaching. She looked up to see a female guard striding towards her bars and staring straight at her.

For a woman, the guard was unusually tall, with broad shoulders and a muscular frame that almost seemed out of place in her snug prison uniform. Her face was stern and emotionless, lacking any hint of compassion.

She stopped inches from Zoe's bars and handed her a piece of paper, motioning with her head for Zoe to read it.

The subtlety of the guard's gestures suggested to Zoe that she was keen to avoid drawing attention. So Zoe took the parchment without saying a word and studied it closely.

The handwriting was immaculate, with each letter crafted with precision and care. When she looked back up to thank the guard, she had already gone.

Zoe turned back to the letter and began to read.

Dear Ms Zoe,

I must commend the ingenuity displayed by your boyfriend in orchestrating your escape from my establishment. While you briefly managed to elude us, it has come to my attention that our diligent law enforcement has apprehended you both. I am confident that justice will be duly served, and our legal system will administer the appropriate consequences for your audacity and hubris.

I perused the statement you made through those individuals associated with K-Pop. Once again, you have profoundly misunderstood our traditions and history. Fortunately, the Japanese people possess a keen discernment for truth, untainted by your distortions of our world. We are a proud and perceptive nation, well-versed in distinguishing fact from the fiction that you peddle. Nothing you do or say will alter this reality.

Do you truly believe you can enter our country and flout our customs with impunity? Do you presume we will accept your judgement of our ways, made through the lens of your morally compromised Western perspective? Do you imagine you can turn the world against us? You are gravely mistaken.

Your falsehoods will be exposed for what they are—delusions of a woman consumed by hatred and envy. I shall personally oversee this process.

If the legal system doesn't correct you, something else will.

As I told you once before, you do not get to win!

At that moment, Zoe felt extremely vulnerable. If he could get a message to her, perhaps he could come after her in prison. This thought weighed heavily on her mind. She feared for both Jeff and herself.

17

Emi, Zoe's legal advocate, entered the spartan interrogation room and bowed with her hands clasped in front of her. Zoe sat across the table, with a weary but defiant look in her eyes. Their gazes met and the two women sized each other up in a silent dance of assessment.

Zoe watched as Emi pulled out the cold metal chair and sat down without saying anything. She then meticulously arranged a set of files on the table. Each file seemed to magnify the significance of the legal battle ahead.

Zoe waited patiently as this ritual unfolded.

She sensed a quiet resilience emanating from this woman and drew confidence from her professional appearance. Emi was wearing a tailored suit. Her hair was styled in a neat, shoulder-length bob that framed her long oval face and her dark, expressive eyes were outlined by sleek glasses. Her dress style was that of a high-powered office worker, but in her warm complexion, there were subtle freckles that hinted at a connection to the outdoors.

Having sized each other up, the two women's eyes lingered on each other for a few seconds more as a cocktail of desperation and hope mixed between them.

'Zoe-san, my name is Emi Yamada,' she began. 'I'm here to help you navigate this difficult situation. We believe in your innocence, and we're committed to protecting your rights.'

Zoe nodded gently. 'Thank you,' she said quietly. 'When you say "we", who are you referring to?'

'Me and many others who feel that you are being mistreated here in Japan, including some government officials. I took on this case as a volunteer because I believe in your innocence. Those who want to move this process forward have political motives. It is my hope that we can expose these intentions.'

'Will you be representing Jeff, too?' asked Zoe, leaning forward.

'Yes. You will be tried together. I have already met with him. He will be at the initial hearing next Tuesday.'

'How is he doing? I've had no contact with him.'

'He's fine. He's worried about you. He told me to say that he loves you and that he feels that this whole thing will be sorted out soon. He seemed confident about this.'

'And what about you? What do you think about this case?' asked Zoe, unsure if she shared this apparent optimism.

'I don't know for sure. That's why I'm here today. To better understand what happened. There is a lot of political resistance related to your presence here in Japan. It is not going to be easy. There are also so many different versions of your story. I'm here to unravel the truth.'

Emi flipped open her legal pad, ready to delve into the intricacies of Zoe's case. 'I've reviewed the charges against you, Zoe-san. It's essential that we understand the specifics. Can you tell me your side of the story?'

Zoe hesitated, as if contemplating whether to divulge a secret.

'Take your time, and remember, I'm here to support you. We have as much time as you need.'

She began to speak, her voice low and hesitant at first, but gradually gaining strength and conviction: She recounted the events that had led to her arrest, her words laced with regret.

She then moved on to narrating every single thing that had happened in LA, China, and Japan. She even described the letter that she had just received in prison from Kiyotaka Suetake.

Emi's eyes repeatedly focused on Zoe's face. It appeared to Zoe that she was trying to read the emotions that lay beneath her words. Meanwhile, her pen scratched furiously across the notepad, taking down every detail.

When Zoe had finished speaking, Emi smiled reassuringly. She chose her next words carefully. 'Zoe-san, I believe in your innocence,' Emi began, her tone measured and thoughtful. 'Given the circumstances and the nature of the charges, I would strongly advise you to refrain from speaking during the court appearance on Tuesday. The judge may ask you some questions, but I would prefer to respond for you. Our preliminary court procedures are sometimes confusing. This will set the tone for what will follow. We must be very careful. In this case, silence can be a powerful defence strategy. We don't want anything you say to be misconstrued or used against you. In a Japanese courtroom, words carry weight, and we need to be strategic in how we present your case.'

Emi paused to gauge Zoe's response to her statement. She then continued, 'I understand this may be difficult, especially when you have a compelling story to tell, but the court is a complex environment. Let me be your voice. I'll ensure your side of the story is presented in the most effective way possible, while protecting your rights and innocence.'

'But you don't know all of the details,' replied Zoe, fearing that this approach was really a form of censorship. 'I need to explain what happened. How else will they know? It should be in my own words.'

'Everything will come out in good time. There will be depositions, witness testimonies, examinations, cross-examinations, and so much more. As part of this process, the truth will be revealed. I'm suggesting this strategy to you because Japanese courts are very traditional. They follow a very strict protocol.'

Zoe couldn't hide her frustration.

'Why can't I speak out in court? Especially if the judge asks me to speak. We're innocent, for God's sake!' Zoe said.

'Zoe-san, I understand your frustration, but there are legal procedures we must follow,' Emi responded calmly. 'Speaking out emotionally in court may harm our case.'

'Harm our case?' Zoe exploded. 'Jeff and I are the victims here! You heard my story. I was kidnapped by that mob boss, and now they're trying to pin everything on us.'

'Please calm down, Zoe-san,' Emi urged. 'Emotional outbursts like this won't help our defence. In fact, they will do much harm. Please trust the legal process. We will present the evidence and prove your innocence.'

'This all happened to me,' said Zoe, remaining defiant. 'I was forced into this situation! I must make the judge understand that I'm not the criminal here. I'm a reporter. I know how to share the facts. It should be me doing the talking.'

'Zoe-san, I empathize with your situation, but our defence strategy is based on presenting facts, not emotions,' explained Emi, maintaining her composure. 'I know the Japanese legal system. You need to trust me. The right-wing media has described you as a radical. Don't buy into their trap. Getting fired up and aggressive will make it look like they are telling the truth. It will make things much worse.'

'And what about the elderly women who survived the unspeakable—the Japanese military sex slaves?' Zoe asked, her voice rising in frustration. 'I spoke the truth! Japan must acknowledge it properly, and I should be able to say that in court.'

'Zoe-san, I appreciate your passion for the issue, but the court is not the place for political statements,' Emi responded. 'We must focus on the charges against you and present a strong defence. That topic is a time bomb ready to explode. We can't mix these things together if we want to win this case.'

'And Pinky . . .' Zoe pressed on. 'It was because of me that she was murdered. I need to tell the court who killed her and why!'

'Zoe-san, I understand your pain, but emotional testimonies can backfire,' said Emi. 'Just let the evidence speak for itself. We have a strategy to address Pinky's death without compromising our case.'

'This is so frustrating, Emi,' Zoe sighed. 'I feel like I'm being silenced.'

'Zoe-san, remaining calm and collected gives us our best chance,' said Emi, reassuringly. 'Trust me. We'll present a strong case, based on facts not emotion.'

'Fine. I'll trust you. But if this doesn't work, I need you to promise me that we'll find another way to make them hear the truth.'

Emi reached across the table, placing a supportive hand on Zoe's.

'I promise, Zoe-san,' she said.

18

As the police van slowly approached the courthouse, Zoe caught sight of several hundred people gathered in front of the stately building.

There were two opposing crowds, separated by a barrier, each of them chanting and brandishing signs. Most of the signs were in Japanese, but there were a scattered few on one side of the barrier with isolated English expressions—'Justice for the Japanese army sex slaves', 'We stand with you', and 'Free the Jeon-Jiju Two'. She blushed slightly at the reference to Jeff and her, then turned her attention to the other side of the barrier, where an opposing crowd seemed every bit as impassioned.

On this side, Zoe could make out only two signs with English phrases—'Foreigners out' and 'Go back to your country'.

But she didn't need to know what the Japanese signs said, or understand what the crowds were chanting, to realize that the situation could explode into violence at any moment.

The chants intensified as Zoe was escorted out of the police van by a group of officers in full riot gear. Struggling to maintain order as they snaked through the crowd, the police were forced to push the people back as they guided Zoe up the stairs and into the building. Once inside, they continued through the gallery section until they reached the courthouse room assigned for this case. The gallery was packed with spectators, and the mood was electric with anticipation.

Zoe took in her surroundings. The courthouse was a picture of custom and tradition. It had an air of formality and respect for authority, and its staff all wore traditional dress. Zoe felt as though she was walking through a living piece of history.

She was led through a metal detector and security checks before arriving inside the courtroom. In this room, the decor was minimalist, the lighting subdued, and the space surprisingly small, creating an unexpectedly intimate setting. At the front stood an elevated judge's bench and a platform for witnesses. Most of the features were made of wood, but as Zoe looked more closely, she could see signs of technology, such as the leads for audiovisual equipment. At one side of the room, there was a discreet booth, which Zoe recognized from her time as a court reporter to be where the interpreter would sit.

In the rear, there was enough public seating to hold up to forty spectators. Here, in the hushed corners of the courtroom, onlookers quietly immersed themselves in the unfolding legal drama. Not a single seat was empty.

Every eye turned toward Zoe as she progressed down the aisle that divided the room. She noticed Jeff seated at the front table beside Emi, their lawyer. Ben was positioned just behind them.

A few seats away, Ms Fujiwara sat beside an elderly man, who was well into his 90s. To Zoe's shock, Mr Suetake sat in the back row of the courtroom with several of his thugs. When their eyes met, Mr Suetake nodded his head and smiled.

Taking her seat in the courtroom, Zoe refrained from exchanging words with Jeff. Instead, she grasped his hand and squeezed it briefly in a gesture of support. He smiled back at her lovingly.

All they could do now was wait and see what fate had in store for them.

Emi leaned toward Zoe, her voice firm, 'As I told you before, I need you to remain silent throughout this proceeding. No matter what the judge says, it's critical that you keep quiet. Do you understand?'

Jeff and Zoe wore solemn expressions. Their eyes were fixed on Emi. They knew that the outcome of the hearing would change their lives. Both nodded in agreement, fully aware that since all eyes were on them, they needed to act wisely and portray themselves as trustworthy throughout the proceedings.

As they waited for the hearing to begin, a side door opened, and a middle-aged female judge entered the room. She was dressed in a sleek, black judicial robe that flowed as she walked. She had an effortless authority that commanded respect from everyone around her, and a piercing gaze that suggested seriousness and discernment. And despite her relatively young age, she already had wrinkles on her face—evidence of years spent deliberating complicated cases. As the judge made her way to the bench, the entire courtroom rose to their feet, their gazes fixed on her. Her voice was steady and commanding as she gestured for everyone to take their seats.

As the room fell silent, she delivered a lengthy statement in Japanese. Her manner seemed deliberate and measured, and what she was saying appeared to elicit occasional supportive reactions from the audience. Though Jeff and Zoe could not understand her words, they could sense their gravity.

The judge then proceeded to ask Emi a series of direct questions for about twenty minutes. Zoe didn't understand why, although there was an interpreter present, the questions and answers weren't being translated into English. She was about to interrupt the proceedings to request a translation when Jeff stopped her by placing his hand on her arm.

Then the judge turned her attention towards Jeff and Zoe, and their hearts pounded with anticipation. An interpreter stepped forward to translate. Jeff and Zoe sat muted, taking in every word, understanding that the shape of their lives could be decided by what happened in the next few minutes. Their future was in the judge's hands, and they could only hope that their lawyer's advice would be enough to sway the decision in their favour.

'The charges against both of you are grave and supported by substantial evidence,' she began, her eyes fixed on the defendants. 'Troubling accusations have been brought forward, and after careful consideration, I have decided that there will be no bail granted in this case. You will remain in custody until the trial commences in eight months.'

With a resounding thud, the judge brought down her gavel, the finality of her decision echoing through the room.

Zoe's mouth fell open in shock, and she struggled to contain her emotions. The realization that she would be spending the next eight months in jail hit her like a ton of bricks. She couldn't believe that this was happening. As the judge's words sank in, a wave of outrage swept through her, and she rose from her seat, her voice quivering with rage. 'Eight months in jail?' she exclaimed. 'Are you kidding me? This is outrageous! We are innocent! The evidence you possess is nothing but fabricated news!'

Her words ricocheted through the courtroom, and all eyes turned to her.

Jeff and the lawyer tried to calm Zoe, but she was too angry to be soothed.

'What is it about this country?' she demanded, her finger pointed accusingly at the audience, as if blaming them for the injustice that was being done to her. 'Doesn't the truth hold any value to you people? We haven't done anything wrong! This is a blatant miscarriage of justice!'

The judge pounded her gavel, attempting to silence Zoe's defiance. She signalled for the security guards to intervene. From the back of the courtroom, they rushed towards her.

Meanwhile, rattled by Zoe's outburst, several audience members rose to their feet and began shouting angrily at her. Others held out mobile phones, capturing this pandemonium on video to be posted on social media.

'The gangsters responsible for these charges are the real criminals!' Zoe continued, screaming her message of truth through the room for the phone cameras. 'They murdered a girl—her name was Pinky. She was a fourteen-year-old, Korean, high school student, who was tricked and forced into prostitution here in Japan. She was a mere child. They orchestrated this elaborate sham to divert attention from their own trafficking operations, bringing girls from Korea to Japan. And they do the same in the United States! It's the wicked cycle of sex trafficking—of the Japanese military sexual slavery—all over again, and it has never ceased! Your government is complicit, allowing it to persist, even facilitating it. Even now government officials are involved! Until you acknowledge your part in this, you are all guilty!'

Her accusatory gaze settled on Mr Suetake.

'If you want the truth, ask Kiyotaka Suetake. He is the villain in this story. Visit his brothels if you want to know the truth!' Everyone turned towards him as she wagged her finger in his direction. He shook his head gently, playing for the cameras. Clearly, this woman was disturbed, out of her mind. He pitied her; that was his message.

The security guards seized Zoe's arms, their grip firm as they escorted her away. Undeterred, she continued to shout and scream, her words trailing behind her.

Jeff remained silent as he grappled with this traumatic moment. Zoe's response was not unexpected. He had suspected she would be incapable of remaining silent. It was just who she was.

Emi shook her head in disappointment. Jeff, Ben, and others had warned her that this might happen, but it still felt like a punch to the gut. Despite her best efforts, her attempts had proved futile.

* * *

Two agonizing days crawled by before Zoe and Jeff found themselves brought together in a confined room within the courthouse. There was a metallic click as the guard removed their handcuffs. He then stood sentinel by the door, a physical reminder of their constrained freedom.

'What's happening here?' Zoe whispered.

Jeff looked at her with a pained expression. His eyes were dull and tired. Then he let out a heavy sigh. 'I don't know. No one bothers to keep me in the loop. But after your outburst in court, I highly doubt it's anything good.'

Zoe shifted uneasily. Regret and remorse weighed heavily upon her.

Suddenly, the door swung open. One of the government lawyers entered, flanked by two silent figures. The Japanese official, bearing an air of authority, wasted no time in delivering their fate, his tone brisk and decisive, 'You will be relocated to a hotel and placed under house arrest. Leaving the premises of your hotel is strictly prohibited. Your court case has been expedited and is now scheduled in three weeks' time. Refrain from engaging with the media or any activists. It will only serve to harm your chances in court.'

Zoe's voice trembled with confusion as she tried to grasp the situation, 'Why are we being moved? What's happening?'

Before she could finish her question, the lawyer and his two associates abruptly departed, leaving Zoe and Jeff behind, uneasy and afraid, their bewilderment hanging in the air.

'I don't understand,' Zoe muttered, her face screwed up in consternation. 'Why would they choose a hotel over a jail?'

Jeff shrugged his shoulders, his own suspicions creeping in. 'I have no idea. Could be some kind of trick that the government is playing on us. Or Mr Suetake could have something to do with this?'

'I just don't know. This is all so confusing.'

A moment later, they were taken out of the back door of the courthouse and ushered into a car that was waiting to transport them to their new residence. It took them through the busy city centre before dropping them off at a hotel on the edge of town. The establishment overlooked the vast expanse of the ocean, its tranquil presence a welcome contrast to the turbulence of their lives.

Upon arrival, they were greeted by the hotel manager, who quickly checked them in. Then they were escorted to their rooms, which were adjacent to each other. Seeing their suitcases there, neatly arranged within the confines of their quarters, gave them a strange sense of normalcy amid the chaos. It almost felt like being on holiday.

Zoe's gaze swept across the room, her eyes landing on her prized possession—Meera's journal. To her surprise and relief, it rested undisturbed among her belongings.

Realizing that they had adjoining rooms, they opened the door that separated them. For the first time in what seemed like ages, they were alone together, the uncertainty of their future looming over them.

Zoe and Jeff stood locked in a tight embrace, their bodies pressing against each other with a bittersweet urgency. The sun was setting, and the only sound was their breathing and the occasional sniffle as Zoe wept softly. She felt terrible for putting Jeff's future at risk, and she knew she had to say something to him. But it was hard for her to admit defeat and to apologize to anyone.

Zoe finally spoke up, her voice shaky. 'I'm so sorry about everything,' she said, her words barely audible. 'I'm sorry you got dragged into this mess, and then the trial. I'm sorry for my childish outburst in court. I've been so selfish, so focused on my own problems that I didn't even consider how my actions were affecting you. I just . . . I don't know what to say.'

'It's okay,' Jeff said, offering her a small smile. 'I know things have been tough lately, but we'll get through it together. And who knows, maybe we'll even come out stronger on the other side. All I can say is that there's never a dull moment when it comes to being with you.'

Zoe looked up at him, her eyes filled with gratitude. 'I love you,' she said, her voice barely above a whisper. 'I'm so sorry I treated you so badly. You've been my rock, my bear protecting me through all of this, and I don't know what I would do without you. I'll make all of this up to you somehow.'

Jeff pulled her close again, holding her tightly as she cried. 'I'll always be here for you,' he said, his voice soft and reassuring. 'We'll figure everything out together. Okay?'

'Okay.'

* * *

Throughout the next couple of days, Zoe and Jeff anxiously paced back and forth in the room, obsessively debating and discussing their next steps. They were convinced that the government was watching them.

'I just don't understand what's going on,' Zoe demanded, her voice filled with frustration.

Jeff sighed, shaking his head. 'I don't know. This whole thing is so crazy. The Japanese are incredibly systematic and methodical. Sending any messages without expecting them to be intercepted would be naive.'

'Yeah, they're watching our every move,' Zoe added with fear and anxiety in her voice. 'This isn't going to just disappear, is it?'

A knock on the hotel door startled them. Zoe and Jeff exchanged uncomfortable glances.

'Who do you think it is?' whispered Zoe, concerned.

'I don't know,' Jeff whispered back, as he walked toward the door.

'Wait,' said Zoe. 'See who it is first. What if it's one of Suetake's gangsters?'

'I don't . . .' said Jeff, before being cut off mid-sentence.

'Just do it,' Zoe insisted. 'We have to be careful.'

Jeff peered through the peephole and then opened it. Standing there in silence was Ms Fujiwara. She walked into the room without uttering a word and dropped a handful of newspapers onto the table.

'You've really stirred up quite a storm,' Ms Fujiwara said calmly. 'Despite their attempts to vilify you, it's not working.

It's like half the world has rallied behind your cause. Your courtroom outburst went viral on YouTube. Five million views and counting, or so I hear.'

Zoe picked up the newspapers, scanning the headlines silently, one after another. The words screamed at her: 'Tokyo's G20 Summit Derailed by Comfort Women Protests', 'Korea Withdraws Ambassador Over Sex Slaves Exposé', 'Crowds Demand Release of Jeon-Jiju Two', and 'Comfort Women Activist Makes Stand in Court'.

Zoe looked up at Ms Fujiwara uncertainly. 'Have I become an activist?'

'Yes,' replied Ms Fujiwara with a nod. 'Both sides of the issue are using you as a pawn to further their agendas. It's no longer about you. You've become the poster child for this struggle.'

'What struggle?'

'The struggle between promoters of conservative traditionalist propaganda and those who want Japan to catch up with the rest of the world. This has been going on for a long time. Your court case has just shone a light on it again. As I said, it is no longer about you, it is about something much bigger—who is going to win over the hearts, minds, and souls of the Japanese people.'

'How did you even know we were here?' Zoe asked, a little suspiciously. 'It's the government that's after us. You said you had issues with the government. Why would they tell you anything?'

'Very little happens without my knowledge,' Ms Fujiwara replied with a faint smile. 'I have eyes and ears in the government and all over.'

Zoe's curiosity was piqued.

'But why would they share this information with you? They're the ones pursuing us.'

'That's not entirely true. It's only a few fanatics who are pushing this agenda,' Ms Fujiwara explained. 'There are always a few bad apples in any government. Most government officials are fine.'

Zoe nodded her head in understanding. The topic of government officials reminded her of someone.

'Was the man I saw with you in the courtroom your father?' asked Zoe.

'Yes.'

'Why was he there? Is there a specific reason?'

'No reason in particular,' Ms Fujiwara said, smiling warmly. 'He just enjoys spending time with his daughter. He also has a keen interest in such matters.'

Zoe paused, contemplating their situation.

'And why are you here now?'

'Actually, I'm here to offer my assistance. You've entered a political world that you don't fully understand, and I'd like to help by translating it for you.'

'Are you referring to my courtroom rant?' asked Zoe.

Ms Fujiwara nodded. 'That's part of it.'

A long, embarrassed pause hung in the air, as their circumstances pressed down on them.

'I was just so frustrated. I couldn't help myself,' Zoe finally confessed. 'What the judge said triggered me. I wish I could take it back. I know I acted foolishly. I just can't control my emotions and what I say sometimes.'

'The Japanese people are naturally nonconfrontational,' Ms Fujiwara said softly. 'They rarely embarrass someone directly. Your assertive behaviour was a shock to them.'

'But what about those media articles? They're pretty rude and confrontational too.'

'That's the media. I'm talking about personal interactions. Japanese people seldom express themselves directly.'

'And what about the courtroom? They were hostile towards me there.' Zoe's mind churned, piecing together the scenes from the courtroom. 'Several of them stood up and shouted at me. They were very aggressive.'

'Only after you disrespected the judge. They were defending her honour,' Ms Fujiwara explained.

Zoe absorbed her words in silence, as she digested the cultural differences at play.

'Why did they bring us here?' Zoe said, shifting the conversation.

'Isn't it obvious?' Ms Fujiwara replied knowingly with a coy smile. 'They want you to run away. Look outside. This hotel is beside the ocean. You can walk to the pier. It is only three hundred metres away. Boats arrive there to pick people up throughout the day. It's not an accident that they selected this place.'

'What do you mean?'

'They want you to leave Japan, so that this political mess just disappears,' Ms Fujiwara elaborated. 'They want to avoid losing face. If you manage to escape, they can label you as a criminal, but at the same time, it gets them off the hook. It's the perfect solution to the predicament they find themselves in. The Japanese government doesn't like this negative press, but it also can't be seen as backing down. Don't you see?'

Zoe stared at her in disbelief. 'But why? How could they expect us to come to that conclusion?'

'Because I'm advising you. They assumed you would have left by now. Since you didn't take the bait, I'm here to tell you to escape,' Ms Fujiwara explained matter-of-factly.

Zoe and Jeff exchanged surprised glances before bursting into laughter.

'What about our passports? They haven't been returned to us,' Zoe said.

'You won't need them. Sort that out in Korea. The Canadian consulate can help,' Ms Fujiwara assured them confidently. 'A boat can take you there in a matter of hours. Once there, the consulate will step up. They can't do anything here, but they can help you in another country.'

Zoe struggled to comprehend what she was hearing.

'This is unbelievable. Do you really think this is the best course of action?'

Ms Fujiwara nodded again. 'You have two choices: Get lost in the byzantine Japanese legal system and spend the next few years fighting, or escape. If it were me, I know what I'd choose.'

'Could this be some kind of trick?' Jeff asked.

'No, I don't believe so,' replied Ms Fujiwara. 'A prominent European businessman faced a similar situation. He ran a car company here in Japan and found himself in trouble with the law. After they arrested him, the story took a negative turn. It began to embarrass the government. Eventually, they let him slip away. It worked out for everyone. He regained his freedom, and the government managed to end the PR blitz against them without losing face. In the end, he was convicted *in absentia*, but only after he'd made it to France. Justice was still served. It was a win-win outcome for everyone involved. What is happening here with you two is very similar.'

'Did he escape by boat, too?' asked Jeff.

'No, he used another approach. He was facing charges of financial misconduct and was under house arrest. He escaped by concealing himself inside a large musical instrument case, which was loaded on to a private jet. His associates, likely connected to the Turkish government and private aviation, arranged the logistics. The jet flew from Tokyo to Istanbul, where he was transferred to another plane bound for Beirut, Lebanon, a country without an extradition treaty with Japan. The newspapers all ran stories saying the escape had exposed gaps in Japan's legal and security systems, but the truth is that it was allowed to happen. The government was well aware of what he was doing.'

'Yes, I remember reading about that case,' Zoe admitted. 'I always wondered how he managed to pull it off.'

'Now you know. It was because he had help.'

Zoe's eyes shone with gratitude. 'Wow. Thank you. If you hadn't told us all this, we probably would have remained stuck here forever, just waiting. I agree. I just want to get home. I don't care how I do it.'

Ms Fujiwara smiled reassuringly. 'I know, that's why I'm here. Call this number.' She handed Zoe a small piece of paper that had a name and contact details on it, and an old first-generation Nokia mobile phone. 'Use this phone to make the call. Toss the SIM card away when you are done. Move forward with your lives. You've done a great service to the survivors of Japanese military sexual slavery. Their suffering has been buried for far too long. The younger generation needs to confront our dark past. So many sins have been concealed. What you have done is a good thing. We'll continue to do what we can to keep this movement going. It's only right.'

'Who do you mean by we?' asked Zoe.

'My father and I admire your spirit. Keep doing what you are doing. It will make a difference.'

'Your father?' asked Zoe, curious. 'What does he have to do with any of this?'

'He is one of the few Japanese government officials who has supported the cause of the survivors of Japanese military sexual enslavement and fought to stop sex trafficking in our country. His work over the years has been heroic. He wanted me to express his sincere appreciation for your efforts. He also said he hoped to one day shake your hand to show his true gratitude.'

'Wow,' said Zoe, not knowing how to respond. 'I hope to meet him too.'

There was a short pause.

'There is one more thing. What will happen with Kiyotaka Suetake? Will there be any justice for him?'

'Oh, haven't you heard?' asked Ms Fujiwara. She walked over to the stack of newspapers, opening the city page. She pointed to some text, 'He is on the run. Our judicial system finally caught up with him and his illicit businesses. He hasn't been seen for nearly a week now. I don't think you have to worry about him. He has his own problems to deal with.'

'But he seems to really have it in for me,' Zoe said. 'He even sent me a threatening note in prison saying "I don't get to win". Surely, he's too arrogant to just stop? He is a very proud man.'

'What can he possibly do to you?' asked Ms Fujiwara. 'Soon, you will be out of Japan. He will still be here. Please don't worry about such things. Just focus on getting home to your country.'

'I really don't know how to thank you.'

Zoe reached out to hold Ms Fujiwara's hand.

'No need to thank me.' With those final words, Ms Fujiwara swept out of the room.

19

Two nights had passed since Zoe and Jeff began devising their great escape, and now, their plan was finally in motion. They had been waiting anxiously in their hotel room, watching the clock tick away the minutes until their scheduled pick-up time.

At exactly 10.30 p.m., there was a knock on their door. They gathered their suitcases, made their way to a side exit on the ground floor, and stepped outside, where a small utility van was waiting.

They climbed inside and hid behind boxes of tools and plumbing equipment, as they had expected to. But they were less than thrilled to hear from the driver that the plan had changed. He told them that rather than taking them to the pier near the hotel, he would instead take them to the city of Kanazawa, a municipality on the west coast of Japan, about a six-hour drive away. There, the driver said, a fishing boat would be waiting to take them to Pohang, Korea.

Neither Jeff nor Zoe liked the idea; changing what they had agreed on seemed suspicious, but as they had no alternative, they acquiesced.

It proved an arduous journey. There were no seats inside the van, so they were forced to sit on its hard metal floor, and the heavily tinted windows meant it was difficult to peek outside. Their heavy, nervous breathing left the air stale, and they spent much of the trip wondering if they would make it out of the country alive.

When they finally reached Kanazawa, it was hard for them to believe that they had made it. Surely there was some trick, some kind of treachery, lying in waiting just around the corner. It couldn't be that easy, could it?

Those doubts lingered as they were taken to a secluded coastal area outside the city limits where a Boston Whaler was waiting for them, shimmering in the moonlight that reflected on the dark waters.

The night was still, and all they could hear was the sound of gently lapping waves as they met the weathered captain. He asked no questions before turning the ignition and gently chugging out into the Sea of Japan.

Their boat cruised through the night, bobbing on and swaying in waves that grew more turbulent the farther they got from shore.

The captain was taking them toward a Korean trawler positioned just inside international waters. For what felt like an eternity, they could see its red and green lights on the horizon, not getting any closer. Then suddenly, it was upon them.

As their Boston Whaler drew alongside it, the captain threw two ropes across to the trawler and a crew member tied them together. The same crew member then dropped a rope ladder down to the Whaler and motioned for Zoe and Jeff to climb up. As soon as they had done so, the crew member untied the Whaler and threw back its mooring ropes. The smaller boat then set off without its captain uttering another word. The whole process was over in a matter of minutes.

'There's no turning back now,' Jeff said to Zoe as they watched the Whaler draw away.

They turned to look around their new boat, an old yet robust sixty-foot vessel called 'Dragon's Shadow'.

Built to withstand the demanding conditions of the East Sea, its weathered exterior told the story of countless voyages. Its dull, forest-green paint job was chipped and faded in spots, making it indistinguishable from countless other fishing boats seen along the coast.

Dragon's Shadow was the perfect choice for their journey, not only because its appearance would keep them under the radar, but because beneath the deck, it had endless storage space for its fishing equipment and catches. There were plenty of compartments perfect for storing nets and crates and frozen blocks of fish—and more than enough were left should its captain want to smuggle some contraband, or perhaps a passenger or two who didn't want to be seen.

Most of the crew treated Zoe and Jeff with a mixture of caution and indifference, casting occasional suspicious looks in their direction but largely going about their own business. The crew member who had helped them aboard, however, was altogether more friendly, smiling and gesturing to them to follow him below deck. He was clearly senior to the others and perhaps knew more about what had brought these guests to his ship. He led Zoe and Jeff to the warm galley below and into a cramped room that contained a couple of well-worn couches and an old television set. The pungency of fish permeated the air.

'Well, it's not that luxury cruise that I promised you,' Jeff smiled at Zoe, 'but it's kinda cosy, no?'

Zoe rolled her eyes and slapped his arm with mock anger. In truth, both were grateful for the respite that the room would provide. They had a long journey ahead; at least here, they would be sheltered from the elements on deck. Even better, they could be alone together.

Having shown them the room, the crewman turned to them and said in Korean, 'This is one of our slow boats, it'll be a seven-hour journey. Don't worry, we do this route all the time. You can rest here. There's some water and food in the cabinets, feel free to help yourselves.' Zoe translated for Jeff as they went along.

Jeff settled into the couch and pulled out a book, which he had brought along to pass the time. Zoe retrieved Meera's journal from her bag. The chaos of the previous days had conspired against her, leaving her with no time to finish it until now.

She waited until the crew member shut the door behind him, and then took a seat and dived back into its mysteries.

April 3, 1944

As we both slowly regained consciousness, I was startled to find myself still alive. I looked around, trying to make sense of my surroundings. The room was dark with some light shining through a small window, and the air was thick with the musty smell of old furniture.

I turned to Arah, who was lying next to me, and asked her if she was okay. She seemed dazed and disoriented, struggling to sit up. After a few attempts, she managed to prop herself up on her elbows, looking around with a bewildered expression. It was only then that we noticed the pair of old mattresses that we were lying on, thrown haphazardly across the floor. We were confused and wondered how we had ended up there.

I recalled only fragments of memories from when we were severely ill. The last thing I remembered was being carried into a military ambulance while I repeatedly vomited. Everything else was a blur. I was sure I was dying.

As we looked and walked around the house and then went outside, we realized that we were no longer in Shanghai. Instead, we had been taken to a small Chinese village, with winding alleys and traditional homes. The house we found ourselves in consisted of three, modestly sized rooms and barely any furniture. The walls were made of wood and brick, and the floors were covered with woven bamboo mats.

The toilet was outside, at the back of the house, and was separated from the main building by a small courtyard. The cooking area was also outdoors. The yard was surrounded by a tall cement wall, which provided some privacy from the rest of the village.

As we tried to make sense of our surroundings, we went back inside and an elderly Chinese woman entered the room, her face weathered with age and wisdom. She was dressed in a traditional Chinese outfit, with her hair tied back in a bun. She moved effortlessly as she carried a tray with two steaming cups of tea. Without uttering a word, she placed the cups down before us and gestured for us to drink. The fragrant aroma of the tea filled the room, and we felt comfort in her simple gesture.

My efforts to communicate with the woman, and determine our location and her identity were futile. She simply shook her head and indicated that she did not understand us, despite our best efforts to speak with her in Korean.

At this point, a middle-aged Chinese man entered the room and introduced himself as Pastor Lee. Speaking to us in Korean, he sat down beside us and began to explain the situation. He told us that we had been brought to his home the previous night, and he assured us that we would be feeling better soon since the drugs that we had taken were no longer in our bodies. Pastor Lee went on to explain that Masuki, a bright young man with a talent for solving seemingly impossible problems, had approached him two days earlier seeking shelter for the both of us. Despite his initial reservations, Pastor Lee had agreed to take us in and ensure our safety.

I asked him where we were. He said we were in his home, miles from the city and far away from any soldiers. But he said we needed to be very cautious and that any misstep could lead to dire consequences. We were to remain hidden within his house as long as the war continued. He earnestly prayed for our protection.

I asked Pastor Lee how he knew Masuki. He told me that Masuki's father and him had been stationed nearby. It turned out that both Masuki and Lee had received tutoring from the same Canadian missionary, Mackenzie. When Mackenzie left the mission, Masuki continued to correspond with Pastor Lee.

When I heard this, all I could think about was seeing Masuki again. Would he come to the house? I had to ask Pastor Lee But the pastor couldn't tell me. He said that Masuki had been expected to visit that very night but had not shown up.

Days passed, and then weeks, but still, there was no sign of Masuki. Pastor Lee remained hopeful, suggesting that things would fall into place over time, but they never did. The mystery of Masuki's disappearance left me with a heavy heart. I wondered what could have happened to him.

With little else to do, Arah and I waited for the war to end. To occupy our time, we spent hours learning both English and Chinese. Books became our companions, offering an escape from the confines of our hidden existence, and much of our simple lives were lived in silence.

On two occasions, Japanese soldiers came to the house. But the neighbours tipped us off. This gave us time to hide behind false walls built by Pastor Lee and evade capture.

Time passed, but Masuki never returned. I wondered if he had perished in the battlefields, like so many others. The war was a brutal and unforgiving reality, where death was just another part of life. It was a constant reminder that any day, anyone could be gone, never to return.

Learning that Masuki had died would have broken my heart, but not knowing was a torture of its own, a slow suffocation of the little hope I had left.

It was when the war ended, and it was finally safe for Arah and I to leave the mission, that I realized that neither of us would ever be truly free again. Despite our liberation, we shared wounds that would never heal and a sadness that could have no end. To this day, a part of me wishes that I had died from that poison. It would have allowed me to escape the demons that torment me. Instead, I face them every day.

Even as I write these words, countless years later, feelings of shame, guilt, and powerlessness stalk me night and day. When that soldier took me as his property, he ruined not only my body, but my mind and soul. He stole away my ability to trust, condemning me to be forever alone. I stepped away from the world that day, cocooning myself away in a chrysalis of grief that no human could penetrate; no lover, no husband, no family. From then on, my only companions would be the books that I read.

And there I remained, my life suspended. Years would pass yet still I endured. And for what? I asked. I was an empty shell of a woman, too broken to live but too strong to die.

For many years, I stayed trapped in that private world of my own creation, unable to see a way out. But in time, I came to find meaning, strength, and nourishment in my books. Reading was a way to understand people and events in history from different perspectives. It expanded my mind and allowed me to be somebody else.

The more I read, the more I understood. And the more I understood, the stronger I became. But my real strength came in the realization that I could harness the power I derived from my books to bear witness to my journey. That in writing, I could set my truth free.

And that is why I have spent my last days on this journal, laying bare my shame so that others might see and understand.

Every word chips away at the wall of that chrysalis, exposing to the light the truth within.

Help me, dear reader. Set it free.

After reading the last page of the journal, Zoe was overcome with sadness. Tears streamed down her cheeks, and her chest heaved with sobs, as she tried to catch her breath. Jeff looked up and saw her crying with her face buried in her hands. He shifted close to her on the couch.

'Zoe, what's wrong?' he asked gently, placing a hand on her shoulder. 'Why are you crying? We are going home. You should be happy!'

'It's Meera's journal. The one I told you about at the hotel. It is so tragic what happened to her.'

Zoe gasped for air and wiped her tears away, setting the journal aside. She looked up at Jeff and tried to compose herself, but the emotions were still raw and painful.

'It's just . . . so much,' she said, her voice trembling. 'Reading through this journal, it's like I'm reliving all of these moments with Meera. She suffered so much silently—we never knew. I wish I had been able to talk to her about it. It hurts to think about how we never had the chance to sit together and just *share*.'

Jeff nodded understandingly and put his arm around her, pulling her close. 'I know it's hard, Zoe,' he said softly. 'But remember, Meera wouldn't want you to be sad forever. She would want you to live your life to the fullest. And you have so much to be grateful for.'

Zoe leaned into Jeff's embrace, feeling comforted by his words. She knew he was right, and she tried to focus on the good things in her life. But the ache in her heart remained. It would take time to heal.

'There are so many people suffering in this world. Meera, the former military sex slaves, the trafficked girls. There are so many. I wanted to help, but I wasn't able to do anything. And now, I'm just exhausted. On top of that, I got you into such a mess. I'm sorry that I treated you so poorly. Thank you for everything you have done for me. I'm forever grateful. But will you ever forgive me?'

Moved by her vulnerability, Jeff spoke gently. 'Don't blame yourself for any of this, Zoe,' he said. 'Have you seen the news? People from all around the world are stepping up to demand action for the sex slaves for the Japanese army during World War II, and against trafficking. You, Zoe, you lit the match.'

'I don't even have the strength to care anymore. I just need some rest,' said Zoe.

'We can do that,' Jeff said, his voice filled with optimism. 'We're so close to being free. Just a few more hours, and we'll be out of danger. I promise, the nightmare will soon be over, okay?'

Zoe nodded weakly, her eyes heavy with exhaustion and her voice dropping to a whisper. 'Just hold on for a little longer,' she mumbled.

* * *

Four hours slipped away, seemingly in the blink of an eye. Suddenly, the boat jolted forward unexpectedly, its engines no longer a soft murmur but roaring. Zoe and Jeff, who had fallen asleep in each other's arms, awoke with a start.

Zoe, visibly shaken, asked, 'What was that?'

Jeff, equally perplexed, shook his head, 'I have no idea.'

Their questions were soon answered when the senior crew member rushed down the staircase into the galley. His face was flushed, and his breathing laboured.

'Ms Fujiwara called,' he said, trying to catch his breath. 'Bad men . . . they're coming. They're right behind us in a fast boat. Stay down here. Don't come up. Stay here. Stay, just stay.' He turned and ran up the stairs.

Zoe and Jeff ignored his warning and approached the bridge where the captain was standing with a worried look on his face. When he saw them, he waved them away, annoyed that they hadn't followed his order.

'What's happening?' Zoe asked in Korean, her voice betraying her fear. 'What did Ms Fujiwara say?'

The captain's sombre gaze bore into them, and his voice was heavy with a grave tone when he spoke. 'I'm afraid we're all in danger,' he admitted, his words echoing around the deck. 'We need to go faster, much faster. Suetake and his men are coming after us in a faster boat, and they mean business. You need to go back downstairs and stay out of sight. Look for a place to hide until we can get out of this mess.'

'Can't we turn back?' Zoe pleaded.

'It's too late,' the captain responded sternly. 'Turning back now would lead us straight to them.'

Zoe and Jeff exchanged a worried glance, silently acknowledging the captain's words. They were stranded in the middle of the sea with a vengeful crime lord bearing down on them in a deadly game of cat and mouse.

A sense of dread twisted their insides as they retreated to the galley, where they paced back and forth, grappling with the terrifying uncertainty that loomed over them.

'What do we do?' Zoe's voice trembled.

Jeff sighed. 'Nothing. All we can do is hope that our boat is faster, that we can outmanoeuvre them.'

Zoe rushed toward Jeff, embracing him tightly with a sudden need for connection and love.

'I'm so sorry I got you into this mess,' she said.

Jeff gently cupped her face. 'It wasn't you,' he insisted. 'I came here on my own. I love you, Zoe. I wanted to be here to protect you. I'm the one who should feel sorry. I feel like I let you down.'

Zoe shook her head. 'Don't feel that way,' she reassured him. 'We just need to find a way to overcome this. We are so close to being free. Mr Suetake doesn't get to win.'

'What do you mean by that?' asked Jeff.

'It was just something he said to me, back at the brothel, and then in the letter that he sent to me at the prison. It is stuck in my mind.'

'You're right,' Jeff said. 'He doesn't get to win.'

* * *

In the darkness of night, Mr Suetake's yacht had closed in on the trawler. As it attempted to draw alongside, some of the trawler's crew hurled buoys and fishing nets overboard, in a bid to fend off their pursuers.

But their resistance was short-lived. Mr Suetake's men responded with a volley of bullets across the trawler's bow and the captain knew the game was up. He brought the trawler to a stop, and the crew raised their hands in surrender.

Suetake's thugs tied the boats together and then climbed aboard the trawler. They searched every inch of the upper deck. Unsuccessful, four of them went downstairs into the galley. After ripping the place apart, they found Zoe and Jeff hiding behind a false wall and dragged them onto the deck where Mr Suetake was waiting.

Dawn had begun to break, painting the sky with a vast array of hues of red, yellow, and gold.

'Bring her to me,' Mr Suetake commanded. Two of his men pulled Zoe towards the front of the boat.

Jeff attempted to intervene, but a brutal punch landed on his face, knocking him out. Zoe frantically tried to see if Jeff was okay, but the thugs only firmed their grip and continued to drag her forward. Then they pushed her to the ground in front of Mr Suetake.

'So, we meet again,' he uttered in English, ensuring the Korean crew wouldn't understand.

'What do you want with us?' Zoe retorted.

'What do you think? Did you honestly believe you could escape from me? I've already made it clear—you don't get to win,' Mr Suetake sneered.

'They know we're out here. You won't get away with this,' Zoe snarled back.

'Both of you are fugitives, attempting to flee and break the law,' replied Mr Suetake with a smug expression. 'Who would care if anything were to happen to you? Most people would believe you got what you deserved—justice. And you know the interesting thing about news—people move on. Tomorrow, there'll be something else. A new issue. Nobody cares,' he said, gesturing to the trawler and sniggering. 'In fact, who would even know what happened to you? You think the people who allowed you to escape are going to explain to the public how you got all the way out here? You're very mistaken Ms Zoe. They will be glad to forget you.'

Zoe spat at his feet.

'Look what's happening worldwide. People are rising against you and your kind,' Zoe countered. 'They'll expose you and shut down your brothels. I read they are already looking for you. You are a fugitive too, just like us. You can't stop that.'

'That's true. All this chaos has been a bit of a pain for me, but I've been through things like this before. I'll give it some time and then fix whatever needs fixing,' Mr Suetake replied dismissively, with a shrug and an air of nonchalance. 'It's amazing what money can buy. This is just a temporary hiccup, a passing trend, you know? People are easily influenced into just following the crowd and moving on to the next shiny thing. It's human nature. Once you're out of the picture, this whole thing will die down.'

'So you're just going to kill all of us?' said Zoe, not knowing what else to say. 'Isn't that the coward's way out?'

'What do you think? If you were to escape, I can only imagine the lies you'd spread across the world. I can't allow that to happen. What choice do I have?' Mr Suetake replied.

'You can't just go around killing people,' Zoe pressed. 'What about the evidence?'

'What evidence?' Mr Suetake scoffed, turning from side to side. 'Does it look like anyone is around to witness anything here? People go missing at sea all the time. Who would know?'

'Then just answer me this one thing,' said Zoe, trying to buy time. 'You came all the way out here. Why didn't you just wait for us to escape? Then you could have fixed things, like you said. I don't understand why you bothered.'

'Because I can, and because you shouldn't have poked your nose into things that weren't your business,' Mr Suetake sneered. 'Remember the old saying, "you reap what you sow"? You're going to be a lesson for anyone who thinks about crossing me. Your actions brought shame upon my family and me. It's a matter of honour.'

'The others on this boat are innocent. Let them go,' Zoe pleaded.

'Come now, Ms Zoe, you know that nobody is truly innocent,' Mr Suetake taunted. 'The mere fact that they're here with you implicates them. They are smugglers. Criminals. They too deserve justice. Right? You must know we can't allow anyone to go free. We'll set this boat ablaze and sink it. No one will ever know.'

A moment of silence passed, Mr Suetake's threats hanging in the air like a heavy fog. To further intimidate her, he bent down towards her and whispered, 'You should have never tried to run. Their blood is on your hands, just like Pinky's. Let me tell you how that went. I heard she cried like a baby before we pushed her off. It was so pathetic. I wonder if you will go the same way. I guess we'll soon find out.'

Zoe lunged at Mr Suetake, slapping him hard across the face. Two of his men jumped up to restrain her. Without showing any emotion, Mr Suetake stood back straight and put his hand on his cheek, grinning.

There was a long pause.

'You'll never get away with this. I swear to God, this will not happen,' Zoe vowed fiercely.

'Naive girl. To the world, you'll simply vanish. I am the winner!' said Mr Suetake.

'You forget, I have your ledger,' Zoe shouted. 'If you do anything to us, it will come out. They will know all your dirty secrets.'

Mr Suetake maintained eye contact, apparently unflustered.

'Silly girl,' he responded. 'That ledger, as you call it, has no real meaning. It was just a simple accounting document. Nothing more. And even if it surfaces, I'll just buy it back.'

At that moment, Mr Suetake held out his right hand. One of his men walked over and handed him a knife.

'In the old days, when a person dishonoured a superior, they would have the right to take vengeance. You slapped my face. This is a shameful act. Because of this, it is within my right to demand restitution for this insult. Wouldn't you agree?'

He bent down and placed the blade against her skin. He then twisted the knife quickly, resulting in a small cut across her cheek.

Zoe screamed and pressed the wound on her cheek. The shock delayed her reaction, the tears rolling down her face a few minutes later.

'It is time that you learn some manners, Ms Zoe. It is time that I demonstrate that you have no power in my country. It is time that you learn your place.'

As this exchange between Zoe and Mr Suetake had unfolded, the first rays of the new rising sun had begun to cast a warm, golden glow over the still waters. Somewhere in the distance, a boat horn echoed through the air, catching the attention of everyone aboard the trawler. Their gazes followed the direction of the sound to the west, where a line of fog shrouded the horizon.

For a few seconds, there was no sound. Then, the horn sounded again. And then, for a third time. It was getting closer.

Zoe was the first to spot it—a single boat piercing through the veil of fog several miles in the distance.

Slowly but steadily, it appeared to be heading straight in their direction. Within a minute, two more boats emerged from the mist, followed by another four, six, eight, and then ten. Minutes later, the number doubled and then tripled.

A hushed silence fell over the onlookers, a stillness that only nature could offer in the heart of the vast, open sea. Every eye was locked on the horizon, where a magnificent spectacle was unfurling before them. The sunrays danced on the gently rocking waves as the approaching flotilla completely broke through the morning mist.

The fleet was a motley crew of vessels, ranging from humble fishing trawlers to sleek, swift motorboats. At the front were smaller, nimble vessels, big enough for perhaps only one or two people. Behind them, emerging from the shadows of the fog were opulent yachts with sleek lines and gleaming exteriors that spoke to the importance and grandeur of their owners. Bringing up the rear were the rugged, weathered fishing boats, the powerhouses of the pack.

As the fleet drew closer, Zoe could make out figures on the decks. They seemed to be shouting and cheering, though she could not decipher the words. She wondered what so many vessels were doing together in the middle of the ocean. Was this a race, a celebration, or what?

As the boats drew nearer, a chant, initially indistinguishable, began to take form. The words coalesced into something discernible, and Zoe could hear her own name being called. The realization hit her like a burst of sunlight through the fog: They were coming to her rescue. There was no other explanation. These people, with hearts as vast as the ocean they sailed on, were reaching out to Zoe and Jeff in their time of need.

Many of them were not only chanting and shouting, but also brandishing posters and banners, and setting off flares. Others were dancing and banging drums, and there appeared to be at least one film crew among them. It was like a floating carnival on the sea.

As Mr Suetake observed the approaching fleet, a look of growing disdain spread across his face. His men exchanged puzzled glances, looking to him for direction. He barked back at them, as if scolding his wayward children, 'Move! Let's get out of here.' He strode towards the bridge to his own vessel.

Once aboard, he turned around and his gaze locked with Zoe's. 'We will meet again,' he said.

His henchmen were following suit, leaping from the trawler onto Mr Suetake's yacht before it accelerated away.

Zoe rushed to Jeff's side, her heart pounding. Jeff was conscious but remained on the ground, disoriented by the sudden turn of events, unable to grasp what had just transpired.

'Are you hurt?' Zoe inquired, gently touching his cheeks to inspect his injury. Apart from a black eye that had already begun to swell, he appeared relatively unharmed.

Jeff spoke uncertainly. 'What is going on? What are all these boats doing in the distance?' With a wary glance around, he rose to his feet, trying to make sense of the surreal scene unfolding before him.

'They're here for us, Jeff. They're here to rescue us. We're safe now,' said Zoe, exhilarated.

They watched as the approaching flotilla closed in on their humble trawler. Most of the boats stopped within about fifty feet, but one of the larger vessels drew closer and glided alongside them with a grace that belied its size.

Two women disembarked from it and climbed aboard the trawler.

'Are you Zoe?' one of them asked in a concerned tone.

'We received a message from Ms Fujiwara, who informed us of the emergency you're facing. When we heard this, we put out a call for help from anyone who had a boat. Look at the outcome. All these people came to help. Can you believe it?'

'Thank you,' said Zoe. 'But who are you?'

'We are activists, just like you, dedicated to the fight against sex trafficking. It's an honour to meet you both.'

The two women extended their hands, like fans meeting their idols.

'Please, come aboard our boat,' another woman beckoned from one of the neighbouring vessels. 'It's faster and safer than the one you're on. We'll get you home safe.'

One of the women looked over at Zoe's cheek and said, 'Are you okay? Your face is bleeding.'

Zoe's hand reached up to touch the wound, and she then looked at the blood on her fingers. 'Yes, it is nothing. Just a scratch.'

Jeff and Zoe stepped onto the boat, struggling to comprehend all that was happening. As they looked back, they saw the fading silhouette of Mr Suetake's yacht, and realized that this was the end of their harrowing journey and the beginning of a new chapter in their lives.

For the next two hours, Zoe and Jeff clung to each other, their fingers intertwined in a pledge that no force could sever.

They fielded a barrage of questions from the eager activists, whose curiosity seemed insatiable: how did they endure the confines of prison, what did they think of the Japanese government, who planned their heart-pounding escape from Japan? As the couple spoke, an intimate audience of about twenty activists stood transfixed, as if under a spell, hanging on to every word. Intermittently, other vessels would glide up to disembark a few more eager faces.

As the flotilla collectively headed in the direction of South Korea, Jeff and Zoe joined their voices with those of the other passengers and, together, they sailed forward, determined to make a difference in the world. Chants and cheers echoed across the water: 'Save our women', 'Support the comfort women', and 'Justice for all'.

* * *

A large crowd greeted the fleet of boats as it arrived back at the docks in Korea. People cheered and reached out to touch Zoe and Jeff, eager to show their support.

Amidst the excitement, a determined young Korean woman approached them, her voice filled with assurance. 'Follow me. I've been tasked with escorting you to safety. You're in good hands. We have a car waiting for you.'

As they made their way through the crowd, well-wishers showered them with praise and encouragement.

'You are both heroes!'

'We stand with you!'

'You inspire us!'

At some point, they were encircled by a group of university students, one of whom requested a few words from Zoe and Jeff.

'We all want to hear from you!' the student exclaimed.

Grateful for the support, Zoe stood on a crate to address the eager crowd. 'We are immensely grateful to you all,' she began, her voice filled with appreciation. 'The Korean women on those boats quite literally saved our lives.'

Zoe glanced at Jeff, seeking his encouragement, as they both grappled uneasily with the rock star treatment they were receiving.

'I want to use this platform to shed light on the plight of the countless Korean and other Asian women who suffer at the hands of criminal gangs, who deceive them and sell them into sex slavery,' Zoe continued. 'It is like the horrors suffered by the victims of Japanese military forced prostitution in World War II are happening all over again, echoing through time. These atrocities must come to an end. We must not allow history to repeat itself.'

Zoe's words struck a chord with the crowd and were met with cheers and applause. She was taken aback by the fervour of their response.

The crowd continued to hum as she stood down from the crate and stepped into Jeff's arms. Then they were led to the end of the docks where a black SUV was waiting.

To their surprise, Ms Fujiwara and her elderly father stepped out of the vehicle.

'I'm deeply sorry to hear about the close call. Are both of you alright?' Ms Fujiwara enquired. 'What happened?'

'Mr Suetake happened,' said Jeff. He added, smiling, 'But then I guess you know that already.'

Ms Fujiwara nodded solemnly. 'Yes, we received a tip-off about Mr Suetake's plan to pursue you at sea. But we didn't know the extent of it.'

'So, did you organize all those boats?' Zoe asked in astonishment.

'No, it was my father,' Ms Fujiwara replied, nodding toward the elderly man beside her. 'He has many dear friends here in Korea.'

Zoe turned her attention to the elderly man, seeing him properly for the first time. 'Thank you for your invaluable help,' she said. 'If it weren't for you, we wouldn't be standing here today.'

A faint smile graced the old man's lips. 'I'm relieved to see both of you safe,' he responded. 'The idea for this strategy came from a remarkable rescue that took place during World War II in Dunkirk. I'm an avid history reader, you see. When the British soldiers were trapped in France, Churchill rallied ordinary people to bring their boats and help rescue them. An incredible armada crossed the English Channel, saving hundreds of thousands of lives. It must have been a sight to behold.'

'It was indeed,' said Zoe, thinking of the flotilla that had come to her own aid. 'Your friends were our saviours. Thank you from the bottom of our hearts.'

'It was my great honour. You see, I would do anything to support Meera's great-niece,' the old man said earnestly.

'Meera?' Zoe asked, taken aback. 'How do you know her?'

'My name is Masuki Fujiwara,' he replied, matter-of-factly.

'Masuki?' Zoe repeated in disbelief. 'Are you the person about whom my aunt wrote in her journal?'

'Journal?' asked Masuki, clearly puzzled.

'My aunt kept a journal,' Zoe said with a sudden pang of nostalgia. 'She gave it to me before . . .' her voice trailed off, the unspoken words hanging in the air. 'It mentioned how you two met and how you saved her. I even found letters from you.'

Masuki's expression softened, and his eyes grew misty.

'What happened to you after you saved her in China?' Zoe asked.

'Somehow my father found me that same day,' Masuki said. 'He had me arrested and sent back to Japan. Years later, when I tracked down Meera, she refused to meet me. She felt consumed by shame.'

Zoe's voice softened. 'Did you hear about her passing?' she gently enquired.

A veil of sorrow descended over Masuki as he bowed his head and turned away. 'Yes, I'm deeply sorry,' he murmured.

'You both need to leave Korea,' Ms Fujiwara interjected, warm but firm. 'It's not safe for you here. There are people who consider you a threat, particularly the criminal gangs. We've arranged tickets to Canada for Jeff and you. We'll take you to the airport immediately.'

Zoe's brow furrowed. 'But how will we board?' she asked. 'We don't have our passports.'

'Oh yes you do,' said Ms Fujiwara, producing two temporary passports. 'We have contacts here with the Canadian embassy. We started this process several days ago. That's why we're here in Korea today. Now we really need to go now. You can ride with my father, and I'll be behind you in a second car. We can say our goodbyes at the airport.'

As Zoe accepted the documents, a flash of hope sparkled in her eyes. The fresh start that she had been yearning for was finally in her grasp.

* * *

As they drove together to the airport, Masuki shared sentimental stories about his time with Meera.

'Meera was my first love,' he began. 'I don't know what she might have said about me in her journal, but for a long time, we were inseparable friends. In a world torn apart by war and rife with hardships, we became each other's pillars of support. Despite coming from vastly different backgrounds, we became very close during that terrible period. She was my rock, my confidante, and my dearest friend. I loved her deeply.'

Zoe nodded in understanding. 'Actually, Meera spoke highly of you in her journal. She even wrote that you two were in love.' She paused. 'Do you remember the day she last saw you in Korea? She gave you a butterfly pin. Whatever happened to it?'

Without hesitation, Masuki retrieved the pin from his pocket and presented it to Zoe. The pin had an antique quality, bearing a patina that indicated its age.

'I've carried this pin with me through the years,' Masuki explained, with tenderness in his eyes. 'It's been my constant companion, my lucky charm. It's been with me through the trials of war, my university days, the early stages of my career, and even my time as a government official.'

His eyes rested lovingly on the pin for a few moments before he continued.

'Did she write about the day I found her in that comfort women station?'

'Yes.'

'That day, I told her she was still my little butterfly.'

'She mentioned this.'

'After I said that to her, she said she was nothing more than a fallen butterfly,' he continued. 'Those words have stuck with me all these years. Through the years, I realized that she was one of so many fallen butterflies. There were too many other women who suffered the same wicked fate. They were somebody's mother, wife, or sister. What happened back then was so wrong.'

'What compelled you to reach out to Meera?' Zoe asked.

'I wanted to marry her,' Masuki said. 'I wanted her to be my wife because I loved her deeply. She had been the most significant friend in my life. When I finally discovered her whereabouts, I made every effort to reconnect with her. I tried everything I could, but for the longest time, there was no response. Then, she sent me a message, urging me never to contact her again. I understood her decision. It was my family and me who were responsible for her being taken away.'

Zoe put her hand on his shoulder, 'I don't believe she blamed you. I think she carried a profound sense of shame for what she endured, making her reluctant to be with you or anyone else.'

Masuki's eyes became watery as he responded, 'There was no reason for her to bear any shame. She was a victim of the war, just like countless others who suffered, including myself.'

Zoe pressed on, 'Why didn't you go to Canada to find her?'

'I did,' said Masuki. 'Twice. But all I had was a post office box address, and I was never able to locate her exact residence. I tried tirelessly. Back then, there was no internet. Finding a person without an address was nearly impossible.'

He continued with a touch of melancholy, 'I remained single for a long, long time. It was only after I had given up all hope of finding her that I finally married and started a family. My wife was a quiet companion, and she passed away during childbirth. I raised our daughter as a single parent, and I never remarried.'

'Why did you decide to help us?' Zoe asked. 'Won't it create problems for you back in Japan?'

Masuki looked at her wisely. 'I am now an elder statesman, and people show great respect for me. In the Japanese culture, age and seniority carry gravitas, and I am regarded as untouchable. I share your determination to obtain a genuine apology for the survivors of military sexual enslavement from my government, although I remain sceptical that it will ever happen. I am also committed to pushing our justice system to address the problems surrounding prostitution and trafficking in our country. We must do everything within our power to put an end to this suffering. If there's ever anything I can do to assist you, please don't hesitate to reach out.'

Just then, the car pulled up at the airport, where a concierge, a representative from the Canadian embassy, and an official from the South Korean immigration office were waiting for them.

'I must bid you farewell for now. These people will take care of you from here,' Masuki told Zoe and Jeff as the concierge opened the car door.

They stepped out into the cold refreshing air and turned around to say their goodbyes to Masuki, but he had already closed the door.

'There is one last thing I wanted to say before you go,' Masuki told them after rolling down the window. 'I wanted to tell you both how profoundly grateful I am for what you have done. Thank you for setting the truth free.'

Zoe stared in astonishment, wanting to speak but found that her lips wouldn't move. Masuki rolled up his window, tapped the driver on the shoulder, and the car pulled away.

20

After Zoe and Jeff returned to Canada, they sought refuge together in Zoe's apartment. For nearly a week, they remained barricaded within its walls, recuperating from their ordeal.

Back in Japan, the government made a show of outrage at their escape, which put them back in the headlines for a couple of days, but the public's interest soon waned, and the press moved on to the next big sensation.

In Tokyo's corridors of power, government spin doctors privately congratulated themselves on their handling of the affair. They saw it as a win: Zoe had left the country, things were returning to normal, and they had avoided losing face.

The campaign to secure an apology from the Japanese government for their system of Imperial military forced prostitution persisted for a few more weeks, until that too began to fade, as did the pressure on the government to intervene in the fight against human trafficking. Perhaps Suetake was right. The public was indeed fickle.

Zoe, though, had enough experience to know that she needed to play the long game. The massive exposure she had received during her arrest had boosted her online followers to two million, so she would have a strong platform to campaign from next time around. *Media issues are like cicadas*, she mused, *one brood swarming the press one minute, then disappearing the next as a new brood takes over. But the issues never really go away entirely; they only lay dormant, to reawaken when the time is right.*

So she tended to her followers on social media. She shared updates with links and photos from her life, and she did so just frequently enough to stay on their radar and relevant, but not so frequently that they would tire of her. She also worked the traditional media, fielding requests for interviews and presentations from news outlets, universities, and community organizations, so she could keep her cause in the public eye.

Back at *The Star*, she returned to her reporting work, though she made a conscious decision to concentrate on local stories. She didn't want to get burned out or be pigeon-holed as 'the sex crime correspondent', which she had overheard one of her rivals remark about her. She even started working on the homelessness pitch that Ben had been banging on about for as long as she could remember. To her surprise, she actually enjoyed the assignment, and it was nominated for a string of awards.

And, for a while, she was happy like that. But as time passed, a persistent itch grew within her, an urge that she couldn't ignore, telling her that she had unfinished business to attend to. The world needed to once again raise their voice for justice for the survivors of Japanese military sexual slavery and their modern counterparts: 6.3 million victims of sex trafficking around the world. It needed to wake up.

* * *

Three months after Zoe's return from Korea, a package arrived from China. It was from Arah and it contained Mr Suetake's ledger.

Zoe didn't even think about what she needed to do, her dormant instinct now fully roused. She threw herself into her work, combing through the contents of the ledger, joining up the dots, tracing the flows of money, and pinpointing the shell companies it was going through. She worked her contacts in finance, government, and police, and followed up every tip from her now formidable network of followers. When she was done, she began to write like a woman possessed, drafting and redrafting, spiking and starting afresh. Through the nights she worked, no longer even feeling the need for sleep—she had slept too long!—and on she went until she was done.

* * *

The dossier made a satisfying 'thwack' as she threw it onto Ben's desk.

'Did you get that story I emailed you?' Zoe asked her surprised boss. 'Here are all the documents, sources, and statements that back it up. Let me know if you need anything else,' she grinned triumphantly at him.

Ben closed his eyes and rubbed his forehead. He sensed a long evening ahead of him. 'I'm guessing this isn't a follow-up to that council meeting on pedestrian fatalities,' he said drily.

'No. No, it's not,' said Zoe.

The series of three front-page articles were among the finest *The Star* had ever published. In them, Zoe methodically stripped down the workings of Mr Suetake's crime ring, taking the reader on a journey that followed one of his victims—under the pseudonym 'Pinky'—from the streets of Korea to his brothel in Japan. Intertwined with Pinky's narrative were interviews with other trafficked girls, families who had lost their children to Mr Suetake, good cops who had tried to put him behind bars, and bad cops once in his employ who had now turned against him. On a follow-up double-page spread inside, where the text continued, there was a giant flow chart detailing where Mr Suetake got his money and how he laundered it. Several government figures were among the clients that Zoe identified as having visited his brothels and several firms that were household names appeared to have received his dirty money.

* * *

The story sent shockwaves through Japan, as government figures and billion-dollar firms fell over themselves trying to distance themselves from Mr Suetake. Many threatened to sue *The Star*, but Ben held firm and stood behind his reporter's story. It was watertight and he knew it. And when the Japanese public saw that he was standing behind it, they knew it too.

The pressure on the Japanese government to act was immense. Realizing that demonizing *The Star* wouldn't work, the government tried a new tack, going all in on pursuing Mr Suetake instead.

The problem was, each time the authorities closed in on him, he managed to slip away, as if vanishing into thin air.

Zoe, however, refused to be deterred. She focused on what she could do. Her groundbreaking story was echoing through newspapers, radio channels, and television screens the world over, giving her the ideal platform to speak out about the atrocities suffered by the victims of Japanese military sexual slavery and to get across her message that, even today, similar crimes were being committed.

One of Zoe's finest moments was when she stood tall before a sea of faces gathered for her keynote speech to the United Nations.

'We refuse to relent until the Japanese government fully acknowledges its crimes against humanity in enslaving hundreds of thousands of women and girls across the Asia Pacific. And we will not surrender until the world opens its eyes to the countless women and girls who remain in sexual slavery today. Until that day comes, the leaders among you in this room should not rest easy. You should not congratulate yourselves, nor feel good about what you have done. For in failing to act, you are complicit in rape and sexual violence during the war.'

The applause thundered.

* * *

Zoe stormed into Ben's office, with a determined look on her face. She had made up her mind, and nothing he could say would sway her. She found him sitting behind his desk, a stack of printed emails and letters in his hands. He stood up and handed them to her.

'You can't go to China,' Ben told her firmly, as if there were nothing to discuss.

Zoe arched an eyebrow, glancing at the pile of messages before her. 'Let me guess, more hate mail?' she asked cynically.

As she skimmed through the messages, she noticed that they all came from two countries. A bitter smile played on her lips.

'These are from Japan and Korea. I'm going to China where the supporters outweigh the trolls.'

Ben's face contorted. 'Zoe, it's serious,' he insisted. 'These threats are real. Remember what happened on that boat? These people are bad dudes—they mean business.'

Zoe's eyes flickered with memories of when she had faced the wrath of Suetake's henchmen. She swallowed hard. 'I'm going,' she declared defiantly. 'The opening of the museum for comfort women in Nanjing is important. We're gaining momentum, Ben. We can't afford to back down now.'

Ben sighed. 'I let you do these talks because they sell papers,' he said, exasperated. 'But enough is enough. We're not in the activism business. We run a newspaper.'

Zoe looked Ben squarely in the eye. She knew her next move could change the course of her life. 'Then I guess I have to quit.'

'Not before I fire you,' Ben shot back.

A small, knowing smile crept onto Zoe's face. She rose from her seat.

'Then let's get it over with. I have things to do. I don't have time for this nonsense. If you are going to fire me, then fire me. Otherwise, I have a trip to prepare for.'

There was no response. Without another word, Zoe turned on her heels and walked out of the room, leaving Ben to stew over what had just transpired.

She had always thought quitting would be scary, but she felt amazing. While she wasn't sure if she had actually quit or been fired, or if her job was still intact, she felt liberated. She had chosen her path and to hell with the consequences. She was on fire. Nothing could stop her.

* * *

Zoe and Jeff sat together in the hushed atmosphere of the speakers' waiting room in a state of nervous anticipation. The auditorium beyond the closed doors was a cavernous space, filled to the brim with more than a thousand eager faces.

An audio technician approached Zoe, carrying a remote microphone, which she carefully affixed to Zoe's belt. 'You're good to go,' the technician said, offering a final instruction. 'Just hit this little red switch when you get on stage. Be cautious, though, sometimes it can trigger if you move the wrong way.'

Zoe chuckled, her eyes twinkling. 'I had that happen to me once before,' she confessed, with a grin. 'The microphone was on, and I was in the washroom. You can imagine how embarrassing that was. Let's just say, I'm lactose intolerant!'

The three of them laughed.

After the technician departed, Zoe rose from her seat and made her way to the water cooler. As her leg brushed against one of the chairs, it caught the microphone switch, turning it on.

'Ben won't let me go to China,' Zoe's voice rang out at 150 decibels, unbeknownst to her. There was a wave of murmuring as people in the audience looked around, confused by the disembodied voice coming from the speakers.

'He says it's too dangerous.'

'Actually, I agree with Ben on this one,' Jeff said. 'Going there would be a mistake.'

Zoe was annoyed. 'I don't care what you say. This is important. These women need us. If they are willing to fight, I'm going to stand beside them. The visit will help raise awareness and . . .'

Before she could finish her sentence, the audio technician burst into the room looking apologetic. Hastily, she reached Zoe and swiftly silenced the activated microphone.

'So, sorry,' the technician uttered sheepishly. 'I told you, it sometimes turns on.'

Zoe turned red with embarrassment. 'Did everyone hear me?' she asked, mortified.

The technician thought for a moment. 'Well, I'm not sure about *every*one.'

Zoe rolled her eyes; Jeff tried to stifle a grin.

'They are ready for you now,' the technician continued, trying to alleviate the awkwardness before hurriedly leaving the room.

Zoe tried to put it out of her mind. She summoned her courage and made her way into the auditorium through the door, awaiting her introduction. As the event's host called her name, the audience erupted into thunderous applause.

When it had eventually died down, the host addressed the audience again. 'Before we proceed, I have a question for all of you,' the host paused for effect. 'Who here believes Zoe should visit China?'

The room exploded in a second round of thunderous applause.

Zoe, now on stage, looked over at the vast crowd and soaking up its appreciation.

'I suppose I have my answer,' she told them. 'If all of you want me to go, how can I say no? I'd better brush up on my Mandarin.'

* * *

One afternoon a few days later, as Zoe was returning from her lunch break, Winnie approached her with an air of excitement.

'Zoe, there are some flowers waiting for you on your desk,' Winnie exclaimed, a note of intrigue in her voice.

That's curious, Zoe thought.

'Who are they from?'

'I don't know, but there's a card,' Winnie replied.

Had Jeff suddenly learned how to be romantic? Zoe wondered. *Somehow that seemed unlikely. Perhaps she had a secret admirer somewhere? How exciting that would be.* Then she had a disturbing thought. *What if it was Dave from accounts on the second floor? He was so . . . icky. Oh God, that's it.*

However, as soon as she spotted the collection of nine, white lilies wrapped in pristine white paper on her desk, her smile began to drop. Elegant though the flowers were, something about them was not quite right.

As Zoe reached for the card, she remembered her mother explaining to her as a child that in Asian culture, white flowers were associated with funerals and bad luck. Then she read the chilling message.

Dear Ms Zoe,

It seems that you're determined to spread false news regarding the comfort women and me. While you may believe it will make a difference, let me assure you, it won't. As I've said before, people simply don't care. Soon, I'll be back in Tokyo, running my business as if nothing happened. However, you may want to watch your back. You never know when a fall down the stairs or an unfortunate road accident might befall you. What you've done to me is unforgivable, and it will not go unpunished. I warned you, you don't get to win.

To her horror, she found a photograph within the envelope. It showed Pinky's lifeless body, in a pool of blood. While she couldn't see her face, she knew it was her by the clothes she was wearing. Zoe dropped the gruesome photo in shock and vomited.

When she had recovered her senses, she threw the flowers into the waste basket and called security to take the letter as evidence. She planned to take it to the police.

That image would stick with Zoe for months, tormenting her. But there was more to come from Mr Suetake. In the following weeks, she received two more deliveries. One included a collection of intricately embroidered handkerchiefs, a nod to a Korean belief that using handkerchiefs—associated with wiping away tears of sadness or sickness—can prevent loved ones from experiencing sorrow, illness, or death.

Another time, she received a card, written in vivid red ink. Its ominous message read:

> I wonder what you are doing now. I wonder if you know where I am. I can be anywhere. Watch your back. I'm coming for you. You don't get to win.

Zoe knew that in Korea, red ink, especially when used to write a person's name, symbolized death. It harked back to an age-old belief that writing someone's name in blood would bring about their demise. She knew a note like this would make any Korean shudder, so deeply engrained was the custom. And she knew, too, that this was exactly how Mr Suetake wanted her to feel.

She told herself that she wasn't going to let that happen. She wasn't going to play his game. She was going to China, come what may. Mr Suetake wouldn't get to win.

21

Zoe and Jeff arrived at the Nanjing Museum of the Site of the Lijixiang Comfort Stations in Nanjing, China, where they were greeted by the museum coordinators and a group of local government VIPs. Amidst the flurry of handshakes and camera flashes, Zoe felt pride and gratitude. She knew it was a tremendous honour to be one of the keynote speakers for the event.

Before going to the auditorium for the speech, they were given a quick tour of the premises by the director. He began with a short introduction: 'The Nanjing Museum comprises eight large buildings. By the end of 1937, after Japanese troops occupied Nanjing, they repurposed several structures into two main military brothels known as the 'Shinonome Comfort Station' and the 'Kokyono Comfort Station'. One of these rooms was where the late Pak Yong-sim, a North Korean survivor of Japanese military sexual slavery, was forced to serve Japanese soldiers for three years from the age of seventeen. Eighty-two-year-old Pak made a pilgrimage to this comfort station to find closure and bear witness to being compelled into sexual slavery, alongside many other young, Korean girls, for up to thirty Japanese soldiers a day. It remains one of the few verified comfort station sites.'

The museum was divided into three exhibition spaces: a general exhibit on the 'comfort women' system of sexual slavery put in place by the Japanese military, a recreation of the site, and a thematic exhibit. On display were thousands of articles, photos, and other visual materials.

Then, the event staff guided Jeff to the VIP section near the front of the outdoor speaking area. There, he saw Masuki and Ms Fujiwara waving at him and went to join them. As he took his seat, a crowd of a couple of hundred people continued gathering for the opening event. In the front row were eight elderly, Chinese survivors of Japanese wartime sexual slavery.

Meanwhile, Zoe was escorted to the speaker room. Inside, she found herself alone, awaiting the summons to the main stage for her speech. She paced back and forth nervously, reviewing her notes, mentally rehearsing her speech, and adjusting the microphone unit on her belt.

Suddenly, the door swung open, catching her by surprise. To her astonishment, Mr Suetake and one of his men barged in.

Zoe recoiled, first in shock, then in indignation. Mr Suetake strode towards the centre of the room as his thug stood in front of the door, blocking Zoe's only path of escape.

'So, here we are again,' said Mr Suetake, his voice dripping with menace. 'I warned you that I wasn't finished with you.'

Zoe was scared, but she was not going to let Mr Suetake know.

'What are you doing here?' she asked, keeping her gaze steady and her voice as level as she could.

'You and I have some unfinished business,' said Mr Suetake slyly.

Zoe's hand reached instinctively for the microphone.

On the other side of the door, as the opening ceremony commenced, a local government official stepped forward to deliver his welcome remarks in Mandarin. He had barely got two sentences in when he was interrupted by an unexpected transmission that crackled over the intercom. A familiar voice resonated through the venue, capturing the attention of the room.

'Get out!' Zoe's urgent voice blared out.

'Oh God,' Jeff said, turning to Ms Fujiwara. 'Zoe must have accidentally activated her microphone again. I need to inform her.'

They sprang from their chairs and headed towards the waiting room. But before they could get there, it became clear that this time around, the microphone was the least of Zoe's worries.

Zoe did her best to keep Mr Suetake talking. She was well aware of his vulnerabilities and knew precisely how to provoke him. His pride had always been his Achilles' heel, a weakness that she could exploit to her advantage.

'You've been declared a fugitive because you're a criminal who got caught,' Zoe said boldly, her voice cutting through the air. 'You brought this upon yourself. You reap what you sow. Remember when you said this to me?'

'There's nothing wrong with what I do,' Mr Suetake retorted defiantly.

'Oh, except that it's illegal. Selling human beings is prohibited by the laws of Japan—and every other country, come to think of it.'

'You don't understand a thing,' he shot back, his frustration growing. 'It's our culture, our tradition. I'm providing a public service.'

'Some traditions are inherently wrong. What you do to those girls is disgusting. Why don't you leave them alone? And why can't you leave me alone?'

'I already told you,' Mr Suetake replied, trying to sound as sinister as he possibly could. 'You don't get to win.'

'Yeah, right. So what are you going to do? Shoot me right here? I have to deliver my speech now!'

'Shoot you?' laughed Mr Suetake. 'No, not yet at least. What would be the fun in that? Didn't I say we'd have fun? You're coming with us.'

Zoe felt sick but refused to yield. 'Fun? Don't you think people will notice my absence? I'm supposed to be on stage right now,' she said.

'On stage?' Mr Suetake scoffed dismissively. 'To spew more lies to those ignorant masses out there? They're all just sheep. Chinese, Koreans . . . you're all simpletons. Good-for-nothing toilets and fuck bags. And you wonder why we take you for whores.'

The thug opened the door, and Mr Suetake strode towards it before stopping dead in his tracks.

Standing there, blocking their path, was a group of at least sixty people, including several armed police officers.

Zoe, her heart pounding, looked over Mr Suetake's shoulder. For a moment, the world stood still.

Then the Chinese police officers approached, their guns drawn.

Suddenly, Mr Suetake's menacing air evaporated. He fell quiet and offered no resistance as the officers surrounded his henchman and him, handcuffing them both.

He turned, desperate, to Zoe. 'It's not over,' he said. 'I'll be back. You don't get to win.' It was a limp threat, pathetic even.

Zoe smiled at him. This time, she knew, it was over. 'Good luck in a Chinese jail. I expect your cell mates will be interested in your ideas about sex and race. I'll make sure they hear all about it.'

* * *

Back in the auditorium, it was now Masuki's turn to address the audience as a keynote speaker. As he turned to face the expectant crowd from the podium, a silence fell upon the venue. He looked gently to his right, where the eight elderly women were watching him intently, their eyes filled with a mix of anticipation and uncertainty.

The atmosphere was heavy with the weight of the past, as if the air were laden with their every memory and experience.

Then Masuki looked to his left, where Zoe sat, transfixed.

His gaze lingered on the strikingly beautiful young woman before him and his chest filled with pride. *How strong she looked! How radiant! Just as he remembered her*. Finally, he could smile once more. *Meera! I knew I would see you again.*

Then he began.

'Ladies and gentlemen, esteemed dignitaries, and honoured guests, good morning.'

'It is with great privilege and reverence that we gather here today for the opening of the Nanjing Comfort Women Museum. This remarkable institution honours and preserves the memory of the many women who endured unimaginable suffering in the military brothels of World War II and pays tribute to their indomitable human spirit.'

'Today, as we embark on this solemn and historic journey, we are joined by over a hundred distinguished individuals, including eight brave survivors of the unspeakable sexual servitude for the Imperial Japanese military before and during World War II. Each of you represents a unique blend of knowledge, compassion, and dedication to the cause of justice and human rights. The Nanjing Comfort Women Museum serves as a reminder of the atrocities committed in the past, an educational resource, and a beacon of hope for a future where such horrors are never repeated.'

'As we gather on this hallowed ground, let us remember the past, honour the survivors, and unite to ensure that the atrocities of history remain seared in our memory so that they may never be repeated. The opening of the Nanjing Comfort Women Museum is a profound step in this journey.'

'As a former Japanese Foreign Minister, I stand before you today to ask for your attention, empathy, and resolve to put right not only the wrongs of history, but the wrongs of our present.'

'First and foremost, we cannot ignore the shadows of history that loom over the suffering of those who were forced into sexual servitude during the war. These women and girls, many of them young and vulnerable, were subjected to unimaginable horrors during one of the darkest chapters in our history. It is time for Japan to acknowledge the pain and suffering these individuals endured, and offer a sincere and heartfelt apology.'

'An apology is not a sign of weakness; it shows that we are willing to confront our history honestly.'

'To truly make amends, Japan should support initiatives aimed at preserving the memory of these women and educating future generations. This is why I am here today. By endorsing this museum and others like it, we can take a step towards healing historical wounds and fostering a better understanding between nations.'

'But we must go beyond our past, to acknowledge that sexual slavery is not confined to the history books. It remains alive on our streets today, where traffickers prey on vulnerable young women and girls, stripping them of their freedom, dignity, and humanity.'

'It is an issue that transcends borders and cultures, a scourge that must be eradicated. We must stand together, not just as citizens of China, Japan, and Korea, but as global citizens united against modern-day slavery.'

'We need to take aggressive action to protect the vulnerable from exploitation. Our governments must prioritise anti-trafficking efforts, strengthen law enforcement, and work tirelessly to bring traffickers to justice. But our responsibilities do not end there. We must also invest in education, awareness, and support for survivors, creating a network of compassion that can help them rebuild their lives.'

'If we can do this, then we can build a future where such atrocities are indeed found only in the history books and not in the lives of our fellow human beings.'

'Let Japan slay the demons of its past to become a beacon of hope, a nation that not only recognizes and apologizes for its past misdeeds, but leads the way in learning from them. The time for change is now, and our commitment . . .'

Masuki stopped mid-sentence. With tears in his eyes, he looked out over the crowd. He searched for Meera once again but could see only her great-niece this time.

Staring back up at the audience, he said, 'I'm afraid that these are just words on paper. Sometimes, we need to go beyond words. We need to act.' He left his speech papers on the podium and stepped away. With measured steps, he made his way towards the eight elderly women, pausing before them, his eyes searching their weathered faces. The audience watched, spellbound. He dropped to one knee, then the other, his body bending before them in reverence. His voice, filled with remorse and determination, resonated through the hall as he spoke in Mandarin.

'My name is Masuki Fujiwara,' he began. 'I was once a young soldier in the Japanese army. After the war, I entered government service, eventually rising to the position of Minister of Foreign Affairs after four decades. But today, I kneel before you, as I should have done so long ago.

'I offer my sincere apologies on behalf of myself and my country. The actions committed against you were not only wrong but a crime against humanity. It is my hope that together, the Japanese, Koreans, Chinese, and all those affected by military sex slavery, can work towards ensuring that such atrocities never happen again.'

Masuki bowed deeply and held the position, his aged frame steadfast in its humility. Tears streamed down his face, mingling with the profound depth of his remorse.

Then, with the support of several museum officials, he rose.

Masuki approached each woman, his hand outstretched to gently clasp theirs. As he whispered words of solace and contrition, tears welled in the eyes of each woman, their emotions pouring forth. Their weeping became a collective release, a sign of the utter depths of their suffering and the power of acknowledgment.

The immense significance of Masuki's apology, his willingness to confront the past and offer a genuine olive branch, was not lost on the crowd—many of whom were now weeping openly along with the survivors of Japanese military sexual slavery.

With his task complete, Masuki looked over at Zoe and his daughter. They looked at him with awe and walked towards him with open arms.

'Thank you for your powerful and beautiful apology,' Zoe said. 'I only wish Aunt Meera had been here to see this day. But I know that, wherever she is, she will be proud of you. Thank you for finally setting her free.'

Masuki grew quiet.

'I'm sorry it took so long, my little butterfly.'

* * *

Standing together at the airport a few days later, Masuki, Zoe, and Jeff prepared to say their final goodbyes. Their shared experiences lingered in the air, but the pain was in the past, replaced with a sense of healing and hope for the future.

Masuki held their hands tightly, his eyes conveying his deep appreciation for their visit.

'Both of you, have a safe trip,' he said warmly. 'Thank you for honouring me with your presence and for witnessing the stories of those remarkable women.'

'What you did for those women, and for all of us, was incredibly touching,' Zoe said, her emotions still raw. 'You brought healing to our hearts. I will never forget it. Thank you.'

'My contribution was but a small gesture,' Masuki replied humbly. 'It was you who opened the eyes and hearts of so many people, who shed light on the pain and suffering endured by those brave women.'

Masuki reached into his pocket, producing the silver butterfly hairpin that Meera had given to him. He held it out, pressing it into Zoe's palm with a bittersweet smile.

'What are you doing?' Zoe asked, confused.

'As you know, it's something your great-aunt Meera gave me during our time in Korea,' Masuki explained, a wistful look in his eyes. 'We were just children back then. I've kept it with me all these years.'

Overwhelmed by the significance of the gesture, Zoe hesitated. 'I can't accept this,' she protested gently. 'It's yours, a cherished memory from Meera.'

'When she gave it to me, she said she was my butterfly,' he said, tenderly. 'I asked her what that meant and, with a mischievous smile, she told me I had to find out. So I went to the library and looked it up. In Korean, a butterfly carries two meanings. For many, it represents prosperity and joy. But it also symbolizes harmony between a husband and wife.'

Zoe's eyes shimmered with empathy and understanding. 'She loved you until the end,' she whispered.

Masuki's voice trembled with a lifetime of longing as he continued.

'She was my love, my life, my dearest friend,' he said. 'My little butterfly. Had there been no war, she would have been my wife. But she was taken from me. I never got over that. Even after her rescue, I never saw her again. By apologizing to those women, I found a way to say sorry to Meera, to make amends for the pain we all endured.'

Tears welled up in Zoe's eyes. 'Please, Masuki, keep it,' she pleaded softly.

Masuki declined with a smile. 'I am ninety-seven years old,' he said, turning his head to stare into the distance. 'My apology to those women was about setting me free, too. I can let go now and be one with Meera again. The way a man and wife should be. But for you, Zoe, this pin is a symbol of prosperity and happiness, a blessing for your marriage.'

Moved by his words, Zoe accepted his gift, her heart swelling. As their hands separated, they shared a final moment of connection before Masuki turned and walked away, carrying a lifetime's worth of memories.

Zoe turned to Jeff, clutching the precious hairpin in her hand. She sensed that things had changed, never to be the same again. The ugliness of the past was behind them now, and a beautiful future stretched out in front, as far as the eye could see.

A picture of the victims of forced prostitution under the Japanese military in a brothel in Songshan, China, taken by the Allied forces in 1944. The pregnant woman on the right is North Korean Pak Yong-sim.

Chinese survivors of wartime sex slavery. Photo taken by Sylvia Yu Friedman in 2011.

Sylvia Yu Friedman (left) interviewing wartime sex slavery survivor Ellen van der Ploeg at The Hague in 2008

Sylvia Yu Friedman (left) with survivor Kim Soon-duk in Washington DC after a press conference where Kim spoke about her suffering in a wartime brothel in 2001

A Japanese reconciliation team on a visit to a village in the province of Shanxi. They have been photographed here with two courageous Chinese survivors of wartime sexual slavery (front row, left and middle). From 2008 to 2012, the Japanese visitors felt a deep moral obligation to apologize to the survivors of Imperial Japanese military sex slavery in China, since the Japanese government has failed to sincerely apologize for the human rights violations of the past. Their inspiring stories have been highlighted in the documentary Healing River, co-produced by Sylvia Yu Friedman and Ivy Makelin of 7G - TV.

Acknowledgments

We are incredibly grateful for the love and support of the following individuals, listed in no specific order.

We cannot express enough gratitude towards Nora Nazerene Abu Bakar, the publisher of Penguin Random House SEA. It is her unwavering belief in us and the message of this novel that has made this journey possible. Thank you so very much for your unwavering support.

Andy Raine, thank you for the outstanding editing work you have done. It was exceptional.

We would also like to express gratitude to Cassandra Chia of PRH SEA for editing support.

Audrey Lore, your presence and encouragement have been a constant source of motivation, and we are incredibly grateful for everything that you have done for us. Once again, thank you from the bottom of our hearts.

Chris and Aimee Lee, we would like to express our deep gratitude for the unwavering love, support, and prayers that you have shown us throughout our journey together. It is because of your care that several significant projects, including this book, have been brought to fruition. We cannot thank you enough for being an integral part of this life-changing journey.

Our deepest gratitude to Papa Gideon Chiu for his powerful love, wisdom, and spiritual guidance.

Agnes, Joylynn, and Miranda, thank you for your steadfast prayers; your devotion to God inspires profoundly. All our love to you all.

To our dear lifelong friend, Olivia Kow: we are truly blessed to have you in our lives. Lots of love to you.

Charlene Chu, my kindred spirit, I'm forever thankful for your friendship and the depth of your understanding.

Dorothy Wong, it always feels like we saw each other yesterday whenever we talk on the phone. Thanks for being on the journey together for so many years. Sending so much love to you and your family.

Connie Lam, we are so thankful for your love, wisdom, and powerful prayers. We look forward to walking together in the years to come.

Dennis Miller, thank you so much for your steadfast prayers and uplifting words. You are a special friend to us.

Albert and Wingee, thanks for your unconditional love and for walking together as a family.

Mabel Tai, thank you for your prayers and loving kindness. It's an honour to know you and to journey together—you will change our generation.

Grace Han, thank you for all your wisdom and powerful prayers over the years.

Thanks for your faithful prayers and friendship, Joon Imm and Grace Chae.

Fanny Vermes, thank you for your love and prayers over the decades. You're always in my heart. Also, I'm grateful to the late Nancy Patterson, for inspiring us deeply. She kickstarted the journey to research Japanese military sexual slavery.

Thank you, Frank White, for all your amazing kindness and support over the years.

We are eternally grateful to my (Sylvia's) extraordinary and loving Mom and Dad, and my brilliant, talented, hilarious, charismatic, and dynamic sister and brothers, Jayne, Jae, and Jaemin. I'm so proud of you all. We wrote this book with our nieces, Zoe and Ava, in mind.

Brandon and Damien, you both are always our inspiration.

Thank you to our amazing friends for supporting over the years: our house church family, Nellie Hue, Parin, Kanani, Jenny Lu, Karen Ho, Winnie Chau, Han Shih Toh, Ivan Yuen, Peter Wang, Vivien Tam, Mary Koo and Kenny Chang, friends on the 852 Freedom Campaign WhatsApp group, and many others.

Countless individuals have played a crucial role in our journeys. Your contribution is deeply appreciated, and we want to express our heartfelt gratitude.